CAPTAIN JESUS

by Colette Snowden

Bluemoose

First published in 2021 by
Bluemoose Books Ltd
25 Sackville Street
Hebden Bridge
West Yorkshire
HX7 7DJ

www.bluemoosebooks.com

British Library Cataloguing-in-Publication data
A catalogue record for this book is available from the British Library

Paperback 978-1-910422-69-4

Printed and bound in the UK by Short Run Press

CAPTAIN JESUS

For my boys, Noah and Gideon

ONE

John-Joe said it was my idea, but it wasn't. Not really. It never was. If there was ever a stupid idea it always started with him. I just went along with it, that's all I did, because he said it'd be cool. Because he said the poor dead bird couldn't feel anything anyway.

That's definitely where it all started, though, for sure. And even though it wasn't my idea, that doesn't stop me from being responsible. I was the eldest, I should have stopped it. It wasn't my idea but I still feel like it was my fault. There's a difference and the difference is guilt.

It was going to be the best day too.

We were just back from holiday. We'd had a week in a cottage in Yorkshire for Easter and it had rained most days but then the sun had come out the day before we left. By the time we got home, it was ice cream and picnic weather. We spent Sunday having water pistol fights and Dad even got the paddling pool out, even though I'm really too big for it. We were supposed to be back at school on Monday but John-Joe said he wasn't feeling well and Gabe said he had a sore throat so I said I had a sore throat too. Dad said we'd feel better when we got to school and saw our friends. He felt our foreheads and said he couldn't see any signs of a fever, but I said it hurt to swallow and John-Joe said it was like barbed wire in his throat. I could tell Mum was going to cave.

'They are tired from the trip back, James,' she said. 'And it does seem a shame to miss out on all this lovely sunshine when we had them traipsing up hills in the rain last week. A bit of sun will probably do them good....'

They were doing that thing where they talk like they're whispering so that we won't hear but they have to talk loud enough to hear each other so we can actually hear everything. Mum used to do a really stupid spelling-out thing so it took ages for her to tell Dad anything. He'd just agree with whatever she said to hurry her to the end of the sentence. But once John-Joe and me could spell there wasn't much point in that any more.

Dad said we should be back in school. He said we'd had two weeks off and that should be enough for us and enough for Mum. He reminded Mum that it's really important kids don't miss the first day back, as though he'd been listening in at school assembly when they lectured us about attendance and gave out certificates, like a lame certificate is ever going to be better than a day off.

'I'd have thought you'd be glad to get them out of your hair, Marie. Have you not got enough to do, what with the baby coming and everything?'

John-Joe coughed and gave Mum that look and asked for a drink. I swear he could make himself pale on demand.

Mum ruffled his hair and gave his shoulders a squeeze.

'Look at him, he's not right is he?'

Dad raised his eyebrows. He's not so easily taken in as Mum.

'None of them look right to me.'

She looked across at me and Gabe and Dad looked too. I kind of half coughed. I didn't want to make it too obvious. I've never been as good at that kind of thing as John-Joe. He was the master. He was, like, super faker.

Dad sighed and Mum pulled out the killer blow she'd been hiding up her sleeve.

'Look, James,' she said. 'Once the baby arrives I won't get to hang out with this lot, this might be the last sunny day I get to sit outside with them in the sunshine before I'm up half the night, grumpy as hell and chained to the sofa feeding the baby.'

She could see that Dad was teetering on the brink now and so could we. John-Joe coughed again. 'Can I have a drink please,

Mum?' he muttered, squeezing the words out like he barely had the energy to speak.

'Of course you can, sweetheart.' She patted him on the head and took a cup off the draining board to fill with water.

'See,' she said to Dad, taking her turn to be the one raising her eyebrows. 'They're just not right. And look at the blossom on the cherry tree. And look what a lovely day it is. It's just one day off school. They'll be fine tomorrow. A day in the garden will do them the power of good. And they can help me with the washing. I've got a mountain of washing to do and I can get it all pegged out and dried today. They can help me carry it out so's I'm not lifting. And they can help me peg it. It's tiring you know, carrying this big fat baby around all the time, it'll be much easier with six extra hands on my team.'

She winked at me secretly and Dad was only going through the motions of raising his objections now. She was like the hot-shot lawyer in one of those courtroom dramas. She gave him the logic, she played on the heart strings, she itemised all the good reasons why he should be on her side.

We stood there silently backing her up. A row of Hear no Evil, See no Evil and Speak no Evil monkeys.

'Well, it's up to you.'

John-Joe grinned at me. He knew we'd won.

'If it was me,' Dad continued, 'I'd have them off to school and out of my hair and put my feet up while you've got the chance. But you know best.'

'I know we'd be racing around to get there on time and then I'd be back to school again to collect them before you know it and end up on my feet for ages because all the mums will be chatting and telling me how my bump's got bigger and all of that. And that's best-case scenario, more than likely I'd get a call from school to say they're ill and need picking up early, so I'd end up meeting myself coming back.'

She smiled at John-Joe and laid her hand on his head. He put in one more cough for good measure.

'Fine.' Dad knew he was beaten. 'Fine. I suppose it won't do any harm. If you're happy to have them at home, far be it from me to frogmarch them into school. They'll probably just spend the day writing about what they did in the holidays anyway.'

'Exactly.'

'Okay then.'

'Okay then.'

Dad picked up his car keys.

'Right you lot, look after your Mum and the big fat baby while I'm at work. If anyone comes to the door, try to look vaguely poorly. No face-timing anyone. No playing out on your bikes in the street.'

Mum made a face at him and followed him to the door.

Gabe asked me what a frog march was.

'It's when someone makes you walk so fast that you jump like a frog,' John-Joe answered. He always had an answer for everything but that was fine because I didn't know.

The front door banged shut and Mum came back in the kitchen.

'So,' Mum smiled, looking at all of us. 'Who's for a banana milkshake under the blossom tree?'

Gabe's hand shot up in the air as though he knew the answer at school. John-Joe and me just shouted 'Me!' then 'Jinx' and Mum gave us a banana each to peel and got the milk out of the fridge. We peeled while she called school and smiled at us as she told the receptionist that we must have picked up a chill on holiday because it had rained a lot. 'Nightmare, I know. Hopefully I can sit them out in the garden and get the sunshine to buck them up a bit.'

That's the thing about that day. It was always going to be a day we'd remember because Mum never let us stay off school for no reason and we hardly ever made banana milkshake with real bananas. And the sun was shining and the blossom was just at that point where you could shake a branch and make it snow pink. That's if you could reach a branch. I nearly could because

I was ten and Mum said I was growing like cress on a window ledge, but it was Mum that had shown us how she could make it snow pink on our heads by shaking a branch to make the petals float down.

Gabe covered his ears when Mum switched on the blender to make the milkshakes, so Mum sent him and me off to fetch a couple of blankets to lay out on the lawn for sitting on. 'And bring some books down too,' she shouted up after us. So we came downstairs with books and pens and paper and a jigsaw and a pile of action figures wrapped up in the blankets like Dick Whittington's pack, except not on a stick.

'Can I go and get a blanket?' John-Joe asked when he saw me and Gabe with our blanket parcels.

'I think two's enough, don't you?' Mum said. 'Do you want to put the honey in the milkshake for me? I forgot to put the honey in, we'll need to give it another whizz.'

'I do. I do want to put the honey in but I want my own blanket as well. Gabe and Jim have got a blanket each, why can't I have a blanket?'

John-Joe started to properly go off on one and he really nearly ruined everything. Just because he was eight it didn't stop him from acting like he was five half the time, he could be more of a baby than Gabe sometimes. Mum said if he didn't calm down and stop having such a tantrum over nothing then nobody would have a blanket and nobody would have a milkshake and everyone could go and put their uniform on and we'd head off to school after all.

That shut him up. And then she rubbed her belly like the baby was kicking because it was getting upset with all the crying and shouting. Which it probably was.

'Right,' Mum sighed, and switched on the kettle for a cup of tea. 'Jim and Gabe, you can be in charge of laying out the blankets on the lawn under the cherry blossom and when you've done that you can get some cushions off the sofas in the living room and take them out there too. I'm not sure how

5

me and this big fat baby are going to handle sitting on the floor but we'll give it a go and the cushions might help.'

She was always calling the baby 'this big fat baby,' which I thought was pretty mean. It was quite a big fat tummy she'd got though, so I don't think she was being mean on the baby, I think she just meant she was fat. Which she was. She swayed when she walked like fat people sometimes do, tipping all that weight from one side to the other to move herself forwards.

'And John-Joe, you can help me with the milkshakes and be the milkshake waiter and you can also bend down and take that washing out of the washing machine for me because I might topple over if I try and do it.'

'So I've got the most important jobs?' John-Joe asked.

'Yes, you've got the most important jobs,' Mum said, winking at me when he couldn't see. 'So, what's everyone waiting for? Get busy with your jobs, men!'

She clapped her hands and it kind of woke us all up. Gabe and me went into the garden with our blanket packs and dumped them on the ground and then raced back in to get the cushions. (I let him win – he was only five).

We could hear Mum and John-Joe talking in the kitchen. He was talking about helping her to peg out the washing and telling her that the pegs on the empty washing line looked like birds perching. Gabe and me weren't talking, we had jobs to do and we just got on with them. We took opposite corners of each blanket and held each one up over our heads and wafted it a bit then laid it carefully down on the ground and pulled the edges to make it lie totally flat. When we'd finished, they were perfectly smooth with just a little overlap where the two met. There was a bit of a breeze so we put a book on each corner of the blanket to stop the corners from flipping back. Mum always uses our shoes for that at the beach. Then we scattered cushions all around in a semi-circle with a few pushed up together in the middle as a special seat for Mum.

'We're just going to peg this washing out and then we'll bring the milkshakes out and read some stories,' Mum called over from the washing line. I stood and watched them for a minute. They had a system. John-Joe bent down to take something from the basket and handed it to Mum and she pegged it on the line.

I wished I'd been picked for the washing and the milkshake jobs and he'd gone to get the stupid blanket like he'd wanted.

'Come and look what I've found,' said Gabe.

He'd gone round the back of the tree with the action figures to set up a game while we were waiting for Mum and John-Joe. He was poking his head round the side of the tree like a meerkat and waving his hand at me to come.

So I went. Behind the tree, lying on a few stray petals in the dusty bit right next to the trunk, was a dead magpie. It didn't look dead. It wasn't mashed up or anything. But it wasn't moving and it was lying on the ground so I knew it must be dead.

'Is it dead?' Gabe asked.

'I think so.'

'Shall we check it?'

'No.'

'Shall we tell Mum?'

'No.'

'So what shall we do?'

'Just leave it where it is.'

'Are you sure we should just leave it?'

The problem with being the oldest is that you always have to make all the decisions and you're supposed to be the one that knows everything.

'What are you looking at?' John-Joe ran up and slapped us both on the back at the same time.

'I've found a dead bird,' said Gabe.

'It's a dead magpie,' I corrected.

'But I found it,' Gabe repeated.

'Cool,' said John-Joe. 'Are you sure it's dead?'

'Pretty sure.'

'We're sure,' I said. 'It's definitely dead.'

John-Joe crouched down beside the bird for a closer look. He looked in its eyes. He put his ear to its chest. He prodded it with his index finger and lifted its wings so the feathers splayed out in a perfect arc.

'Yep,' he turned to us solemnly. 'It's definitely dead. What should we do with it?'

'I think we should bury it,' said Gabe.

'Or we should tell Mum,' John-Joe said.

'Where is Mum?' I asked.

'She's going to put some more washing in the machine and then she's going to bring out the milkshakes and some biscuits,' John-Joe said, pleased that he knew what was happening and in what order.

And that's the last thing I remember about who said what because the next thing I remember is handing John-Joe the pegs while he pegged out the poor dead magpie on the washing line. He'd moved the washing from the middle of the line opposite the patio doors and put it at the end so that the magpie would be right there when Mum stepped outside with each of its wings pegged out and pointing to the rest of the washing.

We stood back and looked at it. When the breeze blew softly, moving the washing on the line and making pink snow drift across from the cherry blossom, the bird moved with the line, flying through the snow.

'It's like we've brought it back to life,' said Gabe.

He crossed himself like we do at church.

'Yeah, but it's still dead though,' John-Joe said. 'It's not like Jesus and we're not miracle workers, we can't do a proper resurrection. Look,' he said as he plucked a long feather out of the magpie's tail and held it up and twisted it in the sunshine so that we could see first blues and greens and then all the rainbow colours reflecting out of the dark feather.

'That's the miracle,' he said. 'Look at that. That's amazing, I'm keeping that.' And he tucked it behind his ear and started dancing in a circle and hitting the palm of his hand over his mouth like a witch doctor casting a spell.

John-Joe chased me and Gabe up to top of the garden and then we hid behind the blossom tree and waited for Mum to come outside and see the magpie pretending to be alive on the washing line. We waited in hiding so that we could spring out from behind the tree and laugh at the joke we'd played on her.

But when she came out she screamed and dropped the tray of milkshakes on the floor. And she carried on screaming. And when we ran out laughing she just looked at us and cried and cried. And when John-Joe put his arms around her and the big fat baby and muttered 'Sorry Mummy, we're sorry Mummy, we're sorry,' she just shrugged him off and went back inside the house and sat on the sofa in the living room rubbing her tummy and crying.

They were looking at me like I was Mum or Dad or their teacher or something but I didn't know what to do. I wanted to go inside and say the thing that would make her stop crying so that she could be in charge again and I could just ask *her* what to do.

But I didn't know what the thing was.

She hardly ever cries but, when she does, she never cries just a little bit. It's always like epic crying. Like she did when Nanna died. Like she did when we thought she was going to have a baby and then she didn't.

So we ended up just standing there, for ages. We could see her through the patio doors just sitting on the sofa, letting the tears drop from her cheeks to her T-shirt.

'You should go in and see if you can help her stop crying,' said John-Joe.

'Don't be so stupid. I can't make her stop. How do you expect me to make her stop?' It came out a bit worse than I meant it to and then John-Joe was crying, and because John-Joe was crying then Gabe started crying. I wanted to join in too but Dad

9

always says there's no point crying over the things you can't fix and if you can fix them you're better off just getting on with it.

So I just got on with what I could fix. I unpegged the bird from the washing line and sent John-Joe inside to find the box from the new school shoes he got before the holidays. He didn't even complain for a second. He just did it. I put the magpie on the step while I went inside for the broom and the dustpan and brush and Gabe helped me clear up the mess from the milkshakes.

But there was glass everywhere and the wet milkshake made it stick to the bristles and the more we swept the more we just made everywhere stink of banana. And then John-Joe came back out again, still crying, telling me that he couldn't find the box anywhere and he'd searched everywhere and it just wasn't there so what were we going to do.

I looked at him, and down at the brush in my hand all clogged up with smelly banana and I opened my mouth to speak but instead of my words coming out we heard a voice coming over the gate at the side of the kitchen.

'Hello boys, I thought you'd be at school today. I just popped round to see Mummy is she here? Is she busy?'

It was Jenny from over the road. We always call her Jenny from over the road because Mum has a friend Jenny too and we call her Phoebe's-Mum-Jenny so that nobody gets confused. Except we still do. I do anyway. And Dad definitely does.

Jenny from over the road is kind of old. Older than Mum anyway, but probably not as old as Nanna was before she died. She has two pairs of glasses and she's always got the wrong ones on. She wears tights, even in the summer, the kind of brown see-through ones that make her legs look they have a tan even though her arms are really white. You can see the hairs on her legs all squished up inside them. She pops in whenever she feels like it, sometimes with cakes or biscuits that she's made, and even when she hasn't brought some baking she always smells like warm cake. Sometimes she comes over nearly every day.

Sometimes we hardly see her for ages and Mum says she must be suffering with her nerves again and goes over there with a bunch of flowers. I like it when she brings us cakes but not when she's here every day, because she just stays for ages and talks and talks and talks and tells us what to do like she was an actual relative. Especially since Nanna died, it's like she's decided there was a vacancy in the family and she's given herself the job.

'Mum's not feeling very well,' John-Joe said to Jenny before I could even think of any words to say. 'She's not feeling very well and we've got all this mess to clear up and a dead bird—'

'Dead magpie, actually,' Gabe chipped in.

'We've got a dead magpie,' John-Joe started again...

'And Mum's a bit upset,' I added. I thought we needed to make it clear that Mum wasn't actually ill. I didn't want Jenny ringing an ambulance or sending us off for clean towels and hot water because the baby was about to arrive.

That's what we thought we'd said anyway, but I don't know what it actually sounded like because what Jenny told us she'd heard was 'blah, blah, blah, blah,' and instead of answering us she just opened the gate and walked straight in without even being asked.

'Right boys, what on earth is going on and where's Mummy?'

I hate it when adults say 'Mummy' like that, as though it's their mummy too. Jenny from over the road is way older than Mum and it just sounds stupid.

Gabe dropped the big brush and it clattered really loudly to the ground and then he took Jenny by the hand and led her over to the patio doors, steering her away from the milk and glass so that she could go in to Mum.

I wanted to stop him. I wanted to stop Jenny from seeing my mum all puffy-eyed and red faced but I just stood there holding the dust pan, glad that somebody finally knew what to do.

Jenny went inside and Gabe came back out again. We sat on the steps outside the back door. John-Joe was the last to sit down and he had to move the magpie to make a space for himself but he didn't say anything. He just picked up the bird and sat down and put it in his lap. He was stroking it and making its feathers go all shiny down its back. And I looked down and its black, black, super-black eye was like the bottom of a well, it was just darkness that went on forever.

When Jenny came back out again, Mum was with her, holding her hand like a little girl who'd had a telling off but was ready to be good now.

Jenny let go of Mum's hand and looked at each of us one after the other with her serious face. The one she uses when we have burping competitions. The one she used that time when John-Joe hid in the tree and threw a water bomb at her that hit her right on the forehead.

'The thing is boys,' she said, pausing forever like they do on one of those talent shows when they're about to tell you who's going home. 'The thing is, you've given your mum a bit of a shock and mummies with babies in their tummies shouldn't get shocks. They need calm. They need helpful boys. They need looking after.'

Jenny from over the road hasn't got any children and it shows sometimes. She's not exactly very good at cutting to the chase.

'The thing is, killing that bird and pegging it out like that wasn't very nice…'

'But we didn't kill it!' John-Joe said. And he stood up, holding the magpie in his hand and looking like he was offering it to Jenny and Mum, with it held out in front of him and his fingers just softly touching the back of its head. He was holding it like a tiny baby.

Mum didn't look at John-Joe; she just looked at the bird. Into the blackness of its eye.

I don't know why but I just wanted to stop her from looking at the magpie so I stood up to talk and stepped in front of John-Joe.

'We honestly didn't kill it Mum. We didn't. We just found it and it was already dead. We thought about burying it but we weren't sure how to do it and then we had the idea of making it look alive again…'

I wasn't really sure what I was going to say, I was just talking and hoping the right words would come out but Mum looked at me blankly, like she didn't believe me, or she didn't understand me, or she wasn't even really there.

'We thought it would be like a resurrection,' John-Joe said, stepping out from behind me. He held the bird up and I thought he was going to spread its wings out and throw it to see if it would fly.

'Look Mum,' he said, holding the bird right out to her. 'Look at it, isn't it beautiful? It's so perfect and amazing, look at its feathers and how black they are one minute and then you look at them again and there are so many colours in the black. And even though it lives outside in the rain and walks round on the dirty ground its belly is so white, like school shirts just out of the wash. If you rub up its belly feathers the wrong way, you can see the ones underneath and they're even cleaner and even whiter and the softest thing ever. They're like toothpaste white. Look…'

Jenny pushed his hands away and held them away from Mum with her own hand holding them back and covering the dead bird.

He glared at Jenny like she was hurting him. She didn't look at him, she looked at me.

'Your mother doesn't need to see that, thank you John-Joe. We just need to get rid of it. Jim you take your mum back inside, I think she could do with a little lie down. I'll take the bird and get rid of it in the bin at home. Then I'll come back and help you clear up this mess and keep an eye on you scallywags while your mum has a rest. OK?'

She said the OK like it was a question but it wasn't a question, it was a 'this is how it's going to be'. Jenny can be nice but she can be bossy. I think she might have been a teacher. I might just be making that up because she sounds like a teacher. Like how she sometimes tells us off even though she's not even related to us or anything and we haven't really been naughty.

Jenny put herself in charge. I hate it when she does that.

I don't think Mum liked that either because she said 'Hang on a minute, Jenny.'

Mum reached out to John-Joe's hands and Jenny frowned a bit but moved her hand away.

'Let me have a look then,' she said and she ever so slowly peered into the cradle that John-Joe had made with his hands to look at the dead bird. Gabe and me went over to look too.

'Can you see, Mum, it's like a rainbow?' John-Joe tilted his hands slowly from side to side so that the light could catch on the bird's feathers and show the shiny hidden colours.

Mum reached out and stroked the feathers, so then Gabe did and I did too. 'It's called iridescence,' she said. 'You're right, it is amazing.'

'It's like when a car has leaked in a puddle,' I suggested, wishing I was holding the bird and showing it to Mum.

'You're right Jim, it is like that.'

Jenny from over the road let out a big long breath like she was cross, but we all ignored her.

'And here,' said John-Joe, 'on its belly the feathers are completely different. They're a different colour obviously, but touch them,' he stoked the magpie's tummy with his thumb as he held it out to Mum to feel the white feathers. 'Aren't they soft Mum? Aren't they the softest, nicest thing you've ever felt in your life?'

Mum hesitated and turned to me for a minute so I touched the white feathers first.

'They are really soft. Feel that, you've got to feel that.'

'Awww, soft, soft, super-soft softness,' said Gabe a bit over the top and in Mum's way.

'Well, let Mum have a go then,' John-Joe pulled the bird away from Gabe and offered it to Mum.

She stroked it gently and smiled.

'That is beautifully soft, isn't it? Silky? Do you know what it feels like John-Joe? It feels like your hair when you were a little baby. After you'd gone bald and then your hair grew back it was the softest thing in the world. This is nearly as soft but not quite.'

John-Joe beamed at her and they stroked the bird's belly together, with me and Gabe just watching, wanting to join in, and Jenny stomping around picking up the bigger pieces of glass from the patio.

'Poor little thing,' said Mum. 'I wonder how it died...'

'It wasn't us Mum, it wasn't. It honestly wasn't.' John-Joe just needed her to tell him that she believed him. And so did I.

'I know you wouldn't do that, darling. I know you wouldn't. You just all gave me a bit of a shock that's all. It all looked a bit black magic.'

'What's black magic?' asked Gabe.

'It's magic to do bad things.' John-Joe answered before Mum could even open her mouth and I wondered how he knew that. I didn't know that.

'There are lots of superstitions about magpies,' Jenny added. 'People...some people believe that...'

'It's nothing you need to worry about,' Mum said, and she kind of shivered like you do sometimes when you've been crying lots and then you stop and you've got to shake the last sad thoughts out of you.

She turned to Jenny.

'Jenny, would you mind just seeing if you can find a box or a tin or something that we can put the magpie in to bury it. It doesn't seem right to put it in the bin. It was a living creature. I wouldn't want it to end up in a rubbish bin. I wouldn't want someone to put *me* in the bin.'

Even though we didn't actually hear her 'tut,' we all felt it and saw it flash across her face.

'I think what we need to do then, boys,' Mum said, 'is wait for Daddy to get home and he'll dig a hole to put the magpie in and we can give it a proper send-off and leave it to rest in peace.'

'Because it is one of God's creatures,' added Gabe.

'Exactly,' said Mum.

'And even if we can't resurrect it we can send it to heaven,' John-Joe continued.

'That's right,' smiled Mum, 'bird heaven.'

'I could dig a hole for it Mum,' I said, thinking I could make it all be over quicker that way and we could just have a picnic in the garden. 'I know where my seaside spade is and I'm good at digging.'

'Thanks Jim, but I think we'll wait for your Dad. And Jenny's going to find us a tin or a box or something.'

Jenny hadn't moved. She was still standing there, looking a bit cross and confused.

Mum used that voice that she uses with us when she wants us to think that we have a choice but really we just have to do what we're told.

'Do you think you'll be able to find a suitable container, Jenny? Have you got anything at home or do you want to get Jim to help you look upstairs?'

'We could decorate the box,' Gabe suggested.

'And make some rest in peace cards to put in the hole with it,' John-Joe added.

'Perfect,' said Mum, giving the big fat baby a rub. 'Great ideas, boys. Why don't you go and find some pens and stickers and paper and things while Jim helps Jenny find a box or tin or something and we'll do some arts and crafts till Daddy gets home and digs the hole.'

Jenny rolled her eyes then. I saw her, but Mum didn't. Mum was too busy watching as John-Joe gently pulled the fan of the magpie's wing fully out again so that she could see the white fingers of its wing feathers, outlined neatly in black. John-Joe folded the wing back again and Mum eased her fingers inside his hand cradle to take the magpie from him.

Then it was like someone had fired the gun for the start of a race as John-Joe and Gabe went off to look for the paper and pens and Jenny led me off to her house to look for a container. She couldn't find a box apart from an empty cereal packet and we both agreed that wouldn't do. She got out some Tupperware and plastic boxes and I had more or less chosen a cleaned-out old ice cream tub with a picture of a beach and some seagulls flying but then she remembered a tin that she'd kept after someone had brought her some fudge back from their holidays. She said she didn't like the fudge but she'd kept the tin because it was lovely. She disappeared upstairs muttering 'I just need to remember where I put it. Where is it? It'll be perfect.'

And it was perfect too. Silver on the bottom with a blue lid covered in birds and blossom trees. Even Gabe said it was nice and he hates girly things.

When we all got back to the garden, Mum was sitting with a cup of tea on the special cushions that we'd put out for her and just behind her there was a folded tea towel. I knew that she'd wrapped the magpie in the tea towel and put it there out of the way. Everyone spotted it and walked round it when they needed to get up to get to the felt tips or go in the house for the loo but no-one mentioned it.

And we sat, in the sunshine, making cards and letting the blossom litter the blanket, not really talking much apart from to say can you pass me the red or the blue or have you got the lid for the dark purple. Mum made a card too, hers was the best but she kept stopping what she was doing to admire details on our efforts. She really liked the border I put round the edge of mine. Even Jenny stayed to help for a while and made a card with us but then she said she had to go because of the man coming to service her boiler.

'See Jenny out for me would you, Jim,' Mum said, when Jenny got up to leave. 'It's a long way up from down here with this big fat baby.'

So I got up and walked Jenny to the gate.

'Will you come back later for the funeral?' I asked.

'It's hardly a funeral,' she said, 'it' just a dead magpie. It wasn't even a pet.'

'Well we're calling it a funeral, and you're welcome to come,' I said, 'because you did help with it all, didn't you.'

I felt like I ought to say thank you but I wasn't really sure what I was thanking her for.

'You're welcome,' she replied to the thank you I didn't say.

'See you later then.'

'See you later.'

And she turned and waved to me as she headed back off over the road and I remembered how much I like her sometimes and wished I'd asked her to bake a cake for the funeral.

I headed back to the blossom tree to finish my card with the smell of banana and sour milk wafting over from the patio.

TWO

remember when Nanna died because it was just after Christmas and we'd been helping her put the decorations away. I remember because it was me that killed her really.

When I say we'd been helping her, I mean she'd been watching us mostly, while we did all the putting away. Mum said it was because her legs were bothering her. Dad said it was because she suffered with her nerves and Christmas could be a very stressful time, but I think she just enjoyed playing at being the queen while we got to be the peasants and did as we were told.

I did a bit of 'yes, your Majesty. Of course, your Highness' as she pointed at decorations she thought I'd missed and she seemed to enjoy the game of being the bossy monarch while I bowed and raised my imaginary cap but Mum gave me the look, so I stopped. Nanna said she'd pay me in gold coins if I did a good job, which she made out was actually better than real money, and, even though I wanted to tell her that I understood the difference between actual payment and a small piece of chocolate wrapped in foil, I just joined in the game of working hard for my chocolate wages, because that's what everyone thought I should do.

It was in the days when I was allowed to help and John-Joe mostly just made a mess. I was five I think, or maybe six. It was before Gabe was born and before the baby that was never born was even a thing, and before Mum was pregnant with the big fat baby, obviously, so it was mostly me, Mum and Dad doing the work.

Nanna made out it would be fun taking everything down neatly and putting everything back in the right box ready for next year, and maybe – let's give her the benefit of the doubt, especially with her being dead and everything – perhaps she actually thought it would be. But putting the decorations away isn't exciting like putting them up. There's nothing to look forward to except next Christmas and that's a long way off. It's like packing and unpacking for holidays; when you're packing, you're just about to go somewhere so folding your clothes and deciding what to take with you is the best job ever. But when you get back and all you're doing is deciding what needs to go in the washing machine and what you have to put back in the drawer, it's just really, really boring. And a bit depressing actually. Very depressing if it's raining and you have to go straight back to school the next day. Super depressing if you didn't even get to wear your shorts because it rained the whole time you were away, so you ended up playing cards and visiting boring museums instead of digging on the beach and swimming in the sea.

It had been me, Mum and Dad – and theoretically John-Joe – that had put the decorations up, so in a way, we were only clearing up our own mess, I suppose. But I didn't even really like touching her decorations they felt a bit sticky – a bit furry too, some of them – and smelt funny, a bit like the boys toilets at school or the alley you can cut through to get to the Post Office without having to go up to the main road and then back round again. I made sure I left Nanna's angel to Mum, because it was a scary thing with a porcelain head that looked like it was wearing too much lipstick. Its eyes watched you and one of its hands was missing. Mum said it was very precious because it had been handed down from Nanna's Mum and one day it would be mine to put on the top of my own Christmas tree. Clearly, that will never happen unless I decide to have horror-movie-themed Christmases when I'm older. Me and Dad call it Frankie, short for Frankenstein's Angel. Mum thinks it's called Frankie short for Francesca because Dad thinks she can't handle the truth.

In our house we've always had a real tree. Me, Dad, John-Joe and Gabe have always kept to a tradition of going to get it the second Saturday in December. It started as just me and Dad and then we had to start taking the others because they wanted to come and it wouldn't be fair otherwise. Every year we go to the same place and the trees are all lined up and wrapped in their net blankets so that their branches are squished and you can't tell what they'll look like when you cut off their coats and they're allowed to ping free. They are like soldiers sleeping against a wall in a long line and they smell amazing. It's a lottery Dad says, you never know whether you're going to get one that's handsome and symmetrical or one that's a bit lop-sided with bald patches and bent foliage. But he's taught me how to check for brown bits and sniff the tree to check it's fresh and, even though it's not just me helping him anymore, I'm the eldest so I get to make the final decision on which tree we have.

Mum complains every year that we've chosen a tree that's way too big for the living room. She tuts and shakes her head when Dad cuts the wrapper off and the branches spring open to fill the place where we put it in the bay window. Then every year she stands and smiles at it, breathing in deep to inhale the scent of the pine needles, 'the real smell of Christmas' she calls it. Dad says it's the 'sweet smell of our pagan heritage' but she just sighs at him and puts on the CD of Christmas carols she keeps in the box with the decorations and fairy lights so that we can feel the true meaning of Christmas while we decorate the tree. Then, after me and John-Joe and Gabe have gone to bed, Mum rearranges the baubles and the tinsel so that they're not all hanging on the lowest branches of the tree, just at the front. She thinks we don't notice that she's moved everything and we let her believe that because it's easier than admitting that we've done a less-than-perfect job. While we're asleep she also gets out the chocolates and hangs them up high where she thinks we won't notice and we can't reach. But we know where to look – she hangs them in the same place every year – and I'm actually quite tall when I stand on a chair.

I love our Christmas tree and its real smell of Christmas but I never liked my Nanna's tree or the smell of it either. Her house was small and the carpets made your eyes go funny. When John-Joe was really little he refused to step on her living room carpet because he thought monsters would rise up from the blue and green swirls on the floor and get him. We had to put cushions on the floor as stepping stones to help him get from the hall to the settee. The patterns in the carpet were sharks then, until one day I lay on the carpet and started being the shark and then John-Joe and me took turns being the sharks and Nanna would come in and ask us what all the noise was about and tell us to stop making such a mess and pick the cushions up off the floor.

There were ornaments that would look at you when you came into the room, all along the windowsill and on some shelves near the fireplace, because there was no mantelpiece to put them on, just the gas fire on the wall, which made a funny noise and a funny smell when it was switched on. Most of the ornaments were ladies in fancy dresses dancing or holding a bird on their finger or brushing their hair. Then there were the animals, mostly dogs and cats but there was an elephant too, which John-Joe said had tusks made from real ivory and we shouldn't touch it because it was murder. But he probably made that up. My favourite was a bear, with a really fierce face, baring his teeth and holding up a fish is his claw that still had water dripping on its skin. If I stood up quickly enough from wriggling around on shark duty, the dizziness and the brain fuzz from the patterns on the carpet would convince me that the fish was still wriggling with its escape from the bear's grip still a possibility.

The one that didn't fit into the club with either the fancy ladies or the animals was the sailor that Nanna called Captain

Paddy. He wore a yellow hat and had a tanned and wrinkled face, with a pipe in his mouth and a look on his face that said 'don't mess with me, you'll regret it.' He looked both sad and angry, like someone who has had such a rough time in life that he wants to pass his misery on to everyone else. He watched us like the others and looked like he was watching them too and in charge of all of them, even the bear. He was on the shelf just above the gas fire where he could see the whole room and there was nowhere in that room that I couldn't see him. He didn't have a body, just a head, like he'd been executed and the axe man had left him there as a warning of what could happen if you don't behave. He was supposed to be attached to the wall really, but Mum said the fixing off the back had come off, so he was propped on a shelf instead. His own shelf, all to himself.

I wasn't the only one that knew he was watching us, Nanna knew it too. She would tell me that Captain Paddy had his eye on me and she would point at him if she thought I was being naughty and she needed to leave the room, making it clear that she would know what I'd been up to while she wasn't looking. It was a bit like the way they tell you Jesus is watching when no-one will own up to something at school. Or like the way your mum and dad tell you that Father Christmas is watching and will put you on the naughty list to get coal in your stocking if you misbehave. But Captain Paddy didn't hang out with angels and he wasn't fat and friendly like Father Christmas with lots of elf friends. He was all threat and no reward. I'd be surprised if he'd ever been friends with anyone.

That day we took the Christmas decorations down at Nanna's house, it was me that killed Captain Paddy and it was the destruction of Captain Paddy that killed Nanna.

We'd already taken all the lights off the tree. When I say we, I mean Dad really because Mum wouldn't let me touch the lights even when they'd been unplugged from the wall. She said there could be residual charge that could cause a shock.

So Dad took the lights down while I held the box and John-Joe got the boxes ready for the decorations (his job involved literally nothing except holding a box and waiting but he wanted a job because I had one). Once the lights were away, we put the decorations back in their boxes. They all had a particular place in a particular box and Nanna sat on the sofa telling us when we'd got it wrong and telling John-Joe which box to bring us next. When the tree was completely bare apart from Frankie the evil fairy, Dad said he'd lift me up to take her down. I wasn't keen. I didn't like touching that fairy in case it cast a spell on me and I definitely didn't want to touch its hair because it was such a horrid candyfloss texture; the kind of thing that makes your blood feel fizzy in your veins.

He lifted me up and I reached for the fairy but her dress was hard to grasp. The fabric was delicate and all ripped with age.

Dad said: 'just grab her head, she won't bite you, she's just a Christmas fairy.'

'Angel,' Mum and Nanna corrected in unison as though they'd rehearsed it.

'Just grab the angel's head,' Dad said again, but I couldn't risk touching her hair and I knew he was struggling to keep holding me up even though Nanna's fake tree wasn't nearly as tall as the real ones we get for our house.

I reached for the dress and held on tight to it but as I pulled it away from the top branch, it got caught and I sort of flung it backwards. It fell diagonally across the room towards the fireplace, travelling head first straight for Captain Paddy. It was one of those times when you can see what's about to happen but you can't stop it. Like when you fall down the stairs. The Christmas fairy fell right onto Captain Paddy's head, bashing her heavy head against his clay hat and knocking him off the shelf. And then he fell too, pushed off his watchman's perch by a scruffy fairy, and as he fell his head hit the corner of the gas fire. By the time he reached the carpet, he was in five pieces, with his yellow hat still in place but his face scrambled and one of his

24

eyes, which had taken the full force of the impact, completely destroyed.

I tried to get to it first, thinking that I might be able to hide the damage and put it back together on the shelf so that Nanna would see it wasn't that bad after all, so that she'd believe it was fixable. But Dad was holding me up high and, even though he put me down as soon as Frankie fell, he still had hold of me. And anyway, Nanna flew across the room quicker than I'd ever seen her move anywhere. It was a small room but it seemed like she was kneeling on the carpet picking up the pieces of Captain Paddy's face before the rest of us really knew what was happening.

Her crying was loud and instant. Mum tried to get her to stand up and go back to the sofa but she wouldn't move, like she couldn't hear what Mum was saying or couldn't understand it. She sat sobbing and trying to fit the pieces back together, trying them in different ways like a puzzle as though, if she worked at it enough the right answer would show itself and he would be whole again. But the bits between the pieces in Nanna's hands had been smashed into tiny shards and lost at sea in the thick pile of the carpet so, even if she could hold all five pieces together to bring the face back to life, he would be scarred by the gaps where he'd been broken.

I could see it was hopeless but Dad tried to convince us that it was easy enough to fix. He prised the pieces from her hands and talked to her in his calmest voice, the one he uses when Mum is getting stressed and upset. He persuaded her to go with him into the kitchen where he could assess the damage on the table and see the pieces properly with the light from the window at the back of the house. She let him help her up off the floor and allowed us each to carry a piece of Captain Paddy into the kitchen like a procession taking the host to the alter for a miracle.

But there was no miracle. Dad said it would be possible to fix it back together as a single head with the help of super glue.

25

He said it was amazing that the hat had survived in a single piece and that it would help to keep all the pieces of the face together, but it was clear when he held the bits to show us in the palm of his hand that Captain Paddy would never look the same again. There was a space where his eye should be and instead of seeming angry he just looked sad, and a bit frightened.

We left Captain Paddy's shattered remains on the table and Dad put the kettle on for a cup of tea before following the rest of us back into the living room.

'I'm sure we can get you another one,' Mum said, putting her arm round Nanna's shoulder and patting her at the top of her arm. 'I'll have a look on eBay, there's bound to be the same one out there, or something similar.'

It had never occurred to me that there might be more Captain Paddys in the world. Who else would want one of those?

Nanna shrugged Mum's arm off and stood up.

'Another one, is that what you think? That's just your problem, isn't it, Marie? You destroy one and you just think you can get another one. Straight in the bin with that and on with the next. Well, it's not that simple is it? Real life doesn't work like that. My Uncle Paddy, your Great-uncle Paddy, gave me that. You knocked it off the wall didn't you, do you remember that? You damaged it so that the hook wouldn't fit on the back again. Otherwise it would never have been on that shelf. It would never have been propped there ready to fall at the slightest knock.'

'It's just a thing. It was just an accident,' Mum was crying and she let me hold her hand. I needed her to hold my hand to help her feel better and to stop me from hitting Nanna with it.

'The truth is, Marie, you have never looked after anything or anyone. You have never seen past your own selfishness and this is just the latest example of that attitude of yours where everything and everyone are disposable.'

'But she didn't break Captain Paddy,' I shouted. 'Mum didn't do it. It was me. I broke him.'

Nanna stopped for a moment and the room was bursting with quiet. Even John-Joe said nothing.

She looked around the room at each of us and took a long slow breath, as though she were refuelling before she spoke again.

When she did speak, it was in a low, calm voice, with the words pronounced slowly like a reading from the lectern.

'Your mother did break Captain Paddy, Jim. And you did. And whatever excuses any of you have, I still have those broken pieces on the table and that is all.

'You might think it's trivial. You might think I'm over-reacting and maybe, if I were in your shoes and you were in mine, maybe I would be over-reacting. But those broken pieces are a symptom of what this girl did to my life,' she pointed at my mum now, her hand shaking and her voice quivering nearly as much. 'She took what little I had and carelessly destroyed it and here she is now with all her happy-ever-afters. And look what I've got – a few broken pieces of pottery and a dwindling collection of Christmas cards.'

It was true, I had taken the cards down from the wall and there weren't many of them but it didn't seem like something to get upset about. It was like John-Joe getting upset that I got more chocolate Santas than him when we took the Christmas tree down at home. A little bit annoying but not the end of the world. And John-Joe was just a kid. Nanna was a grown up.

'Frances, let's just all calm down and get this into perspective….' Dad was normally good at calming Nanna down and cheering her up but she held up her hand to him like the lollipop lady stopping the traffic.

'Listen, James, it's OK, I know no-one smashed the thing on purpose. I know I've upset everyone and I should just get over it. Why don't we all just draw a line under it? You and Marie go home, get the boys to bed, we've packed Christmas away for another year, thank you for helping with that. Let's just rewind and move on.'

I looked at Mum, she was looking at the swirls in the carpet and following the patterns with her eyes. I knew what she was doing because I do it sometimes; if you look at something and really concentrate everything else fades out of your head and all you can see is the thing you're looking at.

'But we haven't finished yet,' said John-Joe. 'The decorations are down but the tree's still up. We need to take it apart and put it back in its box ready for next year.'

'He's right,' Dad added. 'And I need to get all of this put away in the loft for you.'

Nanna looked at the tree and smiled a pretty unconvincing smile.

'You're right John-Joe, we can't leave the tree there, it's bad luck. Why don't we all take the tree down together and get it back in its box. Then we can leave everything to go in the loft tomorrow, if your Dad doesn't mind coming back then? It's a bit late to do it tonight and I'm tired and you boys need to get home and get bathed before bed. Isn't that right, Mum?'

She turned to Mum, who looked up from the carpet, straight at me and John-Joe.

'That's definitely right,' Mum said. 'You don't escape soap and water that easily, boys. Let's get this tree back in its box ready for next year and head home.'

So we all pulled the branches off the tree, ripping it apart like vultures picking on a carcass, with John-Joe and me in charge of the lower branches and Dad sorting out the top bit. Even Nanna helped, though she said we'd need to be the ones to bend down to put the pieces in the box. There was only Mum that didn't help, she went back to tracing the swirls on the carpet with her eyes but no-one said anything because we were too busy with our jobs. I think it was only me who noticed.

Once the tree was in its box, Dad said he'd be back tomorrow evening after work to get everything stored away ready for next year and Nanna gave John-Joe and me a Quality Street from her pocket and hugged us, one with each arm, so that I could hardly breathe because it was too warm and smelt of the inside of old wardrobes. Then she hugged Dad and he gave us our coats and let me press the bipper for the car to open it so that we could get in by ourselves.

From the darkness of the car, the window of the house was lit up like a stage and I saw Nanna take a step forward towards Mum and Mum take a half-step backwards. Then Nanna held her arms out to Mum and Mum hugged her. I was trying really hard to see whether Mum was crying or just pulling a face because of the old wardrobe smell but it was too difficult to know for sure from that distance and I thought I'd probably know when Mum got in the car if she'd been crying or not. It turned out I still couldn't tell though, because she got in without turning round and just put her seat belt on and looked straight ahead.

We travelled the whole way home in silence and John-Joe fell asleep. Dad lifted him out of the car and straight up to bed and I pretended to be asleep so that he'd carry me up to bed too.

We didn't see Mum again until morning, when she made us porridge 'to keep the chill out and the old grey matter ticking over' and checked our clean teeth and washed faces as usual, before handing us our lunch bags and telling us to get our coats on and remember our gloves. It was John-Joe's turn to do the bipper and she followed us out with a bag of rubbish for the outside bin.

It was after tea the next day that Dad said he'd pop round to Nanna's to pack all the Christmas things away in the loft and I volunteered to help. Mum was going to say no but Dad pointed out he'd be back quicker with my help so, in the end, she agreed.

The living room light was on when we got there but there was no sign of Nanna and the TV was off. There was no answer when we knocked on the door so Dad let himself in with Mum's key and called out to Nanna. There was no reply.

The heating was off too and it was totally freezing in the house. Dad went to look for Nanna in the kitchen and I said I would see if she was upstairs, maybe she'd gone for a lie down. But there was no-one up there either.

When I got downstairs Dad was on the phone in the hall and he waved me away from the kitchen door, taking the phone away from his face for a moment to bark at me that I should go in the living room and watch TV while he just sorted things out. I did as I was told and I looked round at all of Christmas sitting in boxes as I switched from soap to quiz show to news and back again.

There was no point in me watching the TV because I knew from somewhere deep in my belly what had happened. I wandered up the hall to see the actual news in full colour with no subtitles, broadcast live from the kitchen. Nanna was dead on the kitchen floor with the bottle that used to hold the pink pills for her nerves sitting empty in her hand and the bottle that used to hold the white pills for her legs lying equally empty on the lino beside her. The bottle of brandy that she'd used to pour over the Christmas cake after I'd helped to pierce it with a knitting needle a million years earlier in October was almost empty on the table, next to a tea cup that said Mother on the side in fancy gold writing. I'd never seen her use the tea cup, it was usually on the window ledge in the kitchen between the clay thumb pot I made in nursery and a picture of Nanna and Mum when Mum was a baby.

She was still wearing the same clothes.

Dear Father Christmas

I have been a very good boy this year. I have started to eat broccoli, not all the time but sometimes, and always when Mum says I have to finish it if I want pudding. I have also learned to tie my own shoelaces and I have been helping my friends Jason and Rory at school with theirs because they can't do it yet.

The reason I am writing (I know it's a bit early but this is important and I think you'll be busy and getting a lot of letters), so the reason I'm writing is to ask if you can do anything to bring our baby back. Mum thought she was having a baby and then she wasn't and now she's very sad all the time and doesn't really play with us. She hardly even reads with us – I don't really like reading I like making up stories but I like it when she reads to me and now she mostly doesn't.

I have tried praying about it and I really do believe in Jesus and in you too, and all the elves, but so far the prayers are not working. I know Jesus doesn't really have lots of hard work to get ready for Christmas like you – he's the birthday boy not the organiser – but he does have lots of people praying to him about lots of stuff so it must be hard to hear me and to get through everyone's prayers. It's a bit annoying because I bet lots of people are praying to him about stupid stuff like a broken bike or homework or new football boots and mine is actually really important and vital.

So, I will keep praying to Jesus, if you know him or you see him perhaps you might mention that I am praying to him a lot, really properly with my eyes closed and my hands to heaven and everything. But just in case he's still too busy I thought maybe you could help?

I am sometimes a little bit naughty, I do try not to be but it can be quite hard to be good all the time and sometimes I'm naughty when I don't even think I'm doing anything wrong. Anyway, if it was my fault and you or Jesus or whoever took our baby away because I've been naughty, I'd just like to say I'm really, really a million times sorry and I am really trying extra super hard to be good now to make up for it. Also, if you can do this one thing it's fine to not bring me any presents because this would be a big present for the whole family and that would be better than any toys in the world. Or you could just bring me something small to open, like a selection box or maybe one of those remote control cars that bashes into things that they show on TV.

I hope this letter is not too long and you read all of it because it has taken me AGES to write it and it really is VERY IMPORTANT AND THE MOST IMPORTANT LETTER EVER.

Please, please, please Father Christmas can you bring our baby back or have a word with Jesus.

Thank you and happy Christmas (we will leave you a mince pie and a carrot for Rudolf).

Lots of love and best wishes

From Jim.

PS. Some of my friends say they don't believe in you but I know you are actually real

THREE

The house smelled of Sundays and warm butter by the time Dad got home from work that day that we found the dead magpie in the garden. Mum had made shortbread and we'd all had turns at rolling out the dough and choosing which cutters to use.

Our kitchen is big. Bigger than the living room. Mum and Dad had it made bigger so that we could have a sofa in there and a TV and a humungous worktop where Mum can see us in the garden while she's cooking the dinner and a big table where Mum can sit with us drinking coffee while we do our homework. Our kitchen is like kitchens on TV with a gazillion white cupboards and a giant fridge, except it's much messier. There are always letters and postcards stuck to the fridge with magnets that fall off when you open the door to get the milk. There are always bags and jigsaws and toy cars on the table, there are always jumpers and books and stuff on the sofa. Dad says he's going to collect up all the stuff in a bin liner and take it to the tip. He never does though. Mum says it's homely and a house that looks lived in is a house full of love. She's always saying stuff like that, where you wonder if it's something she's read in a book.

We were still decorating the biscuits when Dad walked in and Gabe grinned at him with dried icing sugar all round his mouth.

'Aren't you supposed to be decorating them rather than eating them?' said Dad, coming over to look at our biscuits and wiping a splodge of icing off the table with his finger, then licking it.

'We've not eaten any biscuits,' said Gabe, licking his lips. 'Mum said we weren't allowed any biscuits before dinner.' He grinned again. He can always get round Dad. 'But she didn't say anything about not eating the icing!'

Then he got a tonne of icing on a spoon and handed it to Dad. Dad ate it, pulled a funny face and shook his head like a dog that's just run out of the sea all wet.

'That'll be an expensive trip to the dentist! Where's your mother?'

I tried to tell him she'd gone for a rest in the living room but Gabe said 'she's upstairs' while I was speaking so Dad didn't really hear either or us.

'Whoa, whoa, whoa! One at a time,' he said.

John-Joe pointed through the patio doors. 'She's in the garden. Can we go and show her our biscuits?'

I really thought Mum was in the living room and it felt a bit weird that I could be so sure she was in the house when she wasn't. She had folded up the blankets we'd been sitting on and was picking handfuls of blossom petals up off the grass and putting them in a mixing bowl.

Dad watched her for a minute.

'Have you been looking after her boys?'

'Yes,' said John-Joe. 'We made her a special seat with cushions and she's been helping us make cards.'

'Cards?'

'Actually Dad, something happened today,' I said.

'Go on?'

Dad tilted his head and looked at each of our faces. Starting and ending with me.

Gabe stopped dipping his fingers in the icing and looked at me too.

'It's all fine now,' I said, 'but what happened is that—'

'There was this dead bird—' Gabe jumped in.

'Magpie actually,' said John-Joe. 'It was dead already but Mum got upset and we're having a funeral after dinner.'

'I see,' said Dad, looking at Mum through the patio doors. 'Have you finished with the biscuits now? Off you go and get your hands and faces washed upstairs while I go and say hello to your mother.'

'Mine aren't dirty,' I said, holding up my hands to show him.

'Fine, you can get a cloth and wipe the table then.'

He was still watching Mum through the glass.

'Come on boys, scramble!' He smiled at us and as soon as we moved he walked out to the garden.

I could see them through the doors while I was wiping the table but I couldn't hear what they were saying.

Dad took the bowl from Mum and gave her a big hug and carried on hugging her while he was talking. I think she might have been crying again but I don't know. She was kind of smiling and not smiling and pointing to the washing line and to the place under the tree where we'd been sitting while we made the cards.

I wanted to know what they were saying but I couldn't hear from inside the house and I couldn't think of a reason to go out into the garden. So I just wiped the table and tidied the three plates of biscuits onto the worktop.

I thought we might be in trouble with Dad once Mum told him the whole story, but when they came back into the kitchen, Dad was smiling and Mum was just normal.

'Let's have a look at these biscuits then,' Mum said. And while she was admiring the icing-covered dinosaurs and stars and hearts, I must have looked a bit worried because Dad gave me a squeeze on the shoulder and one of those never mind looks.

'Right young man,' he said, 'we've got a hole to dig while your mum makes the dinner.'

'What is for dinner?' Gabe asked from the doorway, with most of the sugar now gone from his face and his hair all damp from the flannel.

'Sausages and carrots and….'

'Yes!' shouted John-Joe, pulling down his fist and then punching the air. John-Joe always wanted it to be sausages for dinner.

'And what's for pudding?' asked Gabe.

'We'll talk about pudding when you've eaten your dinner,' Mum said. Dad sniggered because that's what she always says. 'Now out you go and let me get on with it.'

'But will it be the biscuits we've made though?' Gabe persisted. 'Will you have one of mine? Can I choose one for you and one for Dad?'

'Out,' she snapped back, pretending to be annoyed even though we could see she wasn't really. 'Any more talk of biscuits and me and the big fat baby will eat them all to ourselves with a cup of tea.'

So we went back out into the garden. It was still warm outside and still bright sunshine. It felt too early to be dinner time already and too late to be this sunny.

John-Joe and Gabe didn't really help with digging the hole, they were just messing about scraping the ground with a couple of sticks. I probably didn't help that much either to be honest. Dad let me have a go with the spade but it was really heavy and even when I trod on it like he showed me it was really hard to dig any soil out of the ground.

Dad said it was because the ground near the tree is hard and he was sweating by the time we'd finished.

'Have you even seen the magpie Dad?' asked John-Joe.

'I don't need to see it. I've seen magpies before.'

'Not this close up, I bet. Where is it anyway? Where's the tin?'

'Here it is, behind the tree,' shouted Gabe. He'd been walking round and round the tree hitting it with his stick.

'Let's just leave it there till we're ready shall we boys?' said Dad.

'But don't you want to see it?' John-Joe was already reaching for the tin to show the bird to Dad.

'I said just leave it, John-Joe. It's fine. The bird is dead, you've put it all nicely in its tin now let's go and have our dinner and we'll bury it when everyone has eaten all their carrots.'

It was as if Mum had heard him because she came outside then to call us all in for dinner and John-Joe and Gabe ran across the lawn to get to the table first. Gabe complained that it wasn't fair because John-Joe had a head start but Mum said anyone that whinges gets no biscuits for pudding so he soon shut up.

We were still choosing which biscuits we wanted for pudding when Jenny from over the road turned up with cake. Mum had said we were allowed two biscuits each but then everyone wanted cake as well without giving back either of the biscuits.

'Why don't we just have pudding after the funeral?' Dad suggested, 'It'll be like a proper wake then,' he said, 'We'll have the service and then all come back for a bite to eat and a little drink.'

He winked at Mum who rubbed the big fat baby.

'Or a cup of tea,' he winked again.

'Right,' he said, 'the sooner we get out there, the sooner we get back inside again for cake and biscuits.'

But it took quite a while until we were actually all ready. First Gabe needed a wee and then Mum needed the loo too and then, when we all finally got outside, Jenny said she was cold. By the time Mum had gone back inside to get her a cardigan to borrow for five minutes she probably could have popped home for her own cardigan about six times.

I thought it was going to be Dad that did the actual funeral but it was Mum that went behind the tree to get the tin and the cards. She gave the cards to Dad to hand out to everyone and we all stood there not knowing what was going to happen next.

'As you all know,' Mum started, 'This poor bird died today, we don't know how, but we know that it was here for us to find it and give it a proper goodbye.

'It is one of God's precious creatures so we are very lucky to be the ones who have been trusted with it and you have all done a fantastic job of making beautiful cards to say a special goodbye.'

I looked at John-Joe and he looked into the dark hole that was open in front of us. I don't know what he was thinking. He might just have been thinking about dinosaur biscuits and the cake Jenny had made but I assumed he was feeling guilty for the washing line thing. I was definitely feeling guilty for the washing line thing.

Mum carried on talking. 'What I'd like everyone to do now—'

'Mum?' said John-Joe

'In a minute, John-Joe. What I'd like everyone to do now—'

'But Mum, I've got an idea. Well, more of a thought really.'

'Go on then.'

'I think the magpie should have a name. It doesn't seem right to bury it without a name.'

'It's just a bird,' said Jenny. John-Joe scowled at her and so did Gabe. She so doesn't get stuff sometimes.

'Well what do you want to call it then?' asked Dad.

'Dunno,' said John-Joe. He'd had the idea of naming the bird, not an actual idea for a name.

'How about Blossom?' I suggested, thinking it would be nice to name it after the tree where it was buried.

Mum smiled but Gabe asked how I knew it was a girl bird.

'Yeah, because if it's a boy bird it'd be really mad to be called 'Blossom,' said John-Joe.

'It's just a bird,' Jenny growled. 'And it's dead.'

I don't know why Mum even invited her. I think she was just doing it to be polite.

'OK then, what name do you think would be good?' I asked John-Joe.

He still didn't have an answer.

'How about Captain?' Dad suggested.

'Captain what?' asked Gabe.

'Just Captain,' said Dad. And he explained how some people salute a magpie when they see just one of them on their own and how Granddad always saluted and said 'How Do you do Captain?' whenever he saw a magpie on its own. 'And how's your good lady wife today?'

'That's weird,' said John-Joe.

'It's just superstition,' said Jenny, 'lots of people believe in all kinds of strange stuff. A woman I know thinks—'

'I like it,' Mum interrupted.

'Me too,' I said.

'Me three,' said Gabe.

'OK with you, John-Joe?' Mum asked.

'Perfect.'

'OK then. What I'd like everyone to do now is just to read out their cards and then place them in the ground.'

I didn't mind about putting my card in the ground. I'm not that good at drawing and I thought mine was a bit rubbish anyway. But Gabe wasn't happy. He didn't want to put his in the ground and he can't really read very well yet, so in the end Mum just let him off and said we could put his card up in the house if he wanted.

Jenny didn't seem that keen either, to be honest, even though hers wasn't all that great for a grown up, but she did it.

And then Mum picked up the tin and instead of putting it straight in the ground, she passed it to John-Joe and he passed it to Gabe and he passed it to me and we passed it round until it got back to Mum again. But that's not what she wanted us to do.

'One of you needs to put it in the ground,' she said.

I reached for it and so did John-Joe but he was nearer so she gave it to him. He took off the lid and the magpie looked smaller and kind of more dead than it did before. Its feathers weren't the same.

But John-Joe stroked it anyway. He looked like he was having one last try at bringing it back to life.

'Goodbye Captain,' he said. 'We are really very sorry that you died today and very, very sorry that we pegged you up on the washing line. We wish you peace and hope you fly up to heaven now, leaving the earth behind so that you can soar above the clouds forever and always look down on us from up there….'

'That's enough now John-Joe,' said Dad. 'Put the lid back on please and let's get on with putting Captain to rest.'

John-Joe nodded solemnly and held the open tin up with his arms stretched out.

'Last good byes then,' Joe-Joe said, looking round at us all.

'Goodbye Captain,' Gabe repeated. And then we all said it, like the Amen at the end of a prayer. John-Joe put the lid back on and put the tin in the hole.

Mum handed round the bowl of blossom petals then and we all took a handful and threw them into the hole. Some of them covered the tin and some fluttered around the garden for a bit and flew off into the air.

Mum started saying the Lord's Prayer, while Dad was digging the soil into the hole. And we all started saying it with her. Even Jenny.

But just when she got to the 'and forgive us our trespasses' bit Mum stopped.'

'James?' She said.

Dad stopped digging.

'Are you OK?'

'I'm feeling a bit wobbly. I think…'

And as she spoke a big rush of water came out of her like when you turn on the outside tap and it splutters because no-one's used it for ages.

'Don't worry,' said Jenny. I'll stay here with the boys and get them to bed. Off you go to the hospital.'

And five minutes later Mum and Dad were gone with the bag that had been sitting in the hall and lots of hugs and see-you-tomorrows. And John-Joe and Gabe were in the kitchen eating biscuits and talking to Jenny about whether the big fat baby would be home in time for breakfast.

I went out into the garden and stood scraping soil onto the messy ground where our Captain had been laid to rest but not quite buried yet. The water that the big fat baby had been swimming in all this time had made a big muddy mess next to the blossom tree turning the hard dry ground that had been so difficult to dig into mush.

Fly safe to Heaven little Magpie

Dear magpie, we don't ~~no~~ know how old you were, what you were doing when you died or what you were thinking. We cannot imagine what it must be like to be a magpie or to die but our thoughts and ~~are~~ our hearts are with you.

We wish you were still alive.

We wish we could of saved you.

We are very, very sorry for pegging you on the washing line. I wish we could have brought you back to life and watched you fly away. I wish I could feel what it's like to be you and fly. You are a very ~~beyeutiful~~ beautiful and we will miss you. I have kept one of your feathers, I hope you don't mind. I will use it to think of you and imagine flying.

We hope you will be happy in Heaven with lots of God's creatures and other magpies and our Nanna who died and our baby brother or sister who died in our Mum's tummy. Please say hello to them for us and if people can fly in heaven perhaps you could fly with them.

I hope you like the funeral we are doing for you and this card that I have made.

We are very, very sorry.

Love from John-Joe.

FOUR

When I was a little girl, I used to kneel by my bed to pray every night. I did it for two reasons; firstly because my mum would always ask me had I brushed my teeth and had I said my prayers before she tucked me in. She knew if I lied about my teeth so I was certain she'd know if I lied about my prayers too. Secondly I prayed because I believed that God was listening. It wasn't that I thought he would listen to me ask for stuff – like a new bike or a baby sister – and respond to my requests, it was more a worry that he was listening out for my prayers and waiting to tick me off his list every evening so that he could keep me on his good list.

The house was small and old-fashioned, with lacy net curtains separating me and my mum from the rest of the street. They were held in place by a wire sealed in white plastic and kept taut by little metal hooks screwed into the wooden window frames, and could only be removed long enough to wash them on a high temperature, whites-only cycle.

My view of outside evolved as I grew; when I was very small, the net curtains created a peep-hole that only I could see through because of the way they curved in a frilly arc to reveal the clear glass at the very bottom of the pane. As I got older, my world was completely obscured in a veil for a while until I became tall enough that I could see just the top of everything in the space between the net curtains and the ceiling. By the time I hit my teens, I looked out onto mostly trees and birds and the world at human level was blanked out by a lacy fog.

The front door led directly onto the street and behind it was a cupboard for our shoes, which were removed and replaced by slippers was soon as we came inside. I preferred to be barefoot, especially in the living room where the deep pile of the patterned blue and green carpet felt soft and tickly under foot. But Mum said that sweat and grease off our feet could damage the carpet and encourage dirt and dust to stick to the fibres, so no slippers was a no-no.

I don't remember how old I was when I first started doing jobs around the house but I can't remember a time when I didn't. It started with making my bed before breakfast and putting the bowls and milk out on the table, with the spoon always on the right of the bowl and the milk always on the trivet in the centre, in a jug, not straight from the bottle.

The small, circular table in the corner of our long, rectangular kitchen was naked for breakfast, but dressed with a cloth for tea, ironed by me straight from the wash at the weekend and laid by me straight from the drawer before every evening meal. I would ask for permission to leave the table when we'd both finished eating and clear the plates as I rose from my chair. Then I would wash the plates and the pans while Mum folded the edges of the cloth into the centre and lifted it from the table, taking it out to the back yard for a good shake to remove any crumbs before folding it and putting it back in the drawer ready for the next day. If there were any spills, the cloth would have to go in the wash and a spare one would need to be brought from the upstairs drawers until the everyday cloth was cleaned and ironed again. But I was careful to avoid any spills or untidiness. Mum liked routine, cleanliness and order, so my main job was to make sure everything fitted in her neat little framework.

As I got older, she taught me how to play chess and backgammon; quiet games made for two with pieces that went back in the box at the end. We had one of those wooden sets, where the box folds out with chess markings on one side and backgammon on the other and the pieces fit inside. She would let me decide which game we would play first and, on Sunday afternoons, after Mass then roast dinner, once everything was cleared away and washed up, I would replace the trivet with the wooden box in the centre of the small round table and we would play first one game, then the other. She always insisted on being white because she said black was unlucky for her. She never let me win and I never expected her to.

There are days now when I look back on all that order and routine and I want it back, there's a comfort in knowing what happens next and how to spend the gaps in your schedule. I was never allowed to be bored because being bored was for boring people and, my mum would regularly remind me, boredom was not a luxury that busy people like her could afford. If she was going to be so busy keeping a roof over our heads and looking after me 24/7 she certainly wasn't going to allow me to mope around being bored. Idle hands and all that; she wasn't going to allow the Devil to find work for me to do, she was going to dish out plenty of tasks herself before he got so much as a whiff of a chance.

In the school holidays, she would take me to work with her, at first sitting me in a quiet spot with my colouring books to entertain myself while she cleaned and hoovered each customer's home from top to bottom, then, as I got older, she roped me in as her assistant, in the holidays, at weekends, after school; whenever she needed help to get through the work a bit quicker.

I quite liked cleaning and tidying in other people's houses, seeing how other people lived, what they had, how they spent their time. If I was sent upstairs to Hoover, I would have a little look in drawers and wardrobes while I was there, seeing what was folded and what wasn't, having a nosey at hidden things; passports in knicker drawers, boxes of old photographs stashed away at the back of wardrobes. Some of the people we cleaned for I knew from school or church and I loved knowing that I'd seen bits of their lives that they kept hidden and private, without their knowledge or permission. When I found a vibrator in the

45

knicker drawer of Mrs Wilkes, the stuck-up woman in sensible shoes with the cardboard bob who worked in the office at school and gave out the host at Mass, I knew immediately what it was. After that, I made a point of always taking the host from her on a Sunday and always giving her my 'I know what you've got tucked away in your knicker drawer' smirk. She may not have known what my smirk said, but I did. I also knew that she'd have to rummage to find the vibrator when she wanted it because I moved it – just enough to not be where she'd left it, never enough to put me or my mum under suspicion.

But then I couldn't resist telling a friend at school. Well, not a friend really, more of a reminder that I didn't fit in. Claire had been my friend at primary school and we'd often sat together in church, colouring in pictures of Bible stories and doing Bible-inspired word searches with crayons we'd collected on the way in. We'd knelt together on the floor and used the pew as a table and she would share her sweets with me.

Claire had been chosen as an altar girl when we were about ten, and her selection had begun the change from little girl to centre of the universe. By the time we left primary school she had the attention of all the boys and was the girl all the other girls wanted to be. By the time we were thirteen she had given up being an altar girl and going to church altogether, but she was in my form at school and some of my classes, so I still saw her most days. But I was rarely amongst those sharing a joke or a packet of crisps with her at lunchtime and, even when I was, I was on the end of the punchline. By the time I told Claire about the vibrator when we were fifteen, being friends with her had become social currency at school and I was looking for a way into her inner circle. I was dying to tell someone, and there were other, quieter, more discreet friends I could have chosen, but I was stupid enough to see all the plus points of revealing the secret to Claire without any of the pitfalls.

I told her on the way out of assembly, when our orderly lines had become a swell of randomness in the bottleneck between the hall and the corridor. Mrs Wilkes was directing the traffic of hundreds of teenagers surging forwards towards the fire doors, full of her own importance and sneering at us as though we were stinking cattle.

'Who does that woman think she is?' Claire said to no-one in particular, with me squished up next to her.

'Did you know that my mum's Mrs Wilkes' cleaner?' I whispered. 'I sometimes go with her to help a bit.'

Claire gave me a silent you're-so-boring response.

'I can't help snooping a bit, you know, lead us not into temptation and all that, well, it's too tempting isn't it?'

She looked vaguely interested in something that might be slightly less dull and I had to elbow someone in the ribs to keep my place next to her.

'And?'

'A vibrator. In her knicker drawer. Batteries in. Fully operational.'

Claire guffawed so loud and jolted her torso forwards so that the sea of people temporarily flowed away from her to give space for her outburst.

She grabbed my elbow and wrestled me out through the fire doors and away from the crowd.

'You have got to get it and bring it into school,' she said. 'This is too good. Too fucking good.'

'Come on, boys and girls. Time you were in class. This is not a social club. Get moving,' yelled Mrs Wilkes from the back of the crowd.

We were forced by hard stares and long arms motioning in the direction of classrooms, which were in different parts of the building that morning. As I walked one way to French and she walked backwards in the opposite direction to Geography, Claire called to me.

'Don't forget Marie. Get it next time you're there. Bring it in. We need show and tell. Don't forget.'

I turned to look behind me and waved. My wave was my contract agreeing to take the vibrator from Mrs Wilkes' drawer and bring it into school.

Mrs Wilkes had moved the vibrator to a different drawer when I went to take it a few days later. I'd had to plan ahead. Usually we turned up with nothing but the spare keys and used Mrs Wilkes' cleaning things and Hoover while we were there, so there was no bag I could sneak it into and no way of getting it out of the house without my mum seeing. I had two options: a pocket, where it was unlikely to go undetected, or a bag, which would arouse suspicion from my mum because I never carry a bag unless I'm going to school or helping with the shopping.

'Mum, after we've finished at Mrs Wilkes' today can I go to the library and do some homework?'

'You're asking my permission to do some homework?'

My mum tipped her head to one side in a cartoon gesture of surprise.

'Well some of the girls from school are going to do homework. It's geography, we have to research a South American country of our choice and write something like a travel report as though we'd been there. There might be books I can use and maybe the computer. We thought the librarian might be able to help us too. I'm thinking of maybe choosing Peru, what do you think? Or possibly Argentina? Anyway, can I go because I said I would, and the others are going.'

I could hear myself becoming less and less convincing as the lie became more elaborate and long-winded and had to stop myself from rattling on in case she sensed my dishonesty with her teeth-brushing, prayer-saying instincts. But, delighted no doubt that I was both taking my homework so seriously and meeting up with girls from my class (which never happened, despite her constant assurances that my friends were welcome at our house any time), she was happy to give her permission.

'And what time will this study session be over?'

'Well, the library's open till seven, but it probably won't take all that long. If I help you for an hour at Mrs Wilkes' till five I could do an hour at the library and still be home by 6.30.'

The idea of spending an hour in the library on my own doing homework wasn't very appealing but I had to make it plausible and I really did have to write some blurb about a country in South America for geography so the lie was based on a kind of truth. It was a sin of omission, not an out-and-out lie.

'Ok, sounds fine. Your tea will be ready for half past six, so mind you don't get carried away chatting or lost in some South American rainforest. Grab your stuff, we'll head to Mrs Wilkes in five.'

Even with the bag carefully planned into the trip, I still had to work like a secret agent to get the vibrator out of the house without my mum seeing. I had no excuse for taking the bag upstairs so I had to get the item in question from the drawer in the bedroom to the bag in the hallway unseen and without doing anything out of the ordinary like racing down the stairs or walking backwards with it hidden behind my back.

I took the polish and the Hoover upstairs and while I was polishing I found and extracted the vibrator (moved from the knicker drawer to the bedside table), putting it under the pillow ready to take downstairs. Then I hoovered the bedroom, the office and the landing and, once I'd finished, with my mum safely tucked away cleaning the bathroom, I wrapped the vibrator in the polishing cloth, stuck it firmly under my armpit with the Mr Sheen and carried the Hoover down the stairs. And as I plugged the Hoover into the wall next to my bag I simply slipped the contraband out of the polishing rag and into the bag with my homework. It was a beautifully choreographed manoeuvre worthy of any spy film and I was almost sad that my mum was so busy disinfecting the toilet that she hadn't been there to be hoodwinked by my sleight of hand.

When I tried to tell the girls at school about how ingenious I'd been with the homework excuse and the polishing cloth in the armpit they were just as disinterested as they were in the fact that roasted guinea pig is the national dish of Peru, which I'd found hilarious in the library the night before.

Claire wasn't interested in any preamble. 'So you got it then? Where is it, let's have a look...'

It was form time, before the start of the school day and the teacher had not yet arrived to take the register. I was surrounded by a growing crowd of girls and boys who didn't even know what Claire was asking me to show her but were curious to have a look anyway. I was wishing I'd said no when she told me to take it and bring it in. I was wondering if there was a way that I could back down and say I couldn't find it and I didn't have it after all, without losing face. There wasn't.

I took it out and handed it to Claire.

'Eurrggghh! I don't want to *touch* it, just think where it's been.'

Hysterical laughter from everyone in the crowd.

Claire was creating all the fun and basking in the glow of coolness and I was the one left standing with a vibrator in my hand when the teacher walked into the room chiding the class for the raucous she assured us could be heard all the way from the staff room.

As everyone dispersed to their seats and the teacher set a pile of books on the table, then seated herself behind the desk at the front of the room, I quickly shoved the vibrator into Claire's bag.

She shot me a look, but it was too late for her to take it out again without being seen. She'd wanted it. She'd asked me to bring it into school and then she robbed me of the moment when I could have been the edgy, popular one, so she could have it.

I sat across from her while the teacher took the register but my eyes were so focused on her bag and I was putting so much conscious effort into controlling the sound of my breathing that I didn't even hear my name.

The thing was there, in Claire's bag. The snap decision I'd made to take control of the situation had left me still a thief but with no way of taking my stolen item back or replacing it in the drawer where I'd found it.

'Marie,' the teacher called again. 'Marie Murphy.'

'She's there Miss, just day dreaming as usual,' Claire responded on my behalf, totally cool and relaxed as if nothing was happening. The rest of the class all turned to look at me too and giggled in unison and the pulsing of my brain in my head repeated *someone will tell the teacher, someone will tell her.*

'Actually Miss, I'm not feeling too well. Can I go to the toilets please?'

'Yes fine. Someone go with her. Claire, can you just go with Marie and make sure she's all right and take her to the sick bay if she needs a lie down or something.'

I was at the door before she'd finished speaking and in the corridor before Claire was out of her seat. I walked quickly, past the toilets and through the side door to be outside. If I wasn't in the place where it was happening, it couldn't be happening. I went through the gap in the fence and onto the street. If I wasn't there it hadn't happened. Claire would cover for me. Or she wouldn't. I would go home and be not well and then my mum would cover for me.

Except she wouldn't. When I got home, my mum was just getting ready to go to work so she took my temperature, administered two paracetamols and told me I had nothing that a proper tea and an early night wouldn't cure. By afternoon registration I was back in school and Claire was back in charge, still with the vibrator in her bag, still with an unknown agenda and a face that gave nothing away.

I was nauseous all afternoon with that dryness at the back of the throat that you have when you fall asleep on the sofa. Claire and I had no lessons together that day and no opportunity for me to get the vibrator back from her or even agree a plan. I wrote things down in lessons and turned the pages of the text books in time with the rhythm of the class's collective page turning but I heard nothing of it and I had no idea what I was writing.

When the bell finally rang for the end of school all I could think about was finding Claire and sorting all this out before tomorrow. I could put the vibrator back in Mrs Wilkes' drawer, she'd never notice it was gone; Claire could enjoy the laugh for as long as she liked and I could go back to being invisible.

But as I walked through the corridor I could already see that a crowd had gathered and as I got closer, it was clear that they were watching something on the floor. I saw Mrs Wilkes leave her post at reception to see what all the fuss was about and make her way through the circle of laughing teenage bodies to find her vibrator dancing around the floor, brazenly buzzing away with the sound of its motor hidden only by the giggles and cheers of the crowd.

When she picked it up off the floor, and the amused onlookers dispersed, they didn't know that the vibrator was hers. But Claire did. And I did. And so did Mrs Wilkes. And she clearly knew that there was only one way it could have come to be in school.

'See you tomorrow, Marie,' Claire called to me casually as she wandered past.

'I'll see you home now, Marie,' said Mrs Wilkes. 'You sit there while I get my coat. I think we need to have a chat with your mother.'

'No Miss, I'm sorry. Claire dared me to take it and it was her that put it there to make everyone laugh. I promise. I didn't want to. I'm sorry I took it. I really am sorry. But I only did it because Claire told me to.'

'I'd caution you against digging an even bigger hole for yourself young lady.' She took me by the wrist and led me through the door into the office where she could make sure no-one could hear us behind the closed sliding glass of the reception window.

'Why would you choose Claire to blame? Claire, whom I have known since she was a tiny baby. Claire who was an altar girl for years and always so respectful. Why would you expect me to believe that Claire had any idea that you would take one of my private possessions from my home and bring it into school and put it in the corridor for everyone to see?'

'But Miss,' I pointed out, 'no-one even knows it's yours. Everyone just thought it was funny that someone had left it switched on in the corridor.'

Her eyes widened at me while she thought about it. She exhaled, turned to look through the sliding window at the dribs and drabs of pupils that were still trickling towards the exit.

'You may be right about that, Marie Murphy, but the fact remains that *you* know it belongs to me. *You* took it from my house when I trusted your mother with access to my home to clean in my personal space, never for a minute expecting that her daughter would be rummaging around to see what she could find. How do I know you haven't taken other things? If anything else is missing from my home, Marie, you'll be in the frame for it.'

'I haven't taken anything else, I really haven't.'

'Well I'll have to check every room, won't I? But regardless of whatever else you may or may not have taken, the fact remains that you brought it into school and you put it in the middle of the corridor for the sake of a cheap laugh from your friends.' Her neck had become very red as she spoke and her eyes bulged like the eyes of a toad.

'But I didn't put it in the corridor,' I insisted. 'It wasn't me, it was Claire.'

She stared straight into my eyes when I said this, challenging me to break down and confess. I was hot and I was sure my burning cheeks indicated guilt to her. I had to keep staring at her to show her I wasn't guilty, to make sure she knew I would stand my ground because I was on sure, honest ground.

Eventually it was she who broke the eye contact and paced the room while I waited for her to pronounce my guilt and Claire's blameless character one more time.

'Enough of this Claire nonsense.' Her voice was calm and slow and her words were punctuated by a rhythmic finger pointed towards me and brought down like a gavel to sentence me for my poor judgement. 'I know Claire and I know she wouldn't do that. You're not doing yourself any favours by trying to shift the blame like this. No. Favours. At. All. Marie. I don't like thieves and I don't like liars and I don't like people who try to cover up for their own inadequacies and vile behaviour by blaming someone else.'

Her nodding head and agitation had messed up her hair and she paused to smooth it down and push stray ends back off her face. The colour disappeared from her neck as though someone had pulled a plug to release it. When she spoke again, it was in a calmer, quieter voice, with words gilded in malice.

'The thing is with you, Marie Murphy...'

She paused again, took a chair, placed it in front of me and sat opposite me; her face leant in close to mine.

'Marie. I don't want to blame you. I know your mother's mistakes and past conduct should not influence my opinion of you. But you have to see things from my point of view, Marie. I have shown a very Christian kindness to your mother, allowing her to clean in my house and paying her well for it.'

I hated her for this sentence and dug my nails into the palms of my hand as a physical reminder to keep them by my sides and not lash out.

'But it's clear from this that you have inherited her characteristics, her natural dishonesty, her obsession with sex, her disregard for other people. I fear you are heading down the same path and you need to try to resist it, Marie.'

That's when the pain of the nails in my palms was no longer sufficient to hold back the pain of her words in my ears.

After I'd slapped her once and she stood up suddenly, staring down at me, the impulse to strike her was still strong but she grabbed me by the wrist and said in a hushed, shaking voice:

'Marie, as Jesus taught us, I will not retaliate but neither will I turn the other cheek, and I certainly won't let this behaviour go unpunished.

'The sin that brought you into this world is still, clearly, weighing down on you.'

I had nothing to reply to that, apart from an almost inaudible 'sorry,' which she didn't even acknowledge.

FIVE

There are some days you know you'll remember forever. Dad took lots of photos but I knew we'd never forget anyway. You don't always need a photo to remind you, sometimes you just need to think about it and you're there.

Jenny stayed at our house all night. She said we didn't need to have a bath but she made us wash our faces with a flannel, even though John-Joe and Gabe had already washed theirs after we'd finished icing the biscuits. She even checked behind our ears too to make sure we'd not missed a bit. Then she stood in the bathroom looking at her watch while we brushed our teeth. She said we had to keep brushing until it had been two minutes.

John-Joe said she must have been in the army. I said she must be in the teeth police and then Gabe went and asked what the teeth police was right in front of her.

She let John-Joe and me stay up while she read Gabe a story but we weren't allowed to have the TV on. Mum always lets me stay up to watch till the end of MasterChef but Jenny said you never know what's going to be on so she wanted the TV off while she was out of the room. Just in case.

'Just in case there's a shoot 'em up in the MasterChef kitchen,' John-Joe whispered.

'Or a bomb goes off and all the contestants get it,' I whispered back.

'Or,' he said, laughing so much he could hardly get the words out, 'or, or, there are killer zombie carrots and vampire beetroots that march straight out of the TV and come and get us in the living room.'

We were killing ourselves laughing and Jenny came downstairs to tell us to shush because Gabe was 'never going to be able to get to sleep with all that noise going on'.

John-Joe just pulled a stupid comedy straight face then burst out laughing again right at her.

'Right!' she said, and I thought we were really for it but she stormed off and came back with the big tub of Lego from Gabe's room.

'Just play with that till I get your brother off to sleep,' she plonked it on the floor. 'There'll be a prize for the best model when I get back.'

We kind of knew that it was going to be a really rubbish prize, like a satsuma or something, well, I did anyway, but John-Joe was straight in there to get the best pieces like there was a million pounds at stake.

'What are ya building?'

'I'm not telling you, you'll just copy me.' And he sat with his back to me making his Lego thing and didn't say another word.

I tried to make a Lego cradle because all I could think about was Mum and the big fat baby. But it was a bit rubbish to be honest. It looked more like a coffin than a cradle.

John-Joe made this really cool looking cube thing. It was a different colour on each side. It only had five sides instead of six but when he put it on the table you couldn't tell it had no bottom it just looked perfect.

'Right,' said Jenny, 'are you ready for the judging?'

John-Joe stood up in front of his so that he could step aside and reveal it.

She looked at it without saying a word. Then I showed her mine.

'It's a cradle,' I said, just in case she couldn't see what it was.

'I don't think the baby's going to fit in there!'

I wasn't going to laugh just because she thought she was funny.

'Well,' she said. 'I'm very pleased that you both took the challenge seriously and have been hard at work while I've been reading to Gabe. The winner is….'

She took her bag up off the sofa, fished out her purse and took out five pounds. She wafted it in the air towards John-Joe, then towards me, then towards John-Joe again.

'The winner of the five pound prize is…John-Joe! There you go John-Joe, don't spend it all at once.'

She handed him the money and he looked so pleased that it could actually have been a million pounds.

'Honest? No catch?'

'Of course there's a catch,' said Jenny. 'The catch is that it's time to put the Lego away and go to bed now.'

'But what about the baby?' John-Joe asked.

'We'll get a phone call if there's any news. It could be a while yet. Could be this time tomorrow.'

'It couldn't be that long, surely?'

'Well perhaps not that long, but there's certainly no guarantee it will be here by morning. Now up the stairs, both of you.'

If it had been Mum or Dad there's no way I would have gone to bed at the same time as John-Joe without putting up a fight but there didn't seem much point with Jenny. It's like when someone gets given a job to do at school, like giving out the craft materials or collecting in the homework books, and they get all king-for-the-day on you.

We didn't sleep though. Not for ages anyway. John-Joe put his five pound note under his pillow like it was going to multiply in his sleep or something. Maybe he thought the tooth fairy would come and add a bit more during the night. Maybe he thought I'd nick it if he didn't put it somewhere safe.

Anyway, we talked about stuff. His bed is next to mine with a little table in the middle with a lamp on so we always talked at bedtime unless he was asleep by the time I got up there. Sometimes it annoyed me because I just wanted to sleep, but that night it was like we were holding the fort while Mum and

Dad were at the hospital and Gabe was asleep. We were the grown-ups in charge; Jenny was just visiting.

We talked about all kinds of things; Lego, names for the baby, middle names for the baby. Whether it hurt when you squeeze a baby out. Whether its head would be squished up.

'Do you think the world has to swap one life for another?' said John-Joe.

'What?'

'Well, you know how Captain died today and the big fat baby is being born right now, d'you think it's like a straight swap. Like God saying, ok, that magpie needs to go to make space for that baby.'

'No, that's nuts. The baby wasn't even supposed to come today, Dad said it would be another week or two yet.'

'It's not nuts. It's like when we went on the big wheel and they had to let people out of their seats to let the next people in.'

'Yes but our baby is not a magpie it's a person.'

'Maybe it's reincarcerated though.'

'You mean reincarnated?' I corrected him. 'We don't believe in that.'

'I might.'

'No, you don't.'

'Well, I might decide I do.'

There was never any point arguing with John-Joe. There are some people who always have an answer for everything, like teachers and mums. Even if what he was saying didn't make sense he didn't care. If he believed it, he believed it and there was no talking him round.

'We'd better go to sleep now,' I said, 'we might have to wake up early if there's news.'

'I hope there is news.'

'There will be, the baby has to come out. Now go to sleep.'

He was asleep about a minute later, but it took me ages. I was excited and worried and a bit of something else that I don't have a word for.

I felt like I'd only just gone to sleep when I woke up but it was really sunny outside, John-Joe was out of his bed already and I could smell toast downstairs.

I listened to see if I could work out who was downstairs and my stomach sank when I heard Jenny's voice. She was telling Gabe not to put the butter knife in the jam. Mum never lets him put jam on his own toast, he can't even eat it without getting jam everywhere so you don't want to let him loose with a whole jar full.

Sure enough, by the time I got downstairs, Jenny was wiping the table and Gabe had jam all over his face and his pyjamas.

'You'll never guess what, the baby's here,' Gabe spat jammy toast crumbs and leapt to his feet as I walked into the kitchen.

'Hey, I said I was going to tell him,' John-Joe sniped at Gabe.

'It's here, it's here!' Gabe grinned at me with his mouth still full of jammy toast and his sticky hand pulling the sleeve of my pyjamas, 'but Dad won't tell us whether it's a boy or a girl till everyone's here and Jenny wouldn't let me wake you up.'

He turned to look accusingly at Jenny.

'Toast or cereal?' she said.

'Can I have toast then cereal?' Mum usually makes me choose either/or but I knew Jenny didn't know that.

John-Joe threw me a jealous look. Clearly he'd not taken full advantage of Jenny's sketchy knowledge of our routine.

'You were all in bed late last night,' Jenny said putting a couple of slices of bread in the toaster. 'It's only just gone seven o'clock and your daddy says you can't go and visit your mum and the baby until visiting hours start at twelve anyway. So what's your rush?'

'Because we want to know whether we've got a boy baby or a girl baby,' Gabe said loudly and slowly, punctuating his sentences with chews of his toast. He sounded like he was going to end the sentence by calling her stupid but he didn't, thank goodness.

'So where is Dad?' I asked.

'He's gone to have forty winks,' Jenny said, catching my toast as it popped up.

'So you mean we've got to wait even longer to find out what kind of baby we've got?' John-Joe complained.

'He'll be getting up in time to take you to school so you'll find out soon enough,' Jenny said.

'School?!' we all moaned in unison.

'Surely we don't have to go to school today when our baby is born. That's got to be worth a day off school. We've got to see the baby. We've got to see Mum.'

John-Joe pleaded with Jenny as though she could decide, but there was no use doing that because it was going to be Dad who made us go.

'You already had an extra day off yesterday boys and your Mum needs her rest. She's had a long night.'

She was buttering my toast and putting the jam on for me. She'd clearly learned her lesson from watching Gabe and John-Joe smear jam everywhere but I'm much better at doing stuff like that. I could have easily done my own toast.

'When's Mummy coming back with the baby?' asked Gabe.

'Soon,' said Jenny. 'It's all very exciting isn't it, but you need to make sure you eat a proper breakfast to get ready for such an exciting day.' She looked over to where he'd liberally spread jam on the plate and the place mat as well as the toast. He still had a full slice to eat.

'Eat your toast up, Gabe. Eat up all of you,' she said, handing me a plate with two slices that were a bit too black on one side.

'I don't like it,' Gabe said. 'It's too jammy. Mummy doesn't make it like that. I like Mummy's toast.'

'Mum will be back soon,' said John-Joe. He gave Gabe a piece of his own toast which was only a little less jammy but apparently much more appetising.

Jenny tutted and, without even asking Gabe if he wanted more, she put two more slices of bread in the toaster and put bowls and cereal on the table so that we could all help ourselves.

In the end we had a feast. It was the best breakfast ever. Jenny let us put two kinds of cereal in the same bowl together; a cereal cocktail John-Joe called it. She wouldn't let him put orange juice on it though, she said only milk with cereal but she could make us a hot chocolate on the side.

We'd never been allowed hot chocolate for breakfast before. We'd never even thought to ask for it. John-Joe said it was 'weird and wonderful' but Jenny said that French people have hot chocolate for breakfast all the time so John-Joe decided we should all go and live in France.

'Let's get your mother and the baby home before we start making any big plans to move abroad shall we,' said Dad, patting us each on the head as he came into the kitchen.

'Do you want some hot chocolate Dad?' asked John-Joe. He now had a hot chocolate moustache to go with his jammy beard.

I couldn't believe that he was suddenly more excited about hot chocolate than he was about the baby.

'Never mind the hot chocolate, is it a boy or a girl Dad? What kind of baby did we get?' I asked.

'Well,' said Dad, spinning it out with a massive fake drum roll on the table. 'It's a girl.'

Gabe cried and said it wasn't fair that Mum had had a girl instead of a boy because now he was always going to be the youngest boy and he'd had enough of being the youngest.

'Yes, but you still get to be a big brother,' said John-Joe. 'And you don't even have to give up being Mum's little boy to make way for a new boy either.'

Gabe thought about it for a minute. We'd all been so convinced that the baby would be a boy that we hadn't ever really imagined a sister.

'OK,' said Gabe, as though there might have been an option to send the baby back and swap her for a boy if he hadn't agreed.

'Thank goodness for that,' said Jenny, clearing away plates and bowls. 'Now off to get your uniform on, boys.'

'Do we really have to go to school, Dad?'

'We want to see the baby!'

'Dad, we don't need to go to school today do we? Aren't we going to see the baby?'

'We've already talked about this, boys. Your Mum and the baby need to rest before you lot bombard them with hugs and noise.'

'Jenny's right, boys. Your Mum had a long night last night and she has a tiny baby to look after as well as you rabble. I could do with a bit more kip myself...'

'Well Jenny could look after us while you have a nap. We'll be no trouble and Jenny doesn't mind, do you Jenny?'

Jenny collected the jammy plates off the table with pincer fingers, looking at Dad and saying nothing.

'I think Jenny has done quite enough for us these last couple of days, don't you? Let's let Jenny go home and get you boys to school. You can tell all your friends and your teacher about the baby.'

I kind of knew we were beaten but John-Joe and Gabe were still not budging. Gabe was doing the face he always does to make Mum cave. But it wasn't going to work on Dad. Not this time.

'Look boys, Mum needs a bit of team work from the boys. We need to let her rest today and spread the good news about the baby. She might even be home from hospital by the time you get home from school.'

'D'ya think she will? Will she actually be home?' asked John-Joe.

Dad nodded. He hadn't promised out loud but it was enough to send the others running upstairs to get dressed.

'Do you really think she'd be home by the time we get back from school Dad?' I asked him when they'd gone.

'I see no reason why not. Now vamoosh, I need to you lead the way for the others. If you go to school without a fuss, they'll fall in line.' He stood up and hugged me before I left the kitchen. He smelled funny, not unpleasant but not like him.

'Weird to think that two people went to the hospital and three will be coming home isn't it, Dad?'

'Yes, Jim, it's weird. It is very weird. Uniform, off you go.'

Jenny picked us up from school that day. She wouldn't tell us whether Mum and the baby were home but she drove us back via the supermarket to buy some flowers, which I took as a sure sign they'd be there when we got back.

Sure enough, there was Mum when we ran in, sitting in the living room like Mary in one of those old paintings they have at church, except the hair over her shoulder was blonde and she was wearing pink and green flowery pyjamas instead of a long blue dress. But she had her top open and the baby, who was wearing nothing but a nappy, was lying close against her skin.

Mum looked from the baby up at us and smiled so much that her cheeks looked round and polished like apples.

'Hello boys,' she said. 'Come and say hello to your baby sister.'

We weren't allowed to call the big fat baby the big fat baby any more once it was born. We had to call it Anna.

We weren't supposed to say 'it' either but I kept forgetting and so did John-Joe. John-Joe said we should call her BFB for Big Fat Baby but Dad heard him and gave him the look so he said he'd stop. That's what he always called her when Mum and Dad weren't listening though.

The stupid thing was that Anna turned out to be not that big or fat anyway. Mum said she was the smallest of all four of us. Dad said she popped out like a well-oiled sausage.

'Not exactly,' said Mum.

'Where does the baby come out of?' Gabe asked.

'Out of the mummy's tummy, of course,' said Mum.

'Yeah, but how does it get out?' Gabe asked.

'There's a hole near where the mummy's wee comes out, isn't there Mum?' John-Joe answered before Mum had the chance. 'That's what happens isn't it? I've seen it on the telly.'

'When have you seen that on TV?' Dad looked at Mum and Mum looked at John-Joe.

'On nature programmes, when animals are having babies. It's like when gorillas have babies and the baby gorilla holds on to the mummy with its little hands that's what the big…that's what Anna does with you. But she's less hairy. And we don't pick each other's heads for fleas.'

Mum and Dad laughed and Mum put her arm out to John-Joe to hug him one-handed. It turned out that there's lots of things Mum can do one-handed, like cook the dinner and read a bedtime story and play hide and seek.

Anna was pretty much in Mum's other hand wherever she went. Sometimes Mum put her down or gave her to Dad or let me hold her for a minute but anywhere or anyone else apart from Mum seemed to make her cry in about ten seconds flat, so Mum just kind of kept hold of her all the time just to keep her quiet. Apart from when Anna was asleep. Then we got our two-handed Mum back.

For a couple of weeks, things were pretty crazy. It was just like when Gabe was born, but John-Joe didn't remember that and Gabe didn't either, obviously.

We all got presents from Anna for being the best big brothers in the world. I said she must be the cleverest baby in the universe to have chosen presents for everyone when she was a day old and John-Joe explained that they were from Mum and Dad really; he's pretty clever at most things but he just doesn't get irony. I got a book about super cars, John-Joe got a book about nature and animals and Gabe got a book about tractors. He actually wasn't all that into tractors any more, but he pretended to love it and gave Anna a kiss to say thank you. I don't think he gets irony either.

Dad stayed off work the day after Anna came home and for a couple of weeks after that, but we all had to carry on going to school. John-Joe made us all late nearly every day by insisting on going back upstairs to give Mum and Anna another kiss goodbye before we got in the car.

Gabe's class made a card for the baby and all his friends wrote in it and drew pictures. Most of them were pretty lame, but Mum seemed to like it anyway and she even showed it to Anna, who couldn't have been less interested, to be honest.

All my friends' mums kept coming up to me in the playground and asking how Mum was, how I felt to have a new baby sister, what she was like and whether she was good at sleeping. It got a bit boring answering the same old questions again and again and what was I supposed to say? 'Yeah, it's good having a sister thanks. Yeah she sleeps loads.' Luckily, Mum started dropping us off at school again after a few days and people started asking her all the questions instead. It took ages to get out of the playground at the end of school because everyone was crowding round to see the baby, even the teachers. And by the time they'd finished, John-Joe and Gabe would have climbed a tree and Gabe would have got stuck so I'd have to go and rescue him.

Eventually things got back to what you might call normal though. Dad went back to work. People stopped asking a gazillion questions about the baby and the postman went back to delivering the odd letter every couple of days instead of cards in pink envelopes and parcels full of pink clothes and teddy bears every day.

Once Dad went back to work, Jenny from over the road started coming round sometimes in the morning to help Mum get us ready for school. She stood behind us while we brushed our teeth and made us wash our faces with a flannel whether they were dirty or not. Once she even made Gabe change his school shirt just because he'd got milk on it while he was eating his breakfast. Our school shirts are white, you couldn't even see it.

Things weren't the same but they started to feel normal. Normal-ish anyway. We fell into new routines without even really noticing it. There were kind of two groups now, like there is when you're getting changed for PE at school; boys on one side and girls on the other. Before it was everyone and Mum but she and Anna were like a team of their own now.

Mum was more or less the same though. A bit less in the middle of everything, maybe. A bit more sitting down and watching the rest of us, but otherwise pretty much the same.

The weeks went by without much happening. Half term came and went and we had a picnic in the park and a movie day when it rained and we all got to choose a DVD to watch. Mum made popcorn and closed the curtain to make it feel like we were in a real cinema. Anna got bigger and started smiling so we all started competing with each other to get the best smiles. I told John-Joe that fart noises didn't make babies laugh but she seemed to find them as funny as anything else, which John-Joe said was proof that everyone in the world finds fart noises funny. Except Jenny, who says it's disgusting so, even if Anna was on John-Joe's side I was still able to prove him wrong. There wasn't much of a victory in being right when it meant siding with Jenny though.

The weather got warmer, then rainier and then warmer again and Dad said we might go to France on our holidays if we could get a late booking for a reasonable price. Then, quicker than you thought it was going to be, it was the last day of school.

'So next time you come into school, Jim, you'll be in your final year,' said Mum when she came to pick us up.

'And then there'll just be these two to bring here every day.'

'Until Anna gets big enough,' said John-Joe.

'That will be a while yet,' said Mum, who had the baby strapped to her front with a big long cloth thing. 'But it will be the end of an era when you move up to high school.' She looked like she might cry.

'What's the end of an era?' asked Gabe.

'It's when a big change happens so that things are never the same again,' John-Joe interrupted before Mum even had time to start speaking. She opened her mouth and it was as though he'd caught the words on their way out, before they had chance to become sounds.

'That's right isn't it Mum?'

'You should let Mum answer,' I told him.

'But it's right though, isn't it Mum? Like when all the dinosaurs died, that's the end of an era. Or when they started making films in colour.'

'That's right,' she said. 'Clever boy.'

Then she looked at Gabe and me. 'You're all my clever boys,' she said.

I remember that walk across the playground to the school gates. I remember how we were all chatting and saying goodbye to other kids and their mums and shouting 'see you in September' and 'see you in six weeks' as though we needed to remind ourselves not to turn up again on Monday.

That was the last normal day before everything stopped and everything changed for good. September came round eventually but it wasn't the same.

Nothing was ever the same.

SIX

I wonder whether it's the same for everyone. Whether everyone, if they really thought about it, could pinpoint the one day, the one minute where it all went wrong. If everyone else can trace back through all the debris to that single moment in time that triggered everything. The moment they'd like to go back and carve out of their history like the rotten eye in a potato so that the rest wasn't tainted by the rot. For me, that tiny piece of loose thread that I pulled to trigger the unravelling was when I took the vibrator from Mrs Wilkes' drawer.

Ironically, it was my attempt to make myself more popular, less of an outsider, more happy. I tried to change fate and fate came back at me, baring its teeth, to teach me a lesson. The lesson was that I didn't have it as bad as I thought to begin with.

In hindsight, I was always going to be found out. Who else but my mum and I had access to Mrs Wilkes' bedroom? And once I'd taken it into school, it was always going to go hideously wrong. Claire was never going to let any shit stick to her. She'd been born with greasy shoulders, especially designed so that any blame would simply slide off. She was a rose-scented golden child who'd glowed all in white by the altar and always had her hair tied in a perfect plait.

The dominoes fell slowly, one at a time at first. But when they started to topple they were unstoppable.

Mrs Wilkes walked me all the way home from school the day it happened, with me trudging two steps behind her and her turning every now and again to make sure I was still there.

She didn't say a word to me the whole way, and I didn't say a word back.

Even though I had a key, Mrs Wilkes knocked loudly on the door.

'I want to speak to your mother myself,' she said, breaking our silence. 'I want her to know my version of events and to feel the consequence of your actions.'

My mum opened the door with a smile that fell from her face before a single word was spoken. Mrs Wilkes stood blocking the doorway so that I had to stand behind her on heavy legs for the whole thing.

'I am here to tell you that your services will no longer be required at my home.' She gave my mum no opportunity to interrupt. 'School will take up any further action for what happened today on school grounds with Marie but I am here on a personal basis to express my utter disgust that a person I trusted to enter my home while I am not there has violated that trust in such a manner. Consider yourself fired.'

She turned then and glowered at me as she walked away, leaving no-one to answer my mum's questions but me.

So, in the hallway with my coat still on and my school bag still over my shoulder, my mum asked me her questions and we argued. We argued like we'd never argued before. We said stuff we didn't mean and stuff we'd always wanted to say but never dared. She reeled off how much she'd sacrificed for my sake and I finally unveiled to her how much of a freak and an outcast I was, thanks to her oddness and otherness. How her aversion to socialising with other mums had made me socially excluded from the other girls and ignored by all the boys. How having no money, no new things and no dad was a trinity of obstacles that, piled one on top of the other, was too high for me to step over.

I don't remember most of what was said. It's the tone of it that stays with you, the weight of words that no longer form sentences but still rest heavy as the thick woollen blankets we had on top of the duvet to keep us warm in the winter.

But I do remember the end of the argument, because they were big, unforgettable words. Not the drizzle that gradually soaks you before you've really realised it's raining, but the massive globules that drench you in seconds and hit you right in the eye, blinding you just like that.

'So if she thinks I inherited some kind of sex-crazed nymphomania from you, what exactly is it she reckons I've caught?' I yelled across at my mum, bouncing the words off the banister as I spat them at her.

If we'd not already worked each other up into a delirium of anger and spite, her brain might have been more nimble and she might have thought of something else to say, to avoid telling me the truth. But there's a mania mid-argument when you forget that there is a world beyond the hate and venom of that moment and a time when you'll return to normal, rational thought and your real, human self. In that mania, when the Devil takes you and you spit words from deep within your belly, the love you feel for the other person is so far from your consciousness it doesn't exist and it can't protect them. No amount of love or common sense can protect you or your opponent at a moment like that. The words have a life and a power all of their own and you're conscious being is cowed into submission, trapped in a corner by the need to be right, or hurt them more, or to be the most hurt.

'What did she mean by that?' Mum hissed back at me. She was wild, her arms extended, her height exaggerated as she towered over me gesticulating as though Mrs Wilkes were standing right behind her. 'What did she mean by that? What did she mean? I'll tell you, shall I? I'll tell you what she meant, though a fat lot she really knows about it. It could just as easily have been her if she wasn't such a stuck-up, poisonous bitch.

'What she meant was that you were born out of sin, Marie. You were born thanks to some filthy little shit who offered me

71

a lift home from church after six o'clock Mass because it was dark and raining and he said I shouldn't be walking home by myself. And like an idiot, there I was at sixteen, all trusting and stupid because I was naïve enough to assume that good people who go to church don't do bad things.

'He put the radio on in the car, and the heater. He asked me about school and smiled when I thanked him for giving me a lift. He said it was no trouble. No trouble at all, Frances'

Her tone had changed, she was talking slowly and calmly now. He anger towards me had vanished and it seemed like I had vanished too. She wasn't explaining to me anymore but confessing a secret she'd been carrying round for far too long. She walked into the living room and sat down on her armchair by the fire. She didn't tell me to follow her but I didn't even consider ending it there; the curtain had been pulled back and only she could close it again.

I sat on the sofa and listened while she continued.

'I remember wondering how he knew my name. I didn't know his name. I still don't. I didn't ask him and he didn't offer it. Maybe he had a daughter in my class at school. Or he might have just asked someone, or he might have been eavesdropping and caught my name and thought it might make me trust him more.'

She paused, like a witness giving evidence and trying to remember all the right facts in the right order to be sure of giving an accurate account.

'I did trust him though, even before he used my name. And, even when he parked up round the corner from my house without even asking me where I lived, it didn't occur to me that it was odd. He was just an adult, taking care of me because I was a kid and knowing stuff because that's what adults do.' She looked up from the carpet straight at me, as though she needed to check that I was listening and understanding every word.

'He parked up round the corner from my house so that he could rape me without anyone seeing. He stopped the car, locked the door and climbed on top of me as though it was a perfectly normal thing to do with a girl he was giving a lift to after six o'clock Mass. We were just a couple of minutes' walk from my own front door and he raped me there in his car, with his hand gripped round my ponytail holding me down on the car seat. The radio was still playing the last of the Top Twenty. Before they started counting down the top ten it was all over and he opened the door to let me out. He said: 'You don't mind just walking the last couple of minutes do you, Frances? You'll be home before the rain has chance to get you wet if you run.' So dutifully I ran as fast as I could from his car door to my bedroom door and I stayed in my room all evening with no tea and no TV, like I would if I was being punished for back-chatting or getting in trouble at school.'

I had a million questions to ask but I couldn't find the words for any of them and I couldn't break the spell of her confession. I knew that if I interrupted she might swallow these words down for good. I wanted to hear them and I didn't want to hear them. I needed to let her speak and I wanted to yell 'just shut up now, that's enough' and put my hand over her mouth so that she couldn't say anymore.

'The next day, I tried to convince myself I'd imagined the whole thing. I thought if I could block it out and convince myself it didn't happen, it wouldn't really have happened. Like the tree that falls in a wood. If nobody heard it and nobody saw it, did it still make a noise? Did it still even fall?

'I went to school as normal, I did my homework as normal. I watched all the normal stuff on TV and tried all my usual tricks for getting out of doing the washing up. I even went to church as usual on Sunday and looked out for him at morning Mass and again at six but he wasn't there and his car wasn't in the car park. I didn't ever see him at Mass again. I could believe he was a figment of my imagination. It didn't happen. No tree had fallen after all.

'But then you happened.' It was like she'd just remembered where she was and who she was talking to and she looked up again to accuse me. 'There was no sickness, no real symptoms, just a slightly thicker middle until the day I felt you move.' She smiled. 'You didn't so much kick me as do a full karate routine to alert me to your presence and I knew you'd be a feisty, don't-mess-with-me individual.

'And I remember telling my mum. Trying to break it to her as kindly as I could that someone had taken her daughter's trust and totally destroyed it in the front seat of his Ford Cortina.

'But she screwed her eyes up at me when I told her and asked me who he was, this stranger who'd offered me a lift after Mass. She reminded me that she knew everyone who went to Mass regularly and interrogated me on what he looked like, what his name might be, where he sat in the church, what car he drove, what accent he had. Question, after question after question and not one of them to ask me how I felt or why I hadn't told her before. Not a single word of comfort, just a long, loud sigh when she eventually accepted that she wouldn't be able to figure out who it had been that gave me the lift. And another when I repeated that I hadn't seen him in church since.

'She told me that she'd have to tell my dad, as though I might have assumed we could keep it from him, and that they'd have to work something out. Of course, you were dancing a jig while she wagged her finger at me and gave me a chance to rescind the whole story before she told my father. You were boxing ready for a fight but I was fight-less, I was struggling enough to breathe, let alone fight back.'

It turned out that when my mum's mum had said they'd 'sort something out,' what she actually meant was that they would find someone to take the baby on so that my mum could simply expel the offending article like a troublesome gallstone and make it back to school in September with tales of spending the whole summer selling ice cream in St Ives.

The plan had been for my mum to go down and stay with her auntie Eileen and Uncle Paddy in Cornwall. Auntie Eileen was my Grandma's sister, my great aunt, who'd married a Cornish farmer after a whirlwind holiday romance and had helped him turn his dairy herd into an ice-cream phenomenon by selling various flavours, first out of a refrigerated trailer on the back of a bicycle that she'd ridden around St Ives, then from a van and, eventually from a cabin they'd built on the beach. They had busy lives, Eileen and Paddy. Him still getting up crazy early to 'see to the girls' and make sure they had the maximum yield of the best possible milk, and her devising new recipes and getting them churned into something so addictive that the queues to her Cream of Cornwall hut regularly caused a line of people that limited access across the beach to the sea.

They had busy lives but no children. They'd thrown themselves into their cows and their ice cream to distract them from the absence of raising a family of their own, only to be reminded of the hole in their happiness every time a cow gave birth and with every cone of Cornish Cream Vanilla eagerly grabbed by a delighted boy or girl.

Eileen and Paddy's distant existence and absence of offspring was the perfect scenario for my mum's parents, who packed their increasingly chubby-looking daughter off to Cornwall at the end of the summer term in July. The plan was that she would have the baby at the other end of the country, safely out of sight of neighbours, the priest and the church congregation, leaving it with Eileen and Paddy who would raise it as their own, while my mum returned with tales of Cornish sunshine and how she'd dropped a dress size with all the running around she'd done getting ice cream into holidaymakers' sandy hands.

It had been a perfect plan for all concerned apart from one tiny detail. One seven pounds and nine ounces detail that turned up two weeks late, so that my mum missed the beginning of term, and then wanted to stay with my mum as much as she wanted to stay with me.

'My mum was furious of course,' Mum continued. 'Her plan had been watertight when she packed me off to Cornwall. I would rid myself of the baby, Eileen and Paddy would get the family they'd always wanted and she'd be able to hold her head high without so much as the faintest whiff of shame landing anywhere near her.

'When I came home with her granddaughter, with you, she wouldn't even look at you and she couldn't look me in the eye either. I remember how she drew the curtains, even though it was a long way off being dark, hoping the she could hide you and me away long enough to persuade me to send you back down to Cornwall and just go to sixth form as planned, as though nothing had happened beyond an exciting summer of selling ice cream to holidaymakers.'

Mum's voice had become quieter and slower as she finished her story. The words had exhausted her and the close proximity of memories she'd locked away in a dark, secret place for so long had taken her by surprise. That's the dangerous thing about memories; no matter how well wrapped and hidden we keep them, one small chink of light on the most obscure corners of our carefully archived experience can cast a floodlight so powerful that the drip becomes a trickle and then a torrent before we know it.

It was Uncle Paddy that had made the difference in the end.

'Uncle Paddy told my mum that he didn't want to raise a child that belonged somewhere else because, sooner or later, that child would realise they were in the wrong place and rebel with all the power of its being,' Mum said. 'That was the actual phrase he used, that you would rebel with all the power of your being. He said you had to stay with me because that was your place in the world and that was God's plan. My mum hated the God's plan bit, but what could she do? She could hardly dispute that things had happened beyond her control and, if she wasn't in control, that only left one other obvious candidate pulling the strings.'

Mum fiddled with the crucifix round her neck and retreated inside her own head for a minute. She looked at the deep blue of the carpet, where the patterns swirled and curled around the details of her past, and then up at Captain Paddy, the ornamental head of a Cornish fisherman anchored to the wall by the living room door like a terraced-house equivalent of a cathedral gargoyle, warding off evil spirits and protecting us. Except he wasn't pulling a scary face or baring his teeth but smiling back at her from under his sou'wester, with a twinkle in his eye and his cigarette permanently lit at the side of his mouth.

'It's a shame you never met your great-uncle Paddy,' she said. 'He was a good man, and a wise one.' She smiled back at the floating head of her saviour and nodded, subtly but noticeably, inviting him into the conversation.

With his benediction, she ended her story. There was no continuing saga of how she came to leave Grandma's house or why Grandma had never been to our house. All the questions I'd wanted to ask my whole life but had never dared put into words were still left there, swirling around in the carpet and folded into the net curtains, trying to find a form they couldn't quite muster and becoming lost again.

I never found out what happened to the man who fathered me or whether Grandma had ever opened the curtains to let the world see that I existed. Having said more than she ever would again on the topic, Mum wrapped herself in the comfort of a deep silence where, for long, strange minutes, I ceased to exist, along with everything else in that room and this world.

I wanted to ask questions, of course I did. I formed the sentences in my head but no words could leave my mouth in such a profound silence; it was like being underwater. And once the pause had graduated from a comma to a full stop there was no way I could press play or rewind. She had told the story that was hers to tell. She had decided how much to give me and when to stop, so it seemed greedy to demand more. I repeated my questions silently in my head, storing them up for another day when I might have chance to ask them.

I sat, awkwardly, waiting for some signal that the silence was over. But there was no bell and no music; the deepest of all silences ended with the most pedestrian of sentences.

'Are you making a cup of tea, Marie, or do I need to do it myself?'

SEVEN

When we got home from school on the last day of term, we all had a cup of apple juice and some banana chopped up into slices (because Gabe says sliced banana tastes better than unsliced banana straight from the skin). Anna just had milk from Mum as usual and Mum had a cup of tea and a piece of toast leftover from lunchtime.

Mum had promised us we could play hide and seek in the garden and we'd all agreed that it was OK for her to be the counter for every go because she had to carry Anna around with her so it would be hard for her to hide. Gabe did try to persuade her that she could hide with Anna but Mum said that babies don't really like hiding. I don't know why he was trying to change her mind anyway; hiding is much more fun than counting.

Mum had to count to fifty but Anna needed an urgent nappy change so we got extra time.

It was a good job, too, because we'd only just started to look for somewhere to hide when John-Joe stopped running round and just looked at the house.

'Come on John-Joe, she'll be out again in a minute,' I called to him.

'Look,' he replied, without turning back to me. And when I glanced across to see what he'd found I saw a magpie standing on the window ledge staring into the kitchen.

'Do you think it's Captain come back to life?' asked Gabe, following our gaze towards the kitchen window.

'Don't be silly, it can't be. We buried him, remember?'

'I know we did Jim, I remember that. But Jesus came back after they buried him, didn't he?'

'You can't compare a magpie to Jesus,' I reminded him.

'Well it looks just like Captain.'

'I think you'll find they all look pretty much the same.'

'I think you'll find that's actually Captain's wife,' said John-Joe, as though he was the teacher breaking up the argument at the back of the class.

'Don't be silly, birds don't get married!' Gabe pointed out.

'No, but they do mate for life, don't they Jim?'

'I don't know.'

'Well they do, they definitely do.'

'So, you think she's looking for Captain in the kitchen?' Gabe asked.

'Maybe. Or maybe she's just looking for shiny, pretty things. That's what they like isn't it?'

The sound of Anna crying from the upstairs window reminded us all that we were supposed to be hiding, not bird watching.

'We'd better get hiding before Mum comes out and finds us standing here,' said John-Joe, still looking at the magpie, which was now looking straight back at him.

The reflection in the window made it seem as though there were two magpies standing one just behind the other, one looking straight at us, one looking away. The real magpie let out a cry, like it was shaking something from the back of its throat.

'Well, I know where I'm going, it's the best place ever,' said Gabe, and he ran towards the patio.

'Not as good as mine,' John-Joe shouted after him, as he ran towards the back of the garden.

I hid behind the shed. It was the first time I'd tried it and I had to really breathe in and ease myself along the side next to the fence to get behind it. I wouldn't have been able to hide there without the extra time, because I was really wedged in but I could see nearly the whole garden from there, apart from the bit in front of the shed. No-one could see me though. It was perfect.

Gabe hid behind the plant pots where he nearly always hides. It's true that he's small enough that you can't really see him crouched there, but we all know that's where he'll be. Whoever's counting has to pretend to look for him in other places and look for someone else first, otherwise he gets cross.

He was wearing his Buzz Lightyear costume. Mum had told us all to get changed when we got home so that she could get our uniforms straight in the wash and packed away for the rest of the summer. I changed into some shorts and a T-shirt but John-Joe had dressed up in his Red Indian suit, with his bow and arrows slung over his shoulder. Gabe had refused to wear ordinary clothes if John-Joe was dressing up, so he put his Buzz Lightyear costume on because he didn't have a cowboy outfit and John-Joe said astronauts are a bit like space age cowboys with a rocket instead of a horse, so it kind of matched.

I could hear Gabe messing with his laser gun from his hiding place because he was getting bored behind the plant pots while Mum took ages changing Anna's nappy. He wasn't exactly making it difficult for Mum to find him.

John-Joe hid in the cherry blossom. He'd drawn red stripes on his face with felt tip like warpaint, and the magpie feather he'd kept since we found Captain that day was tucked behind his ear like a pencil.

The blossom was long gone, but there were lots of leaves to hide him. He was high enough to see the whole garden though, and the house. He could even move around in the tree to keep hidden and he'd climbed so high that Mum would have to look right up to find him.

Mum would never have spotted him in a million years if it hadn't been for Gabe.

When she came back outside with the baby, I could see that she'd seen Gabe straight away but she pretended not to see him. Even when he fired his laser gun she still acted as though she didn't know where he was. But after she'd looked in all the usual places, she started to get a bit fed up and Anna was wriggling and being grumpy.

'Come on boys, give me a clue, you're all too good for me.' She walked past where Gabe was crouched behind the plant pots towards the shed and I thought she was going to find me first but Gabe leapt out and fired his gun at her and made her jump!

'You little monkey,' she laughed, 'I can't believe you were there all along! I've got you now though. Help me find the others, will you? They've disappeared for good, I think. They've vanished like the invisible man.'

Gabe put his finger to his lips and motioned to her to follow him with his laser gun.

She put her own finger to her own lips and nodded to him as he led her towards the cherry tree.

I saw the branches move as John-Joe climbed higher, even though he was already out of sight. Then Gabe fired. He fired and fired so that there was no break in the noise and yelled 'You're dead, get out of the tree, we know where you are.'

John-Joe's head appeared from between the leaves.

'That's not fair, you told her where I was. She didn't find me, you just showed her where I was.'

'Yeah, but she can see you now, and I've shot you. You'd better come down or I'm going to shoot you down.'

Gabe shot his gun again but even with the sound of the gun I heard the branch break. I saw panic flash across John-Joe's face and he grasped for something steady. At first it looked like he was going to hold on, but then it was like when someone scores a goal and the TV shows the same thing over and over again from different angles. When it's your team that's let the goal in you can't help hoping that they'll find an angle to show that it didn't happen that way at all. That it wasn't bad news. That the keeper saved it.

But the sound of John-Joe hitting the ground under the tree was too loud to pretend it hadn't happened.

I tried to run to catch him but I was stuck behind the shed. I could see it. It was like I could see it about to happen just before he fell but there was nothing I could do. I had to squeeze myself out of that stupid hiding place and it took forever.

When I got to the tree, John-Joe was lying on the ground with his head split open on a knobbly root and bleeding all over his feather.

Anna was lying on the grass, screaming.

Gabe was shaking John-Joe like you do when you're trying to wake someone up. He put his laser gun in front of him.

'Come on John-Joe, wake up. You can have a go with my gun if you like. I'll let you keep it until tomorrow if you want.

'I think we can say you won that game because Mum saw me first and Jim was cheating so that makes you the winner. John-Joe's the winner isn't he, Mum?'

He looked up for Mum's agreement in declaring the hide & seek winner.

'Isn't he, Mum?'

But Mum wasn't there. She'd gone back into the house and when I went in to find her she was in the kitchen, taking wet washing out of the machine.

'Mum, Mum, John-Joe's hurt you need to come.'

'He's just playing a trick on us, he'll get up when he sees we're not going to fall for it,' she said.

She looked at me. She looked weird. It was still her face but it looked different.

'Do me a favour and pick Anna up, will you. I put her down there to make John-Joe snap out of it but I hate it when she's screaming like that.'

I went up to her and took the wet clothes out of her hand and I think she listened to me because I was crying.

'Mum, John-Joe is properly hurt. I've seen some blood. He's not pretending. Will you come? Please will you come? I think we need to call Dad.'

She got up then and ran across the garden with me running behind her.

When we got to the tree, Anna had stopped crying and was holding the feather. It was all sticky in her little hand. Gabe was still trying to wake John-Joe up and John-Joe was still lying as still as before. In just the same place. Not moving.

'Leave him Gabe,' said Mum, 'let him sleep'. And she took her phone from her pocket and dialled 999.

EIGHT

There was a funny kind of quiet in the house the next day. And every day after that. Even Anna was quiet.

I played lots of games of Guess Who with Gabe. Sometimes I had to let him win but mostly he didn't even complain if he lost.

Dad stayed home from work and Mum stayed in bed a lot, or sat in the kitchen drinking cups of tea that Jenny from over the road made her. Jenny made us orange squash and cheese on toast and chicken nuggets and chips too. She got us ready for bed and read bedtime stories to Gabe and took us out to the park. She was like a nanny. It was as though she were the only person in the house that was allowed to talk in a normal voice and do normal stuff.

Jenny opened the door a lot too. Lots of people came to the house to see Mum and Dad and sometimes even me too. When the police came they wanted to talk to me and Gabe so Jenny made them a cup of tea and Dad sat in the big armchair while Gabe and I sat on the sofa and answered some questions about what happened the day that John-Joe died.

The police officers were nice but I didn't really want to talk to them. It was a man who mostly just sat and nodded whenever we said anything and a police woman who asked all the questions. She had funny eyebrows, they looked like they were in the wrong place, all thin and not hairy enough.

Every time she asked me a question, I looked at her and every time I looked at her I had to try really hard not to stare at her crazy eyebrows.

'She's got funny eyebrows,' I whispered to Gabe.

'Maybe she's a witch?'

'Or an alien?'

He sniggered and the policewoman frowned at us like we weren't allowed to laugh.

I wished John-Joe was there to share the joke.

'So, you were behind the shed Jim? And Gabe was hiding amongst the plant pots?' the police woman asked. I'd just told her the whole story but she was asking questions like it was a reading comprehension, checking I'd understood the story.

'That's right'

'And John-Joe was up the tree?'

'Yes'

'Did he often hide in the tree?'

'No'

'But he had climbed the tree before?'

'He was always climbing trees,' Dad interrupted.

The policeman gave him a look. 'We need the boys to answer the questions, I'm afraid.'

'Dad's right,' I said, 'he was always climbing trees. And he was really good at it too. He never fell, I mean he never usually fell. He'd never fallen before.'

'But he fell this time.'

'Yes.'

'Yes,' Gabe repeated.

'Thank you boys, you've been very brave.'

And that's all they said. They went into the kitchen and spoke to Mum and Dad for a bit and then they left and Mum came and sat with us on the sofa while we watched TV and Dad made lunch.

Father O'Connor came to visit us too. We knew him, of course, but he wasn't like a friend or anything. He'd never been to the house before. He brought cake with him, which he said one of the ladies from church had made. He said he'd brought it because it was important for Mum to keep her strength up at 'this difficult time' which was nice of him but a bit lame really. It reminded me of when the dentist pulls and pokes at your teeth so that your mouth really hurts and then gives you a rubbish little sticker for being brave; it's a kind thought but massively out of proportion to what you actually need. The problem was that what we needed was someone to bring John-Joe back or take us back in time so that we could stop him from falling from the tree. Not even a priest could do that and his cake was his apology for the lack of a miracle.

In between visitors and trips to the park with Jenny, we did a lot of watching TV and a lot of making things out of Lego, even though that mostly made me think of John-Joe and what a Lego genius he was, which made me even more sad about everything than ever. No-one told us not to play outside but we just didn't. Even though it was sunny. Even though it was the school holidays. Jenny said things like 'why don't you boys go and get some fresh air?' and 'what are you two doing indoors on a lovely day like this?' but we didn't move and she didn't make a big deal out of it. She just carried on, playing with Anna, tidying up, chatting away to herself like someone had made her in charge of something until Dad suggested she could take us to the park so that we could let off some steam and Anna could have a sleep and so could Mum.

A few days after it happened, Mum said we had to go shopping for smart clothes.

'The thing is boys,' she said, 'there's going to be a funeral for John-Joe and we have to wear smart clothes to remind everyone how very special he was and how much we miss him.'

She nearly got to the end of the sentence without crying but not quite and Gabe ran over to her and put his arms around her. I wanted to go and do that too but he'd got there first and it felt like I'd just be copying. It felt like it wouldn't be enough anyway.

'We don't need new clothes Mum,' I told her, 'there's no need to go shopping. We can be smart and everyone knows how much we all loved John-Joe. Everyone loved him. He was the best boy in the world, wasn't he Gabe?'

I wanted to ask her how on earth she thought having new clothes or being smart was going to help. It wasn't going to stop him climbing the tree. It wasn't going to stop him from falling. Or dying.

'Think of it like a party,' Jenny explained. 'We're going to celebrate what a great boy John-Joe was and you'd expect to have new clothes for the most important party ever, wouldn't you.'

She looked at Mum but Mum didn't look up. She was staring at the carpet as though she was reading a secret message that only she could see.

'I'm sure they've got stuff they could wear,' Dad said.

Mum looked at him. She looked at us. 'They need something new for the funeral,' she said.

'Well I'll take them then.'

Dad has never taken us shopping in his life. He doesn't even go shopping for his own clothes.

Mum just looked at the carpet again. I wondered if she was counting the little white flecks in the grey.

'Well, anyway,' Jenny tried again, 'going shopping will get your mum and you boys out of the house and give your mum something constructive to do to keep her mind busy. Off you go to the toilet before you go out, boys. Come on.'

'I could go with you,' Dad said.

'I'll take them,' she replied, without looking up from the carpet and the white flecks.

Jenny put her arm on Dad's shoulder. 'Just let her take them out.'

Gabe looked at me like it was up to me to decide whether we should do as we were told or not.

'Are you sure Mum?'

She looked at me and seemed like she was going to say something, then she stopped and turned towards the window.

'Come on now boys,' Jenny repeated.

Mum looked back at me again. Straight into my eyes. 'What else are we going to do?' she said.

And without an answer to give her I just got up to get my shoes on and Gabe followed me.

'Well done lads,' said Dad.

Jenny said Mum could leave Anna with her if she wanted while we went to the shops but Mum practically snarled at her like a wolf.

'They'll all come with me,' she said, 'They'll stay with me.'

So we all did go. Dad came outside to help us all into the car as though we were going on some big trip and he wouldn't see us for week.

I sat with Mum in the front. Anna sat in her baby seat behind me and Gabe sat next to her on his booster seat, letting her grip hold of his finger all the way there, even after she'd fallen asleep.

No-one spoke in the car. The radio was on playing songs we all knew, songs we'd all sung along to before, but no-one sang.

When we got to the shopping centre, I went to get the buggy out of the car for Anna but Mum had brought the big fabric thing and strapped Anna to her front instead.

'Leave that,' she said. 'I prefer this. Now I've got my hands free to hold hands with you two boys.'

She flinched as she said it and I did too. I was used to her saying 'Only two hands for my three boys, it's first come first served, guys.' John-Joe and Gabe would rush forwards to grab a hand each and I'd pretend to be disappointed that I hadn't got there in time, even though Mum and I both knew that I'm really too old to hold her hand now anyway.

I took hold of one hand and Gabe took hold of the other and we marched like that across the car park towards the entrance. We let people move out of our way without the slightest chance of us breaking the seal of fingers to let them pass between us.

Inside it was loud with the sound of the school holidays and children chasing each other round while their mums shopped. We didn't let go of our grip on Mum's fingers.

She took us straight to John Lewis. She said we would find something smart in there. She said we could choose. I really didn't want to choose anything. So we stood in front of a row of shirts, all smart, all nice, and I stared at them wondering which one John-Joe would have liked.

Gabe looked at me, I looked at the shirts and Mum looked somewhere into the back of the shop, way past all the clothes we were supposed to be choosing from.

'Would the one with the cowboys and the horses on be OK Mum?' I asked. 'I think John-Joe would have liked that, what do you think?'

I was going to break my hold on her hand just to reach out and pick one of the shirts off the rail to show her, but when I tried to release my fingers she clenched hers tighter and when I looked up her face was all tight and screwed up too.

I glanced across to see what she was watching and there was a mum in the aisle between the boys' things on our side and the girls' clothes on the other. The mum was looking down at a boy lying on the floor, kicking and screaming and yelling up at her between angry sobs.

'It is your fault,' he shouted to her. 'I was lost and you shouldn't have left me.'

'You wandered off and I couldn't find you, you mean,' the mother replied, hands on her hips, fingers tapping her hip bone.

'No, you just weren't looking after me. You left me. You don't love me.'

And the boy turned away from her and sobbed to the floor.

'Well I was frantic looking all over for you, actually, but now that I've found you I'm beginning to wonder if I should have bothered. You get yourself lost and then you blame me. I'm not having it, Liam. I'm just not having it. People are staring at you because you're behaving like such a baby. You're embarrassing me and you're embarrassing yourself. Now get up. Just get up and let's go.'

She offered him a hand and put her other hand on his shoulder. He turned, looked up at her and let her help him to his feet.

And then they were gone.

We were still standing there. Still holding hands in a human chain. The baby fast asleep against Mum's chest and Mum crying in the middle of John Lewis. Not moving. Not speaking. Not buying us a shirt with cowboys and horses on it.

After a couple of minutes, or maybe much longer, a lady came up and asked if Mum was OK and if she'd found what she was looking for.

Mum looked around as though she had just been teleported to the wrong place by mistake.

'No,' she said. 'We were just leaving.'

'Are you sure you don't need any help?' the lady said. She smiled at me and Gabe and then noticed Anna squashed against Mum's chest.

'Aww, how old is the baby?' she said, reaching out to stroke Anna's head. I was just about to say 'nearly four months' but Mum spoke first.

'We were just leaving,' she said again. She kind of pushed me then so that I would lead the way out and we all walked out of the shop, out of the shopping centre and into the car park, where it had started to rain.

Anna was asleep again by the time we got home. Mum switched off the engine and then just sat in the car, not moving. It felt like we were sitting there for ages.

'Shall we go in, Mum?' I asked. 'You could go for a lie down if you like. Gabe and me will keep an eye on Anna for you and we'll come and get you if she wakes up.'

'Or we could just play with her if she wakes up, couldn't we Jim? She loves it when we do funny faces at her and make farting noises, doesn't she Jim?'

Mum wasn't listening to us. She was listening to something else. I started to listen. It sounded like a giant bluebottle trying to get out of a closed window.

When she opened the car door it sounded louder and when we finally got into the house it was louder still.

'What is the noise Mummy?' asked Gabe.

Mum put Anna down in her car seat in the corner of the living room and we followed her into the kitchen. Jenny was standing by the window, so at first she was blocking our view out to the garden. As we walked into the room Jenny turned to face us. As soon as she moved we could see that the bluebottle was a chainsaw and the chainsaw was making its way through the trunk of the cherry blossom with my dad holding it steady to guide it.

Mum had been so still all this time; in the shopping centre, in the car, in the house. But as soon as she saw Dad with the chainsaw she practically ran across the kitchen and out into the garden towards Dad and the tree.

We couldn't hear her over the noise of the chainsaw but we could see that she was yelling. She was waving and shouting and telling Dad to stop. He had orange things over his ears like a DJ so he couldn't hear Mum either.

'Do you boys want a drink?' asked Jenny. 'And a biscuit? Did you get anything nice at the shops?'

I like Jenny. I do like her. But sometimes I wonder what kind of planet she comes from. The kind of planet where everyone pretends that everything's normal when it's clearly not. The kind of planet where you're supposed to just fill your face with custard creams while your parents yell at each other over the sound of a chainsaw.

The bluebottle noise stopped suddenly. And, as if there had to be a sound to replace it, Anna started crying without a second's silence in between.

'I'll just go and see to your sister,' said Jenny. 'You boys stay here. Chainsaws are dangerous.'

She went to the living room to get Anna and we went straight out into the garden to Mum and Dad.

'It's just a reminder,' Dad said. 'Every time we look out into the garden, it's here to remind us what happened to John-Joe.'

He was still holding the chainsaw against the tree, like he was just taking a break before he carried on cutting.

'So you don't want to be reminded of John-Joe,' she yelled back at him. 'You just want to forget him. You just want to chop down this tree like he was never here and everything will be back to normal.'

He put the chainsaw down. He looked up at the tree. Then over to Mum. Then over to us.

He spoke in a quiet voice.

'I don't want to forget John-Joe, of course I don't. But I don't want to be reminded of how he died either. And neither do the boys.'

We didn't say anything.

'No-one has used the garden since John-Joe fell out of the tree,' Dad continued. 'The boys don't play out here, we don't sit out here. You haven't even pegged the washing out on the line. It's like this tree is stopping anyone from coming into the garden because it's a giant reminder of what happened here.'

'So we need to chop it down to forget.'

She sounded just like John-Joe used to sound when he'd come up with some smart remark for answering back.

'No. We need to chop it down so that we're not always seeing this giant symbol of our son's death every time we look out here or set foot in the garden. I've borrowed the chainsaw, I've made a start, I need you to take the boys back inside and let me get on with it now, Marie. I thought you'd be longer at the shops. I thought I'd have it down before you got back.'

Jenny had come out into the garden, carrying Anna.

'What do you think, Jenny?' said Mum, without even turning round to ask the question.

'Well,' Jenny hesitated. 'I can see an argument for and against chopping it down. I think it could be a painful reminder but, on the other hand, if you chop it down it will leave a gap and the place where the tree used to be might end up being reminder enough.'

I looked at the tree. I don't know how long Dad had been cutting it with the chainsaw but there was a giant scar right across the side of it. Like a mouth that wasn't smiling.

'What do you think boys?'

She turned to look at us and walked up to Jenny to take the baby, who grabbed at her hair and clung onto it.

'I want to keep the tree,' said Gabe. He was trying not to cry. 'Jim?'

'I want to keep it too,' I said. 'Sorry Dad, but John-Joe loved that tree. We all love it. You've already hurt it. You've punished it so we can remember how it was the thing that made John-Joe fall and hurt himself.' I couldn't say die, it seemed wrong to say it out loud. We all knew it anyway.

Mum went over to where the tree had been cut and ran her finger along the line the chainsaw had left.

'If you cut the tree down you're taking away the thing that still connects us here with John-Joe. This is the place where he played his last game and the place where he died. How can you want to destroy his memory like that? Why would you think it would be OK to do that? Without even asking me or the boys? Without even telling me?'

'I was just trying to do the right thing,' Dad said. 'I thought it would help to take the tree away. If this tree had never been here…'

Mum walked to him and gave him a one handed hug.

I could see him sobbing and I wanted to go and hug them too but they looked like they were locked away in a different place from us.

'Didn't you mention biscuits, Jenny?' I asked.

'I'm sure we can find one or two in the cupboard for some hungry boys.'

'Can we have two?' asked Gabe. And we both knew that it was John-Joe who always asked for two before the packet was even opened but I let him take on the task of being the biscuit negotiator.

She grinned at us and led us back into the kitchen where she poured us a cup of milk each and took some chocolate digestives out of the cupboard.

Things seemed a bit more back to normal all round that night. Dad said it didn't matter that we hadn't managed to get anything new to wear for the funeral at the shops because we had plenty of clothes and he was sure we'd look smart.

Mum didn't tell him about the boy who'd lost his mum. She said it was noisy and busy and we couldn't find anything we liked.

We had takeout pizza. Gabe and me got to choose which toppings and we had it delivered in those big boxes, with a free bottle of Coke. Jenny left when the food arrived, even though she was invited to stay, and Gabe and me couldn't believe that anyone would want to leave when there was takeout pizza for dinner.

I helped Mum bath Anna and put her to bed and Mum said I was 'a natural' when I made her laugh while she put the shampoo on.

'You really are the very best big brother anyone could wish for,' she said. It made me get that hot, sharp feeling at the back of your throat from not crying, but I couldn't cry for that. Not in front of Mum. It was stupid to feel like crying at that anyway, because it was a nice thing to say.

Gabe and Anna went to bed at normal time but I was allowed to stay up and watch TV until nine and then read in bed for half an hour after that.

I could hear the TV downstairs, and the washing machine going into its fast spin. I couldn't sleep and, even though it had gone dark outside, it still seemed a bit too light.

I got out of bed to see whether the window was open because I was much too warm to sleep.

As I opened the curtain the moon lit up the garden like a spotlight. I pushed the window to open it wider and let the cool air in. There was a scratching noise coming from the garden.

Under the tree, Mum was kneeling on all fours and digging up soil with her hands. I could see her, with her left side facing the house and her eyes looking down at what she was doing. She glanced quickly towards the house and then back at what she was doing.

As I watched, I saw her find the tin we'd used to bury Captain. She took it out of the ground, filled in the hole and walked towards the house with it.

'I'm just going to put the bins out,' she called to Dad. And I heard the bin rattle as she pulled its wheels down the path at the side of the house and onto the pavement at the front.

NINE

In some people's families, after a row or a heart to heart there's a period of reconciliation or at least an acknowledgement of what's been said. Even if it's a sulk or the slow release of residual emotion, there's something. With my mum and I that never happened. If there was even the slightest sign left behind, perhaps a broken mug that she'd thrown against the wall in her frustration, she or I would quietly sweep it away into the bin without ever referencing how it had come to be there. Or sometimes she had a sore throat from shouting and would pop a cough sweet in her mouth, sucking her way back to the status quo with a hint of eucalyptus; a scent that still carries a whiff of anxiety for me.

The day after Mum's tale of my conception and arrival it was just like that. She was loading washing into the machine when I came downstairs and she slammed the door shut and switched the machine to its usual cycle before turning round to ask me if I wanted toast or cereal for breakfast because there wasn't much milk left, so she'd been waiting for me to decide before she chose what to have herself. There were two things implicit in her question: the first was that she wanted cereal but needed me to absolve her of any guilt by telling her I wanted toast. The second was that yesterday's conversation was now over and there would be no continuation of that dialogue and no further reference to it either. If she never mentioned it again and I never referred to it, then it didn't happen.

So I left the house that day feeling as though nothing had happened because in the context of our house, nothing had;

events had been erased and we were starting again from zero. Except the dad that I had dreamed of all my life had been similarly erased; obliterated by an image of a predatory opportunist, which was going to be much more difficult to delete than the memory of our heated conversation.

But Mrs Wilkes had still fired my mum and was still furious with me. And I was still the girl who had brought a vibrator into school. No-one who was in the corridor when Claire had set the thing down to dance around the floor had forgotten that and Mrs Wilkes wasn't about to forget it either.

Predictably, Claire had been eager to engineer the episode to build on her cool credentials, but when it came to taking the consequences from the deputy head for having 'inappropriate' items in school and causing a 'dangerous disturbance' that had blocked the corridor, there was no way she was going down alone.

The 'item' had been confiscated and was now with Mrs Wilkes for safe keeping, we were informed sternly during morning registration. And we were all to understand that no repeat of that episode would be tolerated. We could rest assured that the culprits were in serious trouble. I looked out of the window at the normalness of the school field, wishing I could be somewhere else.

'Marie. Mar-ree. MARIE!'

I'd tuned the room out, and it seemed I could erase everyone else but I couldn't make myself vanish. I looked away from the empty field to the crowded classroom.

'Marie, Mrs Edgar has asked to see you. You'd better take your things, first bell will be going in a minute.'

So I gathered up my bag and walked slowly to the classroom door with every eye in the room following my usually largely invisible body as I left the room for the deputy head's office.

When I got there, Claire was already sitting outside on a brown plastic chair, with her school bag at her feet and her eyes firmly fixed on the floor.

'Am I supposed to sit here and wait or knock for Mrs Edgar?'

Claire said nothing.

'Claire? What did they say? Do they want me to wait with you or knock and go in?'

She looked up at me, still leaning forward with her elbows on her knees but turning her head like a curious tortoise to sneer at me.

'Look, I'm only sitting here because of you. They're calling my mum because of you. And it looks like I can wave goodbye to Saturday night at Becca's house while her parents are away because of you, when pretty much the only other person who won't be there is you because you weren't invited. So don't go asking me for favours. I'm not in the mood for favours. I'm definitely not in the mood for doing you any favours.'

'I was just asking—' I interrupted

'Well don't. Don't ask me for favours, don't ask me for information, don't ask me for anything. I'm not interested. I'm not listening. I can't even see you.'

She turned her head back to look down at the floor again and twisted a silver ring off the finger of one hand, planted it on the same finger of her other hand and then repeated the exercise. The tops of her right index and middle finger were all scabby and sore where she'd been picking the skin and all her nails, painted bright purple, were bitten down so far that her flesh seemed to bulge over the top of them with a thin red line to mark the boundary between skin and nail. She smelt sweet with a fruity-floral body spray that was half pleasant, half nausea-inducing and the scent followed me as I stepped away from her.

I knocked on the door.

'Come in.'

'Miss, I'm sorry, I wasn't sure if you wanted me to knock or wait outside,' I said, practically falling into the room over the straps of my rucksack, which were dangling on the floor as I heaved it into the room by the loop at the top.

'Claire said she didn't know either, so I thought it was best if I just knocked and asked and if you want me to sit outside I can just go out and sit outside the room on the chairs with Claire till you're ready. But I just didn't want you to think I hadn't turned up. I came as soon as they told me. I came straight here.'

'Just close the door behind you and come and sit down please, Marie. I've already had a chat with Claire so I'd like to hear what you both have to say before I bring her back in.'

Mrs Edgar's voice was calm and comforting, just like it always was. No-one had ever heard her shout or raise her voice even just a little bit. She'd always been kind, like a TV mum who knows the right thing to say and has a glass of juice and a healthy snack ready on the table when the children get home from school. She probably baked and played Scrabble, and gave money to homeless people. She definitely went to church, because I'd seen her there. Not that going to church is a sign of much, but it should be. She almost definitely knitted too, judging by her wardrobe of brightly coloured jumpers and cardigans. Or perhaps she had an elderly mother who still knitted for her little girl, even though her little girl must be pushing fifty. Today she was wearing a home-made cardigan in a mustard-coloured cable knit, with a brown wool skirt that was flat at the front and pleated at the back like a kilt.

'Take a seat Marie, and try not to look so worried.'

It was exactly what she'd said to me the other times I'd been in her office; the time my mum hadn't paid for the school trip to London and she said it was OK because school had money available for situations like this. The time when I'd seen Joe Kirkby and Connor Brady kicking Paul Jessop by the sports equipment storeroom and she'd said it was OK because everything I told her would be confidential. The time I started my periods and had nothing to use and she handed me a bag with some sanitary towels in and gave me an apple out of her handbag because it's important to eat well 'when Aunt Flo's visiting'. I knew she was kind but this time round I wasn't there because something was wrong, I was there because I'd done something wrong. It was hard enough for me to accept kindness at the best of times; being met by kindness now made me feel even more wretched that I had been stupid and thoughtless and dishonest.

I sat down opposite her and she gave me one of her reassuring smiles.

'Now Marie, you know why you're here, don't you?'

'Yes Miss. I'm really sorry Miss.'

'I have no doubt that you're sorry, Marie, students generally are when something they've said or done leads them to be sitting here in my office. Hindsight is a wonderful thing and if more of you could picture the consequences before pushing ahead with the actions I'd spend a lot less time having conversations like this and a lot more time drinking cups of tea with my colleagues in the staff room.'

I said nothing. Sometimes it's obvious when you're expected to listen without speaking.

'As I said, I have already spoken to Claire and she has given me a very clear account of events that suggests she has been your pawn in all of this and has been manipulated and coerced by you to get involved in an enterprise that was at best silly and, at worst, rather cruel.'

'Miss, I—'

'Marie. Remember that I have known you girls for more than four years now. More in fact if you include all the Sundays I have seen you engrossed in a colouring book as a tiny tot with your mother in church. I am also rather less wet behind the ears than children seem to think I am. I think, sometimes, that students imagine I have spent my whole life locked in this room knitting jumpers and reading books. They don't imagine for a minute that I was once a fifteen-year-old who also had to deal with the twists and turns of navigating through adolescent traumas. I have, Marie, and let me tell you that I have learned a thing or two along the way; from my own experience and from all the weird and wonderful fact and fantasy that has been presented to me by students down the years.'

She looked at me for some acknowledgement that I had heard and understood what she'd just said.

'Yes Miss.'

'Now Marie,' she perched herself on the desk facing me, with her legs stretched out in front of her and her hands clutching the edges of the furniture so that her arms were braced as if for impact. 'Claire tells me that you found the vibrator in Mrs Wilkes' drawer while you were in her home accompanying your mother in her work as a cleaner. She tells me that you decided to take the item from Mrs Wilkes' house and bring it into school—'

'Miss, it—'

'Let me finish please, Marie. Claire tells me that you planted the item in her bag without her knowledge and that, as she was leaving school, she reached into her bag to find her bus pass, accidentally switched the item on and brought it out of the bag, placing it on the floor to see what it was and it was at this point that a crowd gathered.

'I have spoken to Mrs Wilkes about this episode and she, as you can imagine, is quite mortified about the whole thing but relieved that the school at large does not know about the connection between her and the item. I would like to call upon you and Claire to keep it that way. I think discretion is the least you owe her under the circumstances.'

'Yes Miss.'

'Mrs Wilkes has also informed me that you did, indeed, have access to her home as she had hired your mother as a cleaner – an arrangement which I believe has now been terminated due to this incident.'

'Yes Miss.'

'So the fact that you took the item does not appear to be in dispute. However, I would like to understand from you the reasons why you took it and what happened after you took it. Can you fill me in on all of that now please Marie?'

It was one of those times when you're completely lost and there are two paths; it's signposted – kind of – but the signs are unclear. I could either end up more lost, more alone and even further up shit creek, or I could take a short, if treacherous road to where I wanted to be; off Claire's blacklist and potentially even part of her crowd of cool and popular. Both paths were riddled with risk and I had just seconds to weigh up my options. I could tell the truth, make sure Claire got her share of the blame and risk incurring her wrath for the whole of the rest of the school year, potentially that meant two more years' of sixth form too; or I could go with Claire's version and hope that she'd see my choice as cool and brave, give me some credit and give me a leg up the social ladder.

'Well, Marie?'

'Could I have a glass of water please Miss?'

Mrs Edgar let out an impatient sigh. 'Stay there. I will be back in one minute.'

I had thought I was buying myself some time to decide but all I'd really done was prolong my indecision while she was out of the room. I hoped, perhaps, the water would loosen the right words in my throat and they would just flow like liquid instead of me having to think them through. I looked out of the window to the dismal playing field where a muddy hockey lesson was coming to an end. A magpie landed on the window ledge and looked out, seemingly examining the same view. I scanned the bookshelves and the walls feeling desperate in case I blurted out the wrong choice when Mrs Edgar came back in with my water. On the shelf next to me was a calendar, one of those where you tear off a page every day. The page it was showing was over a week old and it said: 'A generous person will prosper; whoever refreshes others will be refreshed.' – Proverbs 11:25.

'Water,' said Mrs Edgar, coming back into the room with the silence of a ninja assassin.

'Sorry Marie, I didn't mean to make you jump. I know you must be anxious but we just need to get this bit out of the way and then we can move on and get back to normal. Now have a sip and tell me in your own time.'

She handed me the water and went back to her former position on the desk, looking straight at me as I put the plastic cup shakily to my mouth and took a big gulp.

'Claire is telling the truth, Miss,' I said. 'I found the thing in Mrs Wilkes' drawer when I was being nosey in her house while I was helping my mum clean and I thought Claire would find it funny if it appeared in her bag. She's always laughing about that kind of thing, Miss, and I'm always trying to be included and join in with all the banter, you know, but the other girls don't see me like that, they think I'm all buttoned up and boring. I just wanted to be a bit less boring and a bit more in with the cool crowd for once and I thought Claire would see the funny side and we'd have a laugh and then I could just put it back next time my mum was at Mrs Wilkes'. She's there once a week. She used to be there once a week, I mean.'

It wasn't really a lie, it was more of a part-truth. It was the best way I could find to avoid dropping Claire in it and still try and protect myself from the blame.

'Are you sure that's how it happened, Marie?'

'Yes Miss.'

'You know, you should never feel under pressure to fit in, Marie. I know it's hard. I do know it's hard, but it's important to know who you are and not try to be someone you're not.'

She had started pacing the room and for a moment I thought she was coming over to give me a hug, but she was just moving to help her think what to say. She spotted the calendar, saw that the page on display was from a few days earlier and tore off the spent dates, throwing the pages in the bin as she stepped past the desk.

She sat down again. 'When you try to fit in, instead of focusing on who you are and who you want to be, you're betraying yourself Marie. You're betraying your own heart. And, hard as it may be to believe now, one day you will realise that fitting in with these people in this place is not all that important. This is a moment in time for you. These people are not important, they are not everything you will experience in your life. You are a bright girl, Marie, bright and honest and hard-working, you can go a long way in your life. You can achieve anything you set your mind to. But some of these people you're so keen to fit in with, they don't have that potential – I say this candidly, you understand, Marie: I expect what's said in this room to stay in this room?'

I nodded.

'Don't work too hard at trying to fit in round here,' she waved her arm around the room to include the whole school building and shooed off the magpie in the process. 'There,' she said, emphatically, gesturing out to the playing field where the last of the muddy girls were dragging their hockey sticks behind them as they ambled back to the changing rooms. 'Out there is where you need to make your way, out there where the rules are different and people like you can really shine. In here is not real life, it's a transition, a purgatory where you earn your skills and your battle stripes for the real deal.

'I cannot stress enough Marie that changing who you are to fit in at school is not a good choice. Ten years from now, you will not care who these people are. Twenty years from now you probably won't even remember their names or recognise them if they sat next to you on a bus.

'Having said that, I do understand the pressures on young people, of course I do. And I do appreciate how brave you have been in owning up to your part – your surprisingly and disappointingly large part – in this whole fiasco. Under the circumstances and given that the whole sorry episode has already had an impact on your mother's work and, no doubt, caused some serious conversations for you at home, I see no real reason to escalate the punishment more than necessary.'

She clapped her hands together as though closing a book at the end of a sermon.

Again she walked towards me and I thought she might be coming to give me a hug but she opened the door behind me and called Claire into the room.

'Bring your chair in with you Claire, or there will be nowhere for you to sit.'

Claire struggled into the room, awkwardly trying to fit through the door with her bag extending her girth behind her and the chair taking up space in front.

'Never mind, never mind,' said Mrs Edgar, checking her watch and sighing impatiently. 'This won't take long.'

Claire put the chair back in its place outside Mrs Edgar's office and came into the room. Mrs Edgar gestured for me to stand and took the chair from behind me, moving it into a corner.

Claire glared at me and I looked down at the floor, noticing that the purple nail varnish she'd been wearing earlier was now mostly in flakes on her skirt where she'd chipped it off while she'd been waiting.

'Girls, this is a sorry affair and we need to draw a line under it. You both need to learn from it. Claire, I expect you to be more inclusive of Marie so that she's not tempted to do such foolish things to attract your attention. The two of you have known each other a long time and that's a very valuable commodity. Meanwhile, Marie, I think I have made myself clear already. To put it bluntly, this was a stupid thing to do: you should not be taking anything without permission, no matter how trivial and humorous it might seem at the time. Nor should you be opening someone else's bag or putting anything in their bag without their permission.

'I expect both of you to write a letter of apology to Mrs Wilkes, which I expect you to deliver to me first thing tomorrow morning. After that, as long as Mrs Wilkes is willing to let the matter drop, I suggest we all move on, wisely, kindly and in the spirit of friendship. I shall be keeping my eye on you girls and I don't want to see any more of your shenanigans. Off you go.'

Neither Claire nor I said a word as we picked up our bags to leave. As I put mine over my shoulder I knocked the calendar off the shelf; I picked it up off the floor.

'I'll take that,' said Mrs Edgar. 'Off you go.'

I handed her the calendar. It said: 'Lying lips are an abomination to the Lord, but those who deal faithfully are His delight.' – Proverbs 12:22

TEN

I don't know what time it was when I finally decided to get up. I'd slept. I think I had anyway. It can be hard to tell the difference between asleep and awake in the dark. Sometimes, things you thought were real can turn out to be dreams or just stuff that's been sloshing around your brain while you've been lying in your bed. And sometimes stuff you thought was just a dream turns out to be real.

So I wasn't even sure if I'd seen Mum dig up our magpie. Or if I'd heard her put it in the outside bin. But the idea of it was keeping me awake. It was in my head whirling round and round in a long, unbreakable loop so that I just had to shut it up.

As I got out of bed, I wished I was still small enough to climb into bed with Mum and Dad. Not that long ago I could creep across the landing and open their bedroom door the tiniest bit and Mum would wake up and just lift the duvet to let me in. I never had to tell her what was wrong.

I couldn't even remember what had been wrong all those times. Nothing probably. Nothing much anyway. Not compared to now.

I felt like waking Gabe but then I'd have to explain to him in words. It wouldn't be fair to wake him, but it was so dark and quiet on my own.

First I had to check that I'd not dreamed it. I opened the curtain and looked out. The clouds had smudged some of the brightness out of the moon and I couldn't see the ground to check whether the tin had been dug up or not.

I could go out to the garden and check in the morning, but by that time the bin men might have been and if the tin had been thrown away it would be gone. And anyway, if I waited until morning Mum would be up and I wouldn't be able to get it.

Going out to the bin seemed like a stupid idea but I was awake, I was up and I couldn't let them take Captain to the tip. What would John-Joe say? The dead bird and my dead brother were connected and I couldn't save either of them but I could rescue Captain from the bin, I could at least keep him with me and protect him from any more damage, just like I'd helped to protect the tree.

So I found my slippers and my dressing gown and I crept out of the bedroom. The light was on in Gabe's room; Mum always lets him keep it on at night, even after she and Dad have gone to bed. That's why Mum said John-Joe and me had to share a room instead of John-Joe and Gabe, because the two of them were like Jack Sprat and his wife when it came to the light on in the night; John-Joe always insisted on total darkness.

I could hear the sound of sleep in the super-quiet house but I still made sure I crept slowly down each stair. Then across the hall to the kitchen and across the kitchen to the patio doors.

I kept thinking something would stop me from actually going out there. But the key was in the cutlery drawer where it was supposed to be and it turned in the lock just like you'd expect. And even though the security light came on when I stepped outside and I had to squint to get used to the brightness, nothing happened. No-one came. It was just me and the dark garden.

It was funny being in the garden in the dark. I've lived in the same house all my life but I'd never been alone in the garden in the dark before. It smelt of green and of summer and it sounded like I was a million miles from anywhere. But the tree was still there, with the day's drama illuminated on its trunk for a few seconds before the timer switched the light off again. And underneath, I could just about see Captain's grave. It was clear that Mum had done her best to put it back the way it was before but the stones we'd laid out so carefully to mark the spot hadn't been put back quite right. John-Joe had been so pedantic about lining them up in rows in size order but now they were a bit wonky. A bit more Gabe.

So the tin with the dead bird in it must be in the bin and now I wasn't sure what to do. Perhaps Mum was right, perhaps getting rid of it was for the best. But if we needed to keep the tree, like she said, why didn't we need to keep the poor dead bird where it was?

'John-Joe, what do you think I should do?'

I said the words out loud, not to get an answer, just to feel a bit less alone in the dark.

'What do you think, John-Joe? What's for the best?'

There was silence in the garden. Nothing moved. I didn't hear words but in my head I knew the answer as clearly as though John-Joe had whispered it in my ear.

When I walked round to the front of the house I could see much better because of the streetlight across the road. It wouldn't have mattered anyway though because, when I lifted the bin lid, the tin was just sitting there on top of the black bag of rubbish. I took it out and closed the bin lid really quietly. It was a bit like when John-Joe and I used to play spies and set each other challenges to hide things in Mum and Dad's bedroom or take food out of the kitchen without getting caught. We'd trained for this.

With the magpie in my hand and complete confidence that I was doing the right thing, I made my way back; through the gate into the garden, across the patio under the spotlight of the security light and back into the kitchen, locking the door behind me and putting the key back where it belonged. I crept up the stairs, missing out the one that sometimes creaks if you step in just the right place, and tiptoed slowly across the landing.

The light was still on in Gabe's room, just like always, and I poked my head round the door just to check on him, like Dad sometimes does if he comes home late or he's up in the night. Gabe was asleep, just like he was supposed to be. Just like I was supposed to be.

'What are you doing up?'

Dad had his hand on my shoulder and I shot my head round as though I'd just murdered someone and been caught with a knife in my hand dripping blood.

I thought of about a million lies in the space of a second but I didn't need to use any of them because Dad came up with a reason for me.

'I know it's hard to sleep sometimes. It's hard for me to sleep sometimes too.'

The words 'since John-Joe died' were hidden in the sentence like punctuation that you can only see when something's written down.

'Don't worry about Gabe or Anna, or your Mum or me, everyone's fine. Everyone's going to be fine. You don't need to check.'

'OK Dad.'

I wasn't sure how to move without him seeing the tin. Then I'd have to explain how Mum had dug it up and how I'd been out to the garden and the bin. I'd have to explain why I needed to rescue it. I wasn't sure I even knew why.

'Do you want me to tuck you back in?'

'Can I have a drink of water?'

He sighed, but no parent ever says no to water.

'Ok, you get back in your bed and I'll get you some water.'

He smiled at me and went downstairs to get my drink. In my room I turned on the lamp and put the tin under John-Joe's pillow just in case Dad noticed it under mine.

I was only just under the covers when he reappeared with a glass of water and a biscuit.

'Don't tell your Mum about the biscuit or I'll be in trouble for feeding you sugar in the night.'

'OK Dad, I won't tell.'

And then he sat on my bed and we both ate chocolate digestives.

'Do you know the best thing you can do with a chocolate digestive?'

I shook my head.

'Well, you need two chocolate digestives for each person, actually,' Dad said, pausing with his biscuit in the air like exhibit A.

'The very best thing you can do with them is toast marshmallows on an open fire and then take two chocolate digestives, chocolate sides together, and make a sandwich with the marshmallow in the middle.'

'That does sound nice.'

'It's the best recipe in the world ever. The marshmallow melts the chocolate and the biscuit is just strong enough to hold the marshmallows' squidge in place.'

'When can we do that Dad?'

'Soon, son,' he said. 'One day.'

He looked at his half-eaten biscuit like an alien wondering what is was.

'So do you think you can sleep now that you've got a belly full of biscuit and you've wet your whistle with corporation pop?'

I like it when he talks in Dad-speak. It feels like the world is all lined up in the right order and everyone's following the rules.

'Yes, I'm sure I'll be fine now.'

'Lamp on or off?'

'On. Is that OK? I might read for a bit.'

'That's fine. But no more wandering around, OK?'

'OK.'

I wondered if he knew I'd been outside. I wondered if I'd left any signs in the kitchen. If he knew, he clearly wasn't going to mention it, so that was fine.

'Good night, Jim.'

'Night, Dad.'

I lay in bed listening to him go to the toilet, then back to his and Mum's room. I waited, listening in the quiet for the sound of sleeping.

When I was sure that the whole house was asleep again, I got out of bed and lifted John-Joe's pillow to see the tin. It was a bit dirty but otherwise it was just as it had been that day when we put it into the hole and took turns throwing blossom on top.

I was going to open it to peek inside but then John-Joe told me not to.

'Don't open it,' he said, 'if you open it the soul will fly away and it won't be able to protect you.'

I looked behind me to see him but he wasn't there.

'So what should I do?' I said the words in my head. There was no-one in the room, there didn't seem any point in saying them out loud. Anyway, I couldn't risk waking anyone up.

'Just keep the tin where it is. Keep it hidden. Keep it safe.'

John-Joe was always right about everything. I put the tin back on the bed and put the pillow back on top of it. But that didn't seem enough.

I knelt by the bed and closed my hands to point to heaven like we did at school

'Please Captain, keep everyone safe. Mum and Dad and Gabe and Anna and me. And if it's possible to send John-Joe back, can we have him back please.'

The words said silently inside my head were answered by a thundering emptiness that filled the bedroom. I climbed back into bed and switched off the lamp.

When I woke up in the morning with the sound of the bin truck crunching, then pausing, then crunching again outside, I had to check that the tin with the magpie was still there under John-Joe's pillow. It was.

ELEVEN

I had never been to a funeral before. There was Captain's funeral and funerals on TV but this was the first actual funeral of a real human person and it was my little brother's.

When Nanna died, Dad asked me did I want to go to the funeral, but I didn't. I was only six or so then, and John-Joe and Gabe were staying at home with Jenny because they were too young, so I just decided to stay at home with them. I was a little bit worried that there might be some kind of announcement about how she died, too, and I might have to apologise in front of everyone, so I chickened out

After Mum and Dad had gone, though, I wished I'd gone too. It felt like I'd said no to a special treat; a chance to go out on a trip with just the two of them. When they came home, Dad had a biscuit tin like the ones you have at Christmas. It was full of sandwiches and cakes and we were allowed to choose whatever we wanted. I felt even more like I'd missed out on something special because, if that was just the leftovers, there'd clearly been lots of treats.

John-Joe's funeral was a bit like a party too. There were even balloons on the table when we had something to eat afterwards. But there were no games, there was no music and there were no presents. It looked just like the kind of get together where there would be presents but everyone arrived empty-handed, wearing black or colours that were nearly black. It was like a party that someone had stopped organising half way through.

People still laughed though. People still drank beer and chatted and kissed each other on the cheek. And Dad went round shaking people's hands and thanking them for coming. Some of the people that turned up were parents of our friends from school but not many of their kids came with them. Just Ivan from John-Joe's class and his annoying little sister. John-Joe didn't even like Ivan and Ivan's mum kept apologising that she'd had to bring them because she had no-one to leave them with. Ivan's sister ate a lot of crisps and cake. I think they mostly came for the buffet.

John-Joe's friends David and Damian were there though and I knew he would have been glad about that. He was the only one in the whole class that could tell the twins apart without looking to see which one was right handed and which was left handed. They both came up and shook my hand, David with his right and Damian with his left, and they told me they were sorry for my loss.

That's what the undertaker had said when he arrived to take us to the church, too. John-Joe was in the car in front with flowers spelling out his name on the side of the coffin. The man opened the door of the car behind and stood beside it, waiting for us all to get in so that he could shut the door behind us. Dad put Anna and her car seat in first and then told me to hop in.

'Can't I go in the car with John-Joe?' I asked.

'We're not allowed to do that, Jim,' Dad said, 'we'll all go together in this one.'

'But John-Joe will be travelling there all alone with strangers if we all go in this one and he goes in that one.' I pointed out.

'For goodness sake, Jim, isn't this hard enough?' said Mum. 'There's not even enough room for you to travel in that car.'

'I could sit next to the driver.'

'No, you can't. You can't sit next to the driver, you can sit in this car with me and do as you're told.'

'Dad?'

Dad looked at Mum and then at the undertaker who was still standing by the car door like a statue of a butler, pretending he couldn't hear us.

115

'Would it be possible for my son to travel in the hearse with the…with his brother?' Dad asked.

Mum let out a big sigh like the ones you have to do at the doctor's when he puts the stethoscope on your back to listen to your lungs. She climbed into the car, pulling Gabe in behind her.

The butler finally spoke.

'I'm sure it can be arranged,' he said, winking at me. 'I'll have a word with the boss.'

So I travelled to the church in the hearse, keeping John-Joe company all the way there. If his soul is still floating around feeling attached to his body, I thought, he's bound to be scared. I knew Mum was cross with me for not doing as I was told, especially when she was so stressed and upset and everything, but how could I not stand up for John-Joe now, when he couldn't speak up for himself?

Mum didn't speak to me when we arrived at church. She didn't even look at me. She busied herself getting Anna out of the car and I waited for them at the door but she just walked past me and stood clutching Anna to her chest when Father O'Connor told her he was sorry for her loss.

'I'd thought the next service I'd be doing for your family would be this little one's baptism,' he said, drawing a little cross on Anna's head with his thumb. 'There is nothing harder to process than the loss of a child,' he added. 'Let's get through today and perhaps then you'd like to talk and let me help you find solace in your faith,' he said.

Mum said nothing. But she turned to me then. 'Help us find a seat Jim, that's a good lad.'

Dad had said I wasn't tall enough to help carry the coffin, even though I'm getting nearly as tall as Mum. He carried it in with two of the men from the funeral company, Grandad, Uncle Robert and Dad's friend Mike from when he was at University. I was allowed to walk behind with the flowers that spelt out John-Joe's name and Dad helped me put them down on top of the coffin at the front of the church so that everyone could see. It was like the flower name tag had to be there just in case anyone forgot who was in the box.

It may have been Tuesday lunchtime but the funeral service wasn't really all that different from any old Sunday morning in church. There were hymns, there were readings, we stood up and sat down a lot and we all lined up to take Holy Communion. Except, there in the middle of it, John-Joe was lying dead in a wooden box instead of wriggling on the pew beside me and teasing Gabe because he wasn't old enough to take the host. I kept looking at the coffin and trying to imagine that John-Joe wasn't really inside it because he was in the flowers and the trees and the air all around us just like Mum said he was. But really I knew he was in there. And there was nothing I could do to get him out again.

Dad gave a speech about John-Joe that started with a story about the day he was born. It was a story I'd heard lots of times before and every time I'd heard it I was jealous because there's not much of a story about when I was born. They went to the hospital, I was born and I was the most beautiful thing Mum had ever seen, the end. Boring.

John-Joe's story was much more exciting. Mum was in the supermarket with me when John-Joe decided he was going to arrive early and Mum had had to ask the lady at the fish counter to get help because she couldn't walk back to the car park and she had me and a trolley full of shopping and the battery was dead on her mobile phone.

The store manager said he'd take her to hospital and they left me in the staff room with the lady from the in-store bakery who'd just come off shift. The manager pulled up outside the hospital and ran inside to get help and by the time he came back outside my mum was just bending down to pick up the baby from between her feet on the floor of the car.

'So I missed my son's birth, just like I missed his death,' my Dad said. His eyes were red and he paused to take the deepest of deep breaths. 'John-Joe was an extraordinary boy from the moment he was born. He wasn't ever average and he was constantly delighted to be different.

'We would have preferred it if he'd just lived an uneventful childhood that carried on into a safe and unremarkable adulthood so that he could have died long after us at a ripe old age. But John-Joe was never average, never a boy you could second guess. He packed a lot of living into his eight years and we'll always be grateful for every minute of them.'

Dad only just got to the end of the sentence and Mum was sobbing quietly into the top of Anna's head. He came and sat down with us again and the organ started playing for the next hymn because no-one could say another word that wasn't written down on a sheet in front of us.

There were more handshakes and people saying how sorry they were outside the church and lots of waiting around as though a photographer was going to show up and take family pictures, like they do at a wedding.

But the waiting around was just so that they could get the coffin back out of the church and into the car. There was a graveyard at the church but Mum said we had to go to the cemetery and it all seemed like so much fuss and messing about. I couldn't say that to her though. All I could do was ask her did she think it would be OK if I travelled in the car with John-Joe again and she just hugged me and said that would be fine.

It was sunny in the graveyard. It looked like the kind of place we might go to play football or collect conkers in the autumn and they'd made a space for John-Joe just under a massive horse chestnut tree so that when the conkers start to fall he'll get the best of them.

That's what I was thinking about when they passed me the bag of dirt and waited for me to take out a handful. And, as I took my turn to throw a handful of dirt onto the coffin, I thought how much nicer we had done things for Captain. How much better it would have been if we'd all made cards in the church and put them on top of the coffin instead. Not that John-Joe had anything against dirt, he'd much rather go to bed with a dirty face than a clean one, but it felt wrong to throw soil on top of him. It felt mean.

And that's when it happened for the first time. I thought about how mean it was that we should shower John-Joe's coffin with dirt and, from nowhere, it started to rain. Not just a bit of rain or a drizzle that feels like nothing until you find yourself wet through: this was like someone emptying the mop bucket. We were all drenched within seconds and the soil we'd just thrown onto the coffin just washed off completely.

Nobody moved though. Father O'Connor talked faster and Gabe shivered and complained that he was getting wet, as though no-one else had noticed it was raining, but everyone just stood there, waiting for the priest to stop talking or the rain to stop falling, whichever came first.

I wasn't sure whether John-Joe or Captain had sent the rain, or maybe both of them had. I knew at least one of them was listening to me.

TWELVE

'What just happened in there?'

We had walked in silence with a suitably contrite gait as far as the link corridor that led to the dining hall before either of us had really breathed, let alone uttered a word.

'It looks like she's let us off with just a letter of apology to Mrs Wilkes,' I answered.

Claire stopped suddenly and turned towards me, forcing a girl behind us to swerve round us urgently to avoid a collision.

'You are fucking kidding me?'

'Nope, I'm pretty sure that's the end of that, as long as we write something suitably gushing and sincere in our letters.'

'Marie Murphy, you are the jammiest, most sweet-talking, detention-swerving genius on the planet. How did you manage that?'

We carried on walking to avoid a bottle-neck in the surge of bodies heading towards the dining hall for first break and I explained to Claire how I had confirmed her version of events.

'I gave her some sob story about wanting to fit in and laid it on thick about how my attempts at a light-hearted joke had back fired and she bought it. The whole violin concerto.'

'There is no way she would have let me off if I'd owned up to everything,' said Claire, and we both knew she was right. 'If I'd gone in there and confessed to stealing something from a teacher's house, planting it in someone else's bag and doing it all just to raise a giggle in the classroom, I'd be on my way to a suspension, not writing a measly letter of apology. You must have hypnotised her or something.'

'It's not that,' I hesitated choosing my words carefully. I wanted to explain that I'd not done anything all that rocket science-y, but I didn't want to hand back the Brownie points I'd earned with Claire by offending or upsetting her. 'I think it's just that I'm never in trouble. She sees me as someone who works hard and is, let's say, socially challenged but academically capable at school...'

'Oh yeah, and how does she see me?'

'As someone who's always at the centre of everything,' I answered cautiously, trying to embed compliments in my explanation. 'She sees you as a leader and because you've been in trouble before, she'd assumed that you were to blame and I was the innocent bystander before we even went in there. The world works like that; people make assumptions about other people, opinions get fixed at a moment in time and people don't look past what they think they already know. That's why defendants' criminal records aren't revealed in court until after the verdict...'

'Aren't they?'

'No. The point is, she'd already created a narrative where you were to blame and I was your unwitting accomplice and she'd already decided to throw the book at you and let me off lightly. So when I took the blame for the whole thing—'

'Is that what you did?'

'Yes. When I took the blame for the whole thing, she couldn't throw the book at you any more and she'd already decided to go easy on me so ta-da! We both get off with a gentle rap on the knuckles and a stupid letter to write.'

By this time, we had arrived in the dining hall and, instead of abandoning me to take her seat with the cool kids and the eager boys she usually flirted with and coquettishly stole crisps and chocolate from at lunchtime, Claire had sat down next to me. Her usual crowd was actually openly staring at us.

'So basically, I got let off the hook because you're such a girly-swot-arse-licker?'

'That's not exactly how I like to describe myself but, yes, I suppose, in a nutshell. And because I lied to her and took the blame to save both our skins instead of just my own, even though she's got a full gory Jesus on the cross looking down on you while you're being told off.'

'I know, right? It's a bit like 'God's watching, so tell the truth now.'

And that was the nearest to a thank you I was going to get before she took a sandwich out of her bag, and extracted half from the foil, peeling off the slices of tomato and taking a large bite of the bread and cheese that was left after her inspection.

For the rest of break we talked like ordinary friends. Or rather she talked, often with her mouth full and in the middle of my sentences, and I just kept biting silent congratulations to myself into my apple for making the right choice in Mrs Edgar's office, despite the presence of Jesus and the risk of the full weight of the school's behaviour policy landing on my head. For all the chat I'd given Claire about the equity my previous clean record had given me, it could easily have counted for nothing if Mrs Edgar had been in a tougher and less gullible mood.

'And the best news of all is,' she said, waving her crusts at me, 'the best news of all is that if I'm not getting a phone call home then I won't be grounded and I can still go to Becca's party while her parents are away this weekend. So the big question now is, what am I going to wear?'

Claire grinned at me with a mouthful of crusts, and sneered at the sad looking bits of tomato as though someone else had left them there.

'Christopher Morris will be there, I'm pretty sure he will be anyway.' She looked around the dining hall, apparently scanning for signs of Christopher Morris. 'He fancies you, you know? You probably don't know, do you? You wouldn't spot that a boy fancied you if he lay at your feet naked with a red rose in his mouth. You should come. To Becca's. Saturday night. Do you think your mum would give us a lift? We could go together.

I could do your make up. Go on, what's the worst that can happen? Live a little. COME ON....'

She was like one of those films they show you to warn you about how easy it is to be persuaded to take drugs for the first time.

'I've not been invited.'

'You don't need to be invited Marie, it's a party; anyone that knows it's happening can turn up. Anyway, you'll be with me and I'm invited so you can be my plus one, like at a wedding.'

'But my mum will never let me go.'

'So don't tell her. Actually if you don't tell her then she can't give us a lift. Are you sure she wouldn't let you? She might be chuffed that you're going to a party. You'll be with me. She knows me. She knows my mum. Do you really think she won't want you to go?'

'I don't know. Depends what mood she's in. And don't forget she does know about the whole vibrator thing because the evil Wilkes cow has fired her and given it to her with both barrels so the goodwill and favours cupboard is distinctly bare at home.'

'What?'

'I mean I'm in the dog house. You know, I have some sucking up to do with my mum.'

'So work on it. Look, it's only Tuesday and you have until Saturday to square things at home. Up to you how you play it; if you want to tell her you're staying over at mine, that's fine, my mum won't mind and we can get ready at mine so she thinks we're just having a quiet night in with a family pack of popcorn and a PG-rated film if you like. We'll work out getting there.'

It was weird to think that, only a week ago, Claire wouldn't have acknowledged my existence in the corridor. Now here she was sitting with me at first break instead of her entourage, and not only inviting me to a party but insisting that I come, and finding ways to get round any parental objections.

The bell rang for the end of break.

'Shit, I've got French and she makes you apologise in front of everyone in French if you turn up late,' said Claire, scooping up her bag and coat in what seemed like one seamless motion.

'Just promise me you'll think about it. It's about time you cast off some of that arse-licky butter-wouldn't-meltness and learned to be a proper teenage girl.'

And with that she was gone, chattering to her incredulous friends as she left the dining hall and leaving me wondering what had happened, if it had happened, and what it all meant.

All through Wednesday and Thursday I tied myself in all kinds of complicated knots, looking for an ulterior motive and a plot to pay me back for getting her into trouble. But it was clear from the way she chatted to me at break, called me over to sit with her mates at lunch time and generally treated me like a non-invisible human of the same species that what she'd taken from the whole episode was me getting her off a detention and a phone call home, rather than me being the cause of her waiting for the full force of school justice to fall upon her.

The magical thing about it all was that the change in the way this one person looked at me and talked to me created an instant change in the way everyone else behaved towards me too. It was as though I'd had some overnight metamorphosis and the old, ugly caterpillar me had been replaced by an appealing butterfly without me so much as having a haircut or changing my shoes. When I looked in the mirror, I saw exactly the same dull used-to-be-blonde hair and could do with a hit of vitamin D complexion as before. When the others in my class, and especially the other girls in my class, saw me, they clearly saw something different. Something more like them.

And the more it became clear that they saw me as something like them, the more I was something like them. I made no physical changes to my appearance, but the way I was made me look and feel different. I started to pick my feet up as I walked along corridors in a way that my mum had nagged at me to do for years but I had never quite managed. I stood up to my full height and walked as though I had somewhere to be, instead of ambling along as though following a tour guide round a stately home. The fringe that had been the camouflage behind which I'd made myself invisible all through school became my toolkit for expressing surprise, conveying humour and flirting with boys who flocked round Claire and her friends.

It turned out I was quite funny. It turned out Claire's friends – Becca, Lorna, Fi and Ems – were not that bad and not all that stupid after all. And it was clear that there was a code for entry into this world, like the combination teachers needed for the touchpad to enter the staff room, which I had simply been missing all that time. There was nothing wrong with how I was or what I looked like, I just hadn't unlocked the secret to knowing that until now.

But it wasn't a free pass. With Claire's blessing, I had earned my first step on the ladder to inclusion and belonging, but as the week passed, it became obvious that I had to prove that I belonged there. I had to earn my way up to the next step and the one after.

By Thursday lunchtime Claire was pushing hard about the party and still wondering if I'd persuaded my mum to let me go or if she was going to give us both a lift. It was PE on Thursday afternoon and Claire and I were in the same lesson. We'd been tasked with doing the 1500 metres and pacing ourselves so that we could sprint to be placed by the teacher at the end. The teacher, Mrs Brampton, who looked like she hadn't so much as run for a bus in a long time let alone completed the 1500 metres, was poised at the finishing line with a warm coat, a stop watch and a mug of tea, waiting to mark down everyone's finishing time.

Claire and I paced ourselves by walking at just above stroll pace behind Lorna and Fi. Em, who was good at athletics and all that stuff, was actually running and determined to place in the top five. Becca had produced a note from her mum, hastily forged at lunch time when she realised she'd left her PE kit at home, explaining how a sprained ankle needed to be rested. She was sitting on a bench doing her maths homework.

'My mum doesn't drive, does she, otherwise I'd obviously ask her to take us both,' Claire pointed out by way of excusing her badgering as we meandered along the track. 'Lorna and Ems are going together because they live close to each other and Ems' dad works the night shift so he's going to drop them off on his way to work, and Fi can walk it because she only lives round the corner from Becca.'

'I only live round the corner from Becca,' Fi confirmed, interrupting her own conversation about outfits for Saturday night and how she hadn't decided which shoes yet.

'So if you and me go together that'll work out perfect, you see. Plus I can look out for you and make sure you don't make a complete tit of yourself.'

'Thanks.'

'You're welcome.'

'What if I make a partial tit of myself?'

'I'll create a distraction and we'll pretend it never happened.' She slapped me a little too hard on the arm as a gesture of camaraderie. 'So?'

'Hmmm?'

'Are you fucking coming to Becca's party or not?'

'I just need to find the right time to ask.'

'You mean you've not even asked yet?'

'I've tried to mention it. I have tried. But things have been a bit tense with her and me since I got her the sack from Mrs Wilkes and I think the miserable cow has been putting word around that she sacked Mum because her work wasn't up to scratch because other customers have been giving her a hard time all week.'

'That bitch Wilkes has done that? What a vindictive cow.'

'Yeah, so, there's never really a right time. Especially not for asking for a lift and everything.'

Claire stopped walking, as though coming up with a plan and walking her way to last place in the 1500 metres was too much of a multi-task.

'OK, how about I come to yours tonight? No, tomorrow night. Ask your mum if I can come for tea and when I come round I'll casually drop it into conversation that I've been invited round to Becca's for a sleepover and it would be great if you could come with me and I'll get her to give us a lift.'

'You reckon you can do that do you?' I was walking backwards now to keep talking to Claire without breaking pace.

'Obviously,' she smiled, happy to start walking again now that she'd come up with a plan. 'She'll be putty in my hands, you just watch.'

And it turned out Claire was right. My mum was surprised and disproportionately excited when I asked her if Claire could come for tea on Friday after school and immediately started quizzing me on Claire's favourite foods and what kind of meal would be best for an informal after-school thing. When I was completely clueless and suggested we have fish fingers with mashed potatoes and peas like we usually have on a Friday, Mum sighed as though I'd suggested we serve up mouldy bread and pond water; she reached for the giant book of '101 Family Favourites,' fully illustrated with step-by-step instructions and handy tips for planning ahead for the busy housewife.

'I can pop to the supermarket for some ingredients in between Mrs Anderton's and the Oswald house tomorrow because I have to go past the shops between those two anyway. Then if I'm back here by three, or half three at the latest, there's no reason I can't get something on the table for you by half past five. Would five be all right do you think? What time do you think she normally eats?'

I had no idea when Claire normally ate.

'You're not much help are you? What about a pudding. Should I make a cake? I could do that tonight and then that's one less thing to worry about tomorrow. Or perhaps I should do a fresh fruit salad – some people don't do dessert do they?'

'Dessert?' I repeated. She had never said dessert before in her life; we had afters or pudding in our house, pretty much after every meal.

'Yes, dessert, cake or fruit salad, which do you think?'

'When have we ever had fruit salad?'

'Marie, it's your friend I'm going to all this trouble for, so if you haven't got anything helpful to say, just go and do your homework and leave me to it. It's not like I haven't got enough to do.'

I felt mean then. She was just excited because I never had friends round for tea, not since the days when my mum used to organise play dates with the other mums, based on who she knew and liked rather than who I actually played with in school.

'How about I make a cake this evening and we look through the cook book together to decide what we have tomorrow,' I offered, realising I needed to help before she exploded into a panic. 'I'm sorry I can't help with what Claire likes, I just don't know what she eats at home because I only ever see her eating sandwiches at school so it's a bit hard to tell from that.'

So we looked through the 101 Family favourites together – all 101 of them – and Mum decided she'd make fish pie: pretty much what we usually have on a Friday but all mushed in together and a lot more fuss and trouble. Then we made a chocolate cake together on the basis that 'you can't go wrong with a chocolate cake, Marie' and it was fun. It was like travelling back in time to the days when I was her precious little girl and hers was the only praise and approval I needed. She let me weigh out the ingredients and crack the eggs. She put me on cake-tin greasing duty while she beat the mixture and she even let me lick the bowl while the cake baked. In the morning, when I got up to make my packed lunch for school, she had been like the elves visiting the shoemaker in the night and the cake was there, not plain and brown as I'd left it, but covered in chocolate with a rainbow of Smarties around the edge.

I struggled to hold back tears when I saw the cake, not because it was so amazing I couldn't contain myself; it was just a home-made cake. I was upset for all the moments we'd missed doing stuff together like that because she'd been too busy or I'd been too moody. I was upset because she was so excited that I had a friend coming over and it was such a big deal to her. It was a big deal to her because it was so rare. Because my lack of social status and confidence at school had made it rare. And, most of all, I was upset that I'd failed to give her that pleasure in welcoming her daughter's friends into her home and peeking into my life for so long, and now I was going to do it as part of a plan to manipulate her into letting me go to a party. The cake made me feel nauseous without even taking a bite.

Of course, Mum was putty in Claire's hands, just as Claire had planned it. Claire was clearly less than keen on fish pie, particularly when she found a chunk of boiled egg hidden amongst the salmon and smoked haddock, but she was a master at presenting her disgust as delight.

'Is this a piece of boiled egg? That's amazing. It's so unexpected, isn't it, egg and fish and potato together, but it goes so well. And it's so filling! What a perfect winter warmer. My mum always says you need food that warms up your belly on cold evenings and then you've got central heating for your whole body.'

Claire said all of this while effortlessly hiding the lump of egg under a mound of mashed potato and carefully pushing it to the edge of her plate as her too-full-to-eat-this-bit pile.

I waited for her to mention the party and raise the question of me coming along and Mum giving her a lift, but it was almost like she'd forgotten what she was even doing at our house.

'So you work six days a week? (Could you pass the Ketchup Marie?)'

'Yes, but it's flexible, that's how I ended up doing it really, when Marie was little I could just take her with me and if she was poorly I could just switch my schedule around a little bit to stay at home til she got better. Most people don't care when you come in to clean as long as you're in and out while they're not there and they don't have to do it themselves.'

'But it must play havoc with your hands though?'

'Yes, it can be very drying but, they're always clean and germ free.' Mum showed us her jazz hands and there was a faint whiff of bleach as she waved them.

'Do you know what, that was delicious, probably the best fish pie I've ever had, but Marie tells me there's chocolate cake so I want to make sure I leave room. Is that OK?'

Claire had eaten very little of what was on her plate but she'd done such a good job of distracting Mum while she didn't eat it and smearing it around the plate so that she appeared to have demolished her food enthusiastically that Mum was neither cross nor offended.

It wasn't until she was on her second slice of chocolate cake that Claire casually dropped in a reference to going to Becca's.

'I shouldn't have two pieces really, it's just that it's so delicious. I mean, I should be taking it easy with the sugar and the rich food tonight because we're having a sleepover at Becca's tomorrow night and there's bound to be midnight feasts with a tonne of sweets and chocolate. There usually is, isn't there, Marie?'

Claire looked at me to prompt me to continue a script that she'd not bothered to share with me before the show.

'Are you coming to Becca's sleepover?' she asked

'I...'

'She always gets invited to these things,' Claire lied, 'but for some reason she never comes. Is that because she's not allowed?'

'No, of course not, she's allowed, of course she's allowed to join in with the fun with her friends,' Mum replied to Claire, then turned to me. 'You've never mentioned any sleepovers you wanted to go to, Marie?'

'Oh, hasn't she?' Claire's surprise sounded completely genuine. 'Perhaps it's because she doesn't want to go? Do you want to go to Becca's tomorrow night?'

'Erm, yes. Yes, I do want to go.'

'Well then, that's arranged. Will you need a sleeping bag? Will she need a sleeping bag Claire?'

'Oh, I don't think so, I think there'll be plenty of duvets and blankets and things at Becca's house. Anyway, sleepovers should really be called stay-up-overs shouldn't they?'

We all laughed together even though I was painfully aware that I'd never been to a sleepover and that this wasn't a sleepover anyway, it was a party. It was a lie.

'The only problem is getting there. It's two buses to Becca's house and it'll be dark when we head out and my mum doesn't drive, otherwise she'd probably take us. I'm sure she would.'

'Well I can take you,' gushed my mum, reading straight from the script Claire had written for her.

THIRTEEN

Some kinds of quiet are lovely. Like the quiet you get when a car alarm stops or when you find a perfect picnic spot with no-one else around.

But the quiet in our house when we got back from John-Joe's funeral wasn't lovely. It wasn't something that had come into the house, it was something that had been sucked out of it.

Then there was Jenny. She swept around tidying mess that wasn't there, making cups of tea that nobody drank, talking about the service, the weather, how well behaved Anna had been, how professional the funeral people had been. She talked about everything she did like celebrity chefs do when they're cooking on TV. 'I'm just putting the kettle on.' 'I'm just opening the back door to let some fresh air in.' 'I'm just going to the loo.' She worked really hard to try and make a dent in the silence but with every sentence she made it bigger and bigger.

'Thanks for everything you've done today, Jenny'.

I could tell that Dad was hinting that she should go now but Jenny wasn't getting the message.

'Perhaps you'd like me to put Anna to bed? Or the boys? I could put the boys to bed? Or are you too old for that now boys? Do you still like bedtime stories?'

It was only seven o'clock. Too early for me or Gabe to go to bed and Anna was already asleep in her bouncy chair.

'Thanks Jenny, but it might be a bit early for the boys,' Dad said.

Mum said nothing.

'Well, perhaps I'd better be going,' Jenny smiled at Mum with a fake half-smile, hoping to be asked to stay. It was as though she thought we'd all dissolve if she wasn't there and she didn't keep talking. If no-one could see us and no-one could hear us, did we still exist?

Suddenly, I didn't want her to go. Suddenly I needed her to stay. She was like the TV you leave on when you're not even watching it. She was normal life, carrying on while no-one was looking and if she left then perhaps we might all just topple over and none of us might ever speak again. Perhaps we'd vanish.

'Actually Dad, I am quite tired,' I said.

Gabe looked at me like I'd lost the plot. None of us ever admitted to being tired, not even if we couldn't speak for yawning. It was the law.

The thing is with Gabe, though, he just goes along with whatever you do. He always thinks I'm right, which is sometimes useful, sometimes just annoying. Today it was useful.

'Me too actually, Dad,' Gabe said.

'And we both still like a story at bedtime, don't we Gabe?'

It was true, Gabe still did have a story every night but it must have been at least a year since I'd had a bedtime story. Maybe even more. Mum said I was old enough to read to myself if I wanted a story before sleep. I got to stay up later by not having one. It suited us both.

But that night I didn't want to go to the bedroom and try to sleep by myself. John-Joe was in the ground and in our quiet house there was nowhere more quiet than the bedroom we used to share.

'Are you sure, boys?' Dad looked worried, like we were trying to trick him or something.

Jenny seemed a bit unsure too, even though it had been her idea.

'What do you think, love?'

He was talking to Mum but she seemed not to notice. 'Love?'

She looked up then. She held her hands out to Gabe and me and we went over to her.

'You two have been amazing today,' she said. 'I'm so proud of my boys.'

I remembered how cross she'd been with me about getting in the front seat of the car but I didn't mention it.

'I love you, Mum.'

'And I do.'

'And me,' echoed Dad.

We've never been the kind of family that says I love you all the time. Or any of the time. Dad says that's what they do on American TV and at new age hippy communes, it's not for the suburbs of Northern England. But it seemed right to say it then. It seemed like what we were all saying was that we loved John-Joe. Not that I would ever have said anything of the kind to his face.

Anna started crying. Not her usual can't-really-be-bothered-but-you-need-to-know-I'm-waking-up cry but a full on howling at the top of her lungs.

I could see that Jenny didn't know what to do. Should she pick up the baby, take Gabe and me to bed so that Mum could pick up the baby, or just leave.

In her indecision she did nothing. Dad picked up the baby. Anna carried on crying and Gabe and I took turns to hug Mum goodnight.

'Straight to sleep now boys,' she called after us. 'It's been a long day. One story and then it's lights out.'

In a different voice she said to Jenny, 'Don't let them lead you a merry dance. Thanks Jenny.'

Jenny paused on her way out of the room to go back across to the chair where Mum was sitting and squeeze her on the shoulder. But Mum had already switched off her Mum voice and disappeared from the room again. She said nothing.

Upstairs, we could still hear Anna crying. She cried while I got my pyjamas on, she cried while I brushed my teeth, while

Jenny made us wash our faces with the flannel and while Jenny read a story to Gabe.

I said I'd just listen to Gabe's story instead of having one of my own but I found it hard to listen. Jenny carried on reading about George's Marvellous Medicine as though she couldn't hear the crying from downstairs and Gabe seemed like all he could hear was the story too. But all I could hear was the crying, breaking the silence with a noise so loud and unpleasant that I just wanted the quiet back.

When Jenny got to the end of the chapter there was an awkwardness that we weren't used to. Jenny kind of patted Gabe on the head and said 'night night, God bless' and I just said 'night Gabe. Night Jenny' and left the room.

Anna's crying followed me across the landing along with Dad's voice saying 'shhhhh, shhhhh, shhhh,' Jenny followed me too, right behind me, as though she planned to come into the room and tell me a story even though I'd already told her there was no need.

I didn't want her in the room. I really didn't. This was my room now. Just me and John-Joe and Captain were allowed in. No-one else. Well, maybe Mum and Dad but definitely not Jenny.

'You've done well today,' she said, 'your Mum and Dad are proud of you. I'm proud of you. But it doesn't end here I'm afraid. Your Mum's going to need you, and Gabe, and Anna.'

'And Dad will,' I said. 'Dad will too?'

It seemed an odd idea that my grown up Dad would need me but I didn't want him to be left out.

'And your dad,' Jenny agreed. 'All of them. They'll all need you. But you're not on your own. I'm here. You just let me know if you need me. Remember, I'm only just over the road. Just come and find me if I'm not around when you need me.'

I nodded. She squeezed my shoulder just like she'd done with Mum and she left me at my bedroom door, with the sound of Anna's wailing encouraging me to go inside and sleep there.

Inside the room was the certain knowledge that John-Joe was gone for good, locked underground and never coming back.

Outside the room was the sound of Anna's protests as she just screamed on and on and on, as though she were demanding that someone bring him back, the way that babies just don't get it when the thing they want isn't possible.

I hesitated at the door. I wondered if I really focused, really wished for it, if John-Joe might be sitting up in bed, asking me where I'd been. I said a prayer to ask for him back before I pushed the door open. Father O'Connor says you should never underestimate the power of prayer and that the more often we pray and the more voices God hears all sending him the same message, the more likely we are to get an answer.

But the room was empty. Father O'Connor also says that God doesn't always answer prayers in the way we want or expect. He answered mine with one bed, mine, just how I'd left it that morning, all messed up with the duvet hanging off the edge and touching the floor, and the other, John-Joe's, all neat and tidy, freshly made and uncrumpled.

I reached under his pillow for the tin. It was just where I'd been keeping it for over a week, with the lid still shut tight and the weight of the bird inside it.

I put the tin down on my bed and lifted the duvet off John-Joe's bed. I punched the duvet and screwed it up and put it back nice and untidy. I punched his pillow and gave it a dint where the head would go. Sitting down on my own bed and looking across, you might think he'd just got up to go to the toilet or something.

The tin felt nice in my hands. It was smooth with rounded edges. I sniffed it. It smelt a bit, but not as much as I'd thought it might when I first took it out of the bin. I wondered if it would smell more the longer I kept it in the bedroom. I wished I'd taken it to the cemetery and put it in the ground with John-Joe so that Captain could have kept him company. I wished I'd thought of that amongst all the fuss and hurry of getting to the funeral. Too late now.

'I'm sorry John-Joe, I should have thought of it sooner. I should have thought ahead.'

I didn't know I was crying until I saw a tear fall onto the tin.

'Please Captain, make it all better again.'

I put the tin under my own pillow and lay down to sleep. The sound of Anna's crying seemed to stop as soon as my head touched the pillow and there was silence again. The nice kind that marks the end of noise. The kind that says 'you are in a safe place now and everything will be OK.'

I looked across to John-Joe's bed. Saw him pull his tongue out at me, pulled mine out back at him and fell asleep.

FOURTEEN

Claire stuck her head around the front door, holding up two fingers and mouthing 'two minutes'. We were already five minutes later than planned because my mum had insisted on packing me a bag with spare underwear, a toothbrush and toothpaste, a hair brush and a packet of seven Penguin biscuits as my contribution to any midnight snacking. I had spent the short journey between our house and Claire's with my mind racing between alternate plans. One minute I was considering how to 'accidentally' leave the bag behind in the car so that I didn't have to be the only person at the party with a toothbrush and a packet of biscuits; as we turned the next corner, I was contemplating faking a sudden but reasonably severe bout of sickness. We'd still have to give Claire a lift (because we'd promised) but I'd have to go home because I was (reluctantly) too ill to stay at a sleepover and didn't want to ruin everyone else's night by vomiting over the snacks and chit-chat.

Mum kept the engine running, basing her estimate of how long Claire would take on an adult's generic two minutes which, for her, meant 'I'm just getting my coat and I'll be there'. But Claire's two minutes was clearly an open-ended measurement of time that seemed like two to her because she was busy changing outfits, applying mascara and checking her look in the mirror. To us, sitting in a car on a miserable November evening, watching the neighbours' nets twitching as they surreptitiously peered out to see who was there, it seemed like days might pass with no further signs of life from Claire's house.

Mum switched off the engine. 'You just go and knock, see where she's got to. What time is this Becca expecting you?'

'I think she said half eight but it's pretty relaxed. It's not like her mum's cooking a meal for us or anything. I mean, it's not really a fixed time, more of a get here when you get here kind of a thing.'

'Well it's just rude if you ask me. Rude of Claire to be late for us, rude of you to be late for Becca. Just go and knock will you.'

So I got out and knocked. And heard Claire's mum shouting 'Claire. Door.' Before eventually opening it herself.

'Hello love, do you want to come in and wait?' Claire's mum was wearing a fluffy white dressing gown with pink hearts all over it and had hobbled to the door with a tissue snaked between her toes, which had bright red nails on her right foot, while on the left three were red and two were still unpainted. 'Come on in for a minute, you'll let the heat out.'

So I stepped into the cramped hallway, scented by washing drying on the radiator, conscious of how annoyed my mum would be that I'd been absorbed into the house instead of bringing Claire out as planned.

'She's just doing her make up I think.' Claire's mum smiled at me and then shouted up the stairs. 'Claire! Claaaaire!' She turned back to me. 'I'm sorry about this love. She's always a nightmare about being on time when she goes out.' Then back to the stairs, 'CLAAAAAIIIIRE!' and back to me. 'Takes after her mum. Look at me, I'm supposed to be on the Karaoke by half past eight, belting out a bit of Celine Dion, and here I am with wet toes and no knickers on.'

As though she could actually hear my embarrassment and discomfort call to her from the hallway, Claire appeared at the top of the stairs and posed with her arms outstretched like some Hollywood superstar in the showpiece number of a big budget musical.

'How do I look?'

'Fabulous, love,' Claire's mum beamed. 'You look gorgeous. Now get your skinny arse out of here and let your mother use the bathroom, you're making me late.'

Claire sashayed down the narrow staircase, still in character and I wondered whether her mum had chosen a red carpet specifically so that the two of them could pretend to be celebrities on opening night.

My own costume for the evening had stuck with the sleepover scenario and I'd left the house wearing black jeans, a grey and black stripy jumper with a vest top underneath and ankle boots. Meanwhile, Claire had made no effort to look like she was going anywhere but a party. Or a fashion show. I had risked a bit of mascara, some blusher and a shiny lip balm and here was Claire, her eyes defined with a thick black line that flicked up at the outer edge and extended to a sharp point half way to the eyebrow. Her lips were bright red and matched her dress that was high at the neck and high above the knee, creating the illusion that her long, black tights-clad legs were even longer. She jumped towards me off the bottom step and spun around, revealing the circular section cut out of the back of her dress where her hair – usually tied back in a ponytail – flowed in waves just touching the transition between fabric and flesh.

'What are you wearing?' she beamed at me, opening out the unfastened front of my coat like a pair of curtains to cast a critical eye over my outfit.

'My mum thinks we're going to a sleepover, I thought she might smell a rat if I looked too dressed up,' I said, by way of an excuse for looking disappointingly under-dressed.

'So your mum thinks it's a sleepover does she?' Claire's mum chipped in.

Claire ignored her and turned to check her appearance in the hallway mirror, making imperceptible changes to her hair, pouting and checking her teeth for lipstick. 'Oh yeah, I suppose you're right. You look nice anyway. You look like you.'

Perhaps it was the look on my face that encouraged her to dig an ever deeper hole and fill it with insincere compliments. Perhaps it was the knowledge that she was still dependent on my mum for a lift.

'You look like normal,' she added, turning to her mum to support her pseudo-compliment, 'you know, natural.' She looked from the mirror to me and gave me a kind, patronising smile, perfectly co-ordinated with an identical reassuring smile from her mum, who threw in her own 'Lots of boys love the girl-next-door look' comment into the abyss.

'Anyway, we're all set,' said Claire, 'I'll just grab a coat.' She reached into the cupboard under the stairs for her coat and looked for a minute like she might disappear completely as she rummaged.

'You have a good time love,' said Claire's mum, making for the stairs, 'you look lovely Marie. Claire doesn't really know how to tone it down,' she said, grinning as she glanced towards Claire's long, bent leg sticking out of the cupboard as the rest of her reached in. 'She gets that from her mother.'

'Eh?' Claire asked, re-emerging with a long coat, which she fastened to the top before wrapping a scarf around twice.

'I said have a great time but be good,' her mum replied, now half way up the stairs. 'Don't do anything I wouldn't do and...'

'If you can't be good, be careful,' they chanted in unison. Followed by 'Jinx'. Claire's mum gestured firing a pistol through the fingertips of both hands at her daughter and made a clicking noise with her tongue, then disappeared into the bathroom to get ready for her own night out.

'Don't look so nervous,' said Claire. 'We're going to have a great night. You look more like someone who's about to take a maths exam without a calculator than someone who's off to a party, let's get moving shall we, your mum's waiting.'

Claire was full of apologies as we got into the car but it did little to defrost Mum's irritation at being left waiting. She said nothing, of course: having decided to be delighted about my newly rekindled friendship with Claire and the 'sleepover' arrangement, she couldn't very well kick up stink in front of our passenger – what would that look like?

Instead, as Claire babbled on about how she'd wanted to wear the glittery nail varnish but her mum had borrowed it and not put the lid back on properly so it had dried up and become too thick and sticky to use, my mum shot me looks through the rear view mirror. No bullets of camaraderie here, just the death stare of annoyance and disapproval.

To make matters worse, Becca's house was hard to find. She lived on a sprawling suburban estate full of stout cul-de-sacs, each with five giant houses that were all slightly different but confusingly similar to Claire in the dark as she tried to direct us. We had to make several three-point turns to drive back the way we'd come when faced with dead ends that Claire had thought were definitely the right street this time but proved not to be.

We turned round for the last time outside a double-fronted house that was lit in every room and had a small group of people standing outside the garage smoking and staring at us as the car reversed.

'I'm so sorry about this, they all look the same don't they,' Claire said again. 'And these pathetic excuse for streetlights don't help. It's definitely the next street though. I remember now it's the street with the end house with the giant climbing frame in the garden. Sorry. You could just drop us on the corner and we'll walk up, save you turning round again to get out.'

My mum said nothing and drove us to the corner with the landmark climbing frame, where all the quiet houses in the street had just a light switched on here and there and a car or two on the drive as their only signs of life.

'It's that one, with the red car,' Claire declared as Mum stopped by the kerb. 'That's Becca's dad's car, we can walk it from here. Thank you sooooo much.'

Mum left the engine running while we got out. She'd progressed from a bit frosty to positively Arctic and I didn't have to pretend to accidentally forget to leave my overnight bag in the car because she'd just disengaged. I had been nervous, uncertain if I really wanted to go to the party, pretty much decided on faking feeling unwell so that I could go home, but her irritation with me over something that wasn't my fault made me determined to have a good time and ignore what she might think, just as she was ignoring what I might feel. All her joy and encouragement for me at the social rite of passage was gone and replaced by a resentment that had been present all my life; any time she'd had a bad day or been short of money or allowed envy to creep into our lives.

'Thanks so much for bringing us, you're a complete super star,' Claire gushed, opening the car door. 'Marie, your mum is an absolute star, thanks again.'

Claire stood holding the car door for me.

'Thanks Mum.'

No reply. No eye contact.

'I'm sorry about having to wait for Claire.'

No reply. Frosty stare through the rear view mirror.

'Come on,' Claire bent to see into the back seat of the car and hurry me along. 'It's a bit chilly out here you know and you're letting the heat out of your mum's nice warm car.'

I wanted to make things right before I got out. I wanted my mum to wish me a nice evening. Her words would have been my good luck charm, my benediction, but she said nothing and put the car into gear ready to drive away.

'Bye then, see you tomorrow.'

I climbed out of the car and Claire slammed the door shut and linked arms with me to walk up the street. I didn't look back as Mum drove away.

'Come on,' said Claire, turning sharply as soon as my mum's car had turned the corner. 'It's not this street, it's that last street where we turned round.'

'So why didn't we get out there instead of pissing my mum off by turning round for the six millionth time?'

'Because a quiet little sleepover doesn't involve a house lit up like a Christmas tree and boys having a fag on the driveway. If we'd stopped there she would've been onto you straight away.

'You're so cute, it's like guiding an alien in our human ways.' Claire laughed enthusiastically at her own joke and, as though she genuinely had to guide me, she linked arms with me again and walked me round the corner to Becca's house.

FIFTEEN

Dad had told me that things would get back to normal after the funeral but all the adults carried on acting weird for weeks afterwards.

Jenny was still coming round every day. She tidied up and made lunches and brought shopping to put in our fridge as though she lived with us. She bought the kind of stuff Mum would never get, including stuff we'd seen advertised on TV that Mum said we weren't allowed because it was only one small step up from toxic waste. It turned out it wasn't poisonous after all. In fact we quite liked some of it.

She talked all the time. I mean, *all* the time. She was always asking us stupid questions about football and what we'd been watching on TV. She told us about what'd been happening in the news and about science and history and geography. To fill the gaps in our house she emptied out the contents of her brain into every room and then quizzed us on the things she'd told us to check that we were listening.

She made great scrambled eggs though.

I liked that she was trying to make everything seem normal. It was good of her. But the harder she tried, the less and less normal everything seemed. Sitting at the table for a Sunday lunch of sausage rolls and baked beans while your neighbour tells you all about Henry VIII, global warming and the large hadron collider is not normal. Neither is your Mum having a nap in the middle of the day, even though she got up late and hasn't done much apart from drink tea and look out of the window.

Dad also kept talking to me. Even after he went back to work he kept ringing during the day and coming home early. Then, when we went back to school, Dad would go into work late so that he could take us in and Mum could stay at home with Anna. He would pick us up sometimes, too, but mostly it was Jenny that picked us up and took us home. She'd make us crumpets or toast or some other kind of snack while she quizzed us about school and forced us into letting her help with homework. She even watched kids' TV with us when we hadn't asked her to, and got really interested in the programmes. I caught her watching our programmes all on her own more than once.

Mum was there but not there, like the books on the shelves and the pictures on the walls.

So Dad filled in the spaces Mum had vacated. He got into a routine of popping into my room at bedtime and offering to read me a story. He would sit on John-Joe's bed and look ridiculously large with his ankle crossed over his knee. Or he would lie back on my bed propped up on his elbows with his head against the wall, indicating when it was time for me to go to sleep by saying 'I suppose you want your bed back now, eh Champ?' I was sure he must be able to feel Captain in the tin under the pillow, like the Princess and the Pea. Like when you get a stone in your shoe. But he didn't say anything. I didn't either. Maybe he couldn't feel it. Perhaps it was all part of John-Joe's magic, making the tin disappear when Dad lay back on the pillow. Whether he was ignoring it, didn't feel it or couldn't feel it because it had been magicked away, our chats were all part of our new routine.

He'd also started calling me 'Champ'. I don't know why, I didn't ask him. I didn't really like it but I didn't tell him. It reminded me of dog food and made me wonder why he didn't just call me Jim like he always used to.

'So Champ, how was your day today?' he asked, sitting on John-Joe's bed once Gabe and Anna were asleep and Jenny had finally gone home for the day.

'It was good'. 'It was fine.' And I'd think of something to tell him about what we did at school or what we'd talked about with Jenny to let him know how fine and normal it had all been. The truth was it had been the most boring summer holidays we'd ever had and then, when we went back to school, we just carried on like we always had but John-Joe wasn't there and everyone knew why so no-one asked. No-one mentioned him, so we didn't either.

'Gabe and me played football for a bit after school, but then it was raining so Jenny taught us how to play Twenty-one with the playing cards and gave us Cheese Strings for a snack.'

I made it sound like we'd had a great day, with fresh air, educational games, and exciting new foods to try, but he still looked worried.

'Did Mum play cards with you?'

I shook my head. Telling him she didn't join in felt like a betrayal. I don't know why. Mum's never really played cards with us. No-one's ever really played cards with us until Jenny started turning up every day.

'How did Mummy seem today?'

'I think she was tired. I think she was fine but just, you know, tired. She's up in the night because of Anna isn't she? Jenny says mums get tired all the time, especially when they have little babies.'

Dad smiled at me, but it wasn't a real smile; it was like the smile you do when someone wants to take your photo but you're not in the mood.

'We might teach Mum to play cards tomorrow,' I fake-smiled back at him. 'Jenny says she'll teach us a game called Cheat tomorrow where you just cheat to win and the other people playing have to catch you out.'

I looked at Dad and he was still trying hard but not winning any Oscars. He looked like the Joker; like his smile was tattooed on and he couldn't help it. If I'd only looked at his mouth and not his whole face I might have been convinced but I couldn't help looking at his eyes and trying to read what they were really saying.

I wondered if he was thinking the same as me. That John-Joe would have loved a game called Cheat. Just for the name. John-Joe would have been great at it. He could cheat without you noticing at any game you like. And even if you did work it out, you wouldn't mind.

'I bet John-Joe would have loved the Cheat game.' The words slipped out before I realised.

'I bet he would, Champ,' Dad said. He smiled for real. 'I bet he would. It's OK to miss him you know. It's OK to talk about him.'

'Is it OK to talk *to* him?' I asked.

'Of course it is,' Dad said. 'I talk to him all the time.'

I'm not sure he knew what I was asking really, but that was enough. My Dad had given me permission to talk to John-Joe.

It seemed like he'd given John-Joe permission to come back into the room too, because he was pulling faces behind Dad's back.

'What are you grinning about Champ?'

John-Joe stuck out his tongue at me and made himself cross-eyed.

'I'm just smiling at John-Joe.'

'That's good son, that's great,' he took hold of my shoulder and squeezed it really hard. 'We shouldn't ever stop talking about him and we should always smile when we think about him. He wouldn't want us to be sad, would he Champ? He'd want us to talk about him and remember all the times when he made us laugh. He'd want us to share the joke.'

John-Joe was pulling on the skin under his eyes so that I could see the bottom of his eye-balls. He pushed his tongue into his lower lip to make his chin bulge out, with his head twisted to one side. I stifled a laugh and Dad gave me half a laugh back. I think he thought I was doing a little laugh because he'd made me think of a funny moment and I wished he could see John-Joe with me.

'Dad?'

'Yes, son?'

'Do you think people really do go to heaven when they die?'

'I don't know, Champ. I hope so. I'd like to think so but I'm not sure what heaven means. I think there must be a heaven of some kind but you don't get to find out until it's too late for you to tell anyone.'

'But what do you think it is?'

'I don't know. I really don't. I even wonder if it's the same thing for everyone. We're not all the same are we? Some people's idea of heaven might be a giant holiday resort where they can meet up with all their family and have sunshine and swimming pools and an all-you-can-eat buffet every day.'

'Sounds brilliant' said John-Joe.

Dad made a face. 'But that's more like my idea of hell. I'd like to think of heaven more like a feeling. Like being a bird and just having the freedom to fly anywhere but never get tired or lost…'

'Or have to eat worms!'

'Or have to eat worms,' he smiled. 'I'm pretty sure we don't go up to a fluffy cloud with a man in a long beard anyway.'

'It would have to be a pretty ginormous cloud.'

'Yes it would, son.'

John-Joe was still making faces and trying to interrupt the conversation. He was just as annoying as he'd ever been.

'And do you think people can come back home and just stick around for a bit when they're dead?' I asked

'Like ghosts you mean?'

'Not like ghosts exactly, just like himself, like he's still here, just the same.'

Dad looked straight at John-Joe and smiled and for a minute I thought Dad could see him too. I even thought, for a tiny second, that it had all been some big mix up and none of it had ever happened. Perhaps John-Joe had been here all the time.

But Dad couldn't see him, he was just smiling at what was in his own head.

'Do you know what a gannet is, Jim?'

'Is it a bird that eats a lot? Mum says I'm a gannet when I eat my tea too fast.'

'That's because gannets can swallow a whole fish in one gulp,' Dad explained, 'but that's not what I love about them. They're sea birds. Beautiful big white birds with a kind of golden halo on their heads and long, elegant wings with black tips at the edge.'

Dad stretched his arms out wide and splayed his fingers. John-Joe copied him.

'They have really jet black eyes too, like beads. When you see them out at sea, you can watch them circling high overhead and then suddenly, even from high up, they'll see something under the water and dive. They shoot down so fast like a bullet into the water to catch what they've seen—'

'And then swallow it down in one.'

'Perhaps,' Dad said, looking confused for a minute because I'd derailed his train of thought. 'But the point I'm trying to make is that the gannet can see something that's invisible to us. And perhaps we can see in a way that the gannet can't. We all see things differently and understand what we see differently. But the gannet has such complete faith that what he can see is real that he interrupts his flight and shoots down all the way into the water to catch it.'

'Do you think I'm like a gannet Dad?'

'Perhaps, son.'

'Gannets sound great,' said John-Joe, 'can we search them up on YouTube?'

'Gannets sound great,' I repeated to Dad, 'can we search them up on YouTube, Dad?'

'Perhaps tomorrow. Not now though, it's late.'

'It's only a bit late and it will only take five minutes to watch a couple of videos of birds flying.'

'Jim, you have school in the morning.'

'Yes but it might help me sleep. And anyway we're going to church to look at the Stations of the Cross tomorrow morning so it's not like I have to be all super-concentrated and do a maths test or anything.'

I really wanted John-Joe to see the gannets.

'He's going to cave,' said John-Joe. 'Good work, Jim.'

'Have you brushed your teeth?'

'I think I have.'

'Have you?'

'I might not have.'

'Right, well, you get your teeth brushed while I get the iPad and find a gannet video for us to watch. Just one though.'

'What if the first one we find isn't very good?'

'Maximum of two.'

'OK, maximum of two.'

'Teeth.'

'iPad.' Having John-Joe in the room made me cheekier. I had to say what he would have said because Dad couldn't hear him.

John-Joe's toothbrush was still in the bathroom because no-one had moved it. It was a Star Wars electric toothbrush that he'd got as a reward for being good last time we went to the dentist. One of the buttons made the bristles vibrate, the other played that tune that you hear in the films every time Darth Vader walks down a corridor. John-Joe saw me looking at it and said I could use it, so I did.

When I got back into the bedroom, Dad was already sitting on John-Joe's bed with the iPad ready. I breathed at him as I sat down so that he could smell how minty I was.

'I found this one,' Dad said, 'ready?'

He clicked on the play icon and we watched the camera pan across hundreds of gannets on a rock and zoom in to have a look at them. It showed one of them in close up, its pupil dilated in the sunshine and its long, sharp beak like the blades of a pair of scissors pointing out to sea. And then we saw the gannet launch itself into the sky. It was lifted by the wind and flew without flapping its wings, which really were like Dad's outstretched arms. I looked up to see what John-Joe thought of it but he wasn't there.

'Wait for it,' said Dad.

I looked back at the screen just in time to see the gannet dive, like an arrow shot from a bow, straight down and super-fast. And then, a second later, it came up from the water with a fish in its mouth and the video ended.

Dad clicked on the exit icon and pressed the button to switch off the screen.

'Amazing isn't it?'

I was looking round the room for John-Joe but he'd gone.

'Jim?'

'Yes Dad, amazing. Thanks for showing me. John-Joe would have loved that.'

'Yes he would. He always loved birds didn't he? Even seagulls and magpies.'

'That's why he wanted us to resurrect Captain on the washing line Dad, he just wanted to bring the bird back to life.'

'I know son, but let's not talk about that shall we, it upsets your mother.'

I thought about Mum taking Captain out to the bin and I felt guilty for hiding him under my pillow.

'OK, Dad, we won't.'

'I know you didn't mean any harm by it, Jim. It's just that your Mum was very upset by it; she thinks of it as something that brought bad luck. It's just superstition, she's not really thinking straight after what happened with John-Joe, I'm sure she knows really that you were just playing. You're a good boy. You're all good boys. Now get into bed and get to sleep, you've school in the morning.'

'I suppose a glass of water is out of the question?'

He was about to give me one of those big, impatient parent sighs when he looked at my face and saw that I was joking.

'Yes, you know all the tricks,' he said. I looked for John-Joe, who'd invented more tricks for delaying bedtime than the whole of the rest of the world put together, but he was still gone.

'Are you too old to be tucked in?'

I got under the duvet and lay back on my elbows. There was nothing to tuck.

'No Dad.'

Dad pushed my hair back off my face in the way that's really annoying and kissed me on the forehead.

'It's been nice to chat and watch the gannets together, Champ.'

'Yes Dad, can we do it again another night?'

'If you go straight to sleep. Lamp on or off?'

'Off.'

He switched off the lamp on the table between the two beds and stumbled to the door in the dark. As he turned the door handle, I whispered into the blackness.

'Sometimes I see John-Joe and he talks to me.'

Dad said nothing. I don't know if he heard me.

SIXTEEN

B ecca was a year older than the rest of us at school. She'd had
some rare kind of cancer when she was six or seven and had
missed lots of school from being in hospital or feeling too ill to
learn, so she'd been kept down a year to catch up. You wouldn't
think one year would make that much of a difference but it did
with Becca. Or perhaps it was the way that everyone else saw
her as older and more grown up that made the difference, or
just that she'd cheated death so she was full of life. Whatever
the reason, Becca was a whole different level of cool from Claire
and the fact that her parents seemed completely relaxed about
leaving their just-turned-seventeen-year-old home alone for
the weekend hosting a party in their quite fancy and seriously
massive house ramped up her social status almost to celebrity
level.

She was nowhere to be seen when we arrived at the party,
a boy so tall and thin that he immediately made me think of a
praying mantis opened the door for us, looked us up and down
and walked away without speaking, leaving us to shut the door
behind us ourselves. We stepped into the hallway to the sound
of Chumbawamba singing about whisky drinks and lager drinks,
as though helpfully identifying the mix of smells in the hallway.

The house was like the kind of house I'd only ever seen on
TV, with a staircase in the centre of the huge hallway, doors
leading to rooms either side, and a door open to the kitchen at
the back of the hall. The stairs were covered with people sitting
and chatting or trying to pick out a route up or down without
treading on anyone. There was a mountain of coats on each of

the banisters and a weighted helium balloon on a pink ribbon either side of the stairs; the one to the left said 'happy birthday', the one to the right had a pink '17' on it.

'Oh God, should we have bought her a present? I didn't realise it was Becca's birthday party.'

My general panic at being at a party in an unfamiliar house with an army of strangers was doubled by a surge of new panic that I'd already committed a horrendous social sin by turning up empty-handed.

'Don't be daft. Her birthday was two weeks ago. Anyway, what were you going to bring? You hardly know her. Most of these people hardly know her, do you think they've all brought presents? Obviously not, where would she put all that stuff? What kind of stuff do you think she needs, anyway? Have you seen where she lives? Trust me, there's nothing Becca actually needs and not much she can't have just by asking for it.'

We were still standing by the front door. I was there because I didn't know what else to do and Claire was busy scanning the hall and stairs for someone she knew. The doorbell rang behind us and I let someone in who was carrying four bottles of wine in a hug in front of her.

'Ta,' she smiled, kicking the door shut behind her. 'It's properly cold out there. Grab that, will you?' She nodded towards one of the bottles she was carrying that was slipping and in danger of falling. 'Cheers, no-one wants to be the first to smash a bottle and spend all night stinking of eau-de-red do they? Can you pop it in the kitchen for me?'

She was walking away as she talked and turned to look back towards me. 'It's this way. Cheers. You're a life-saver.' I followed the girl towards the back of the hall and turned to see if Claire would follow but she'd already disappeared.

The kitchen, a space as big as the whole of the downstairs in my house, was also full of people and already full of bottles, on the giant kitchen table and on the work tops. Most were already open and many were already empty. For the second time

I felt embarrassed to have arrived empty-handed. No-one had told me the etiquette of not offering a present but being sure to bring a bottle. As I looked around, everyone else seemed like they knew the rules and completely belonged in that kitchen, in that house, in that universe, while I had just landed in from outer space in the wrong clothes.

But Jesus was smiling on me. Becca walked past just as I was depositing the bottle of wine on the counter.

'Aww, thanks,' she said. 'I'm not a big fan of red wine myself, stains your teeth,' she flashed her perfect Hollywood smile at me, 'but each to their own, it's all part of the communal liquid buffet. There are some crisps somewhere, though. There definitely were some crisps. Have you seen Claire? Someone said they'd seen her arrive?'

'Yes, she arrived with me but she vanished while I was...' I didn't need to worry about how I was going to explain rescuing the bottle from smashing on the tiled hallway floor without letting slip that I hadn't brought it with me, because Becca had already lost interest in my arrival, my bottle, and me, and was back to scouring the room for signs of Claire.

'Thanks,' she said, looking back to flash me another smile as she walked away, the mass of teenage bodies parting for her as she moved effortlessly through the room like a knife through soft butter.

'Are you going to open that?' A tall boy I vaguely remembered from the year above us at school was reaching out for the bottle I was still holding on the kitchen worktop. I realised I was clutching it as though it were some kind of steadying handle to keep me upright as I lurched from not sure what I was doing there to completely sure I'd rather be somewhere else.

'You don't need a corkscrew for that one, see,' the boy reached over and took the bottle. I was about to tell him it wasn't mine and look to the girl who'd asked me to carry it for permission to hand it over, but she'd vanished too.

He took the bottle, unscrewed the top and poured some into the mug he was already carrying. I managed not to fall over.

'Want some?'

He waved the bottle in front of my face. I had never drunk red wine, but I knew that 'I don't know if I like it' would be a ridiculous response.

'I've only just got here, I haven't got anything to drink out of.'

'We'd better fix that then, hadn't we?'

He put down his mug and reached up to open a cupboard behind me, leaning in close as he plunged his arm deep into the cupboard to pull out a mug.

'This'll do you,' he said handing me a mug with a picture of a doe-eyed puppy on it. It seemed appropriate.

'It looks a bit like you actually, no offence, but you do look a bit lost and worried, like that puppy. It's all right, you know, it's just a party, you're not being kidnapped by a cult and trafficked to Outer Mongolia.'

I pointed out that there would be little point trafficking anyone to Outer Mongolia as the whole point of the 'Outer' bit is that there's hardly anyone there.

'Did you want some then?' I dutifully held the mug with both hands to keep it steady while he poured a hefty mugful of wine almost to the brim, reminding myself that geography nerdiness and pedantically correcting throw-away comments was probably in the 'don'ts' column of the flirting rulebook.

'There you go, that should help you feel a bit less like a lost puppy. Hang on to that mug, once you've lost your drinking vessel you'll have a devil of a job finding another. Cheers!' He clinked the bottle against my mug, picked up his own mug of wine and walked away with both.

With nothing better to do and no-one to offer me any guidance on what I was supposed to do next, I took a sip, approaching it with caution as though it were a hot mug of tea that I might blow on.

I stood there for what seemed like an age, just sipping wine out of a mug. Every now and then someone would speak to me to ask me if I'd seen someone-or-other, or did I know where there were any more cups, or was there anything to eat. And from time to time someone would push past me like I was a household obstacle, a lamp or a chair, knocking me out of their way as they aimed for the other side of the kitchen or reached past me to get a drink or deposit an empty bottle.

Eventually, I heard Claire's voice behind me.

'There you are! I've been looking all over for you.' She peered into my mug. 'You're empty, we can't have that,' she scanned the bottles behind me, looking for one with something left in it. 'Is white OK?' she asked, filling up my mug without waiting for an answer to create a pale pink liquid as the white wine mixed with the remnants of the red. 'There you go,' she beamed, 'and even better than that, look who I've found!'

She placed the now empty bottle back on the counter and stepped back to reveal Christopher Morris. She pointed both arms outstretched towards him, palms facing up, like a magician's assistant eliciting applause for the successfully completed illusion.

I must have looked less pleased than she'd anticipated by her big reveal, because the smile fell from her face and she looked hurt and perplexed as though I'd just rejected a gift. This is how cats must feel when their owner grimaces at the half-dead bird or mouse they bring into the house.

'Marie,' she whispered loudly, turning to Christopher and instructing him to 'stay there a minute'. She grabbed me and pushed me a couple of feet away and then talked right into my face, so close that I could feel her words on my skin as she exhaled them more distinctly than I could hear them.

'Listen Marie, you've got a straight choice now. This party is an opportunity for you. You can choose to be the same old butter-wouldn't-melt, buttoned-up, boring Maria von Trapp with no social life and a shitty little halo, or you can just become a normal teenage girl who hangs out with boys, and doesn't think she's better than everyone else, and isn't always asking herself what Jesus would think.'

'I—'

I was going to say 'I don't think I'm better than anyone else' but Claire hadn't finished and I couldn't get the sentence out before she interrupted.

'Because I'll tell you what Jesus would say to you if he were here, he'd say 'you've got one life, Marie, and you can choose to watch it pass you by or you can grab it with both hands and have fun.' Didn't Jesus die so that you can live? Isn't that what you believe? Well now's the time, Marie, and Christopher is right here, like a gift from the heavens especially for you.'

Claire stepped aside with a final meaningful nod to me.

'What'ya drinking?' Asked Christopher.

I looked down at the slightly pink-tinged liquid in my mug and Christopher leaned forward to inspect the contents without waiting for an answer.

'Looks like you'll be needing a top up soon-ish, eh?'

The mug was full, but Christopher had clearly decided on a narrative that involved us going off to hunt for something to drink together. Claire was giving me the sort of encouraging look a teacher gives a kid that's been asked to read out at the front of the class, even though they've got a chronic stammer and the book is shaking in their hands from pure fear.

'I'm pretty sure I saw some full bottles in the conservatory, or whatever that room is next to the conservatory. Anyway, have fun, I told Scott I'd only be two minutes, he'll think I've abandoned him if I don't get back to him soon.' She gave my arm a final squeeze and threw me one last meaningful look of encouragement, marching off to find Scott, who sat opposite me in chemistry and always picked his nose when he thought no-one was looking.

'So, shall we try the conservatory then?' Christopher nodded in the direction of a door to the left of the kitchen and I took a larger than planned sip of almost white wine from my mug. He was quite handsome really but he hadn't quite grown into his body or his face yet so he looked like someone who might be handsome later; maybe in a decade or so. His face was thin with eyes so dark that you could hardly distinguish the pupil from the iris. They looked like black buttons and they were framed by the kind of long dark eyelashes that every tube of mascara promises and none ever delivers. He was brutally aware of the power of those lashes and, when I took a second gulp of wine without moving, he looked at me through a slow blink.

'It's OK if you don't want to hang out with me. I mean, it's no big deal. Claire just thought you might want to, you know, hang out. Y'know, because you don't really, y'know, mix with that many people really, do you? I don't know why though, I think you're really, y'know, I like you. You look nice by the way, very... girl-next-door.'

I grimaced.

'I mean, not girl-next-door,' he corrected himself, 'I mean, like a rock star on their day off, you know, all casually stylish, the I-don't-have-to-try-too-hard-because-I've-just-got-it look.'

I laughed at his awkwardness, at my awkwardness and at the ridiculousness of standing in the kitchen of a friend I barely knew, with a crowd of people she barely knew, drinking wine that was lukewarm and quite unpleasant from a mug with a puppy on the front. As I laughed a light spray of wine came out through my nose and my laughter turned to choking, with Christopher giving me a few futile pats on the back and clearly not sure whether to act concerned or laugh out loud at my complete lack of social skills. In the end, he went for the latter.

'You're a classy bird you, eh?'

'That's right. I learned the snorting wine through your nose trick at my Swiss finishing school. It's a hard skill to master you know, not everyone can do it.'

Perhaps it was the calming effects of the alcohol, or maybe it was the ice-breaking laughter that made me feel less like I was pinned to the spot awaiting execution and more like I was at a party and here to enjoy myself. I had said something funny and Christopher had laughed and the world had carried on around us as though this were completely normal.

'And the other thing they taught us at finishing school is that a gentleman never lets a lady's mug of wine get empty, not even if he has to wade through a kitchen full of people in search of the one remaining bottle that hasn't been drained dry by the hordes of unwashed plebs.'

He laughed again. And played along.

'Yes, my lady, we must get you to a bottle before the etiquette police come and arrest us for crimes of empty mug-dom and drinkless instability.'

After my gulps my mug actually was almost empty and Christopher grabbed my hand and pulled me through the bodies littering Becca's house, several of them by now far too engrossed in each other to even notice when we pushed past them or protest when Christopher picked up the bottle beside them to see whether it still contained anything. By the time we arrived in the conservatory, I was carrying an empty mug and Christopher had the fingers of one hand wrapped tightly round mine, with the necks of three partially full bottles tightly locked together in his other hand.

The conservatory was less crowded than the rest of the house and much quieter, but the comfy chairs were all taken so Christopher and I sat on a window seat. He even pulled open the blind so that we could see into the garden, but there was no romantic clear starry sky, it was just damp and suburban with a view of garden furniture all dressed up in its overcoats ready for winter and an elaborate swing, climbing frame and slide structure that you might expect to see in a park. Behind that was a shed that looked like some kind of woodland holiday cabin.

Now that it was just the two of us, the cocky, confident boy that I knew from the classroom melted away, leaving behind a doppelganger that seemed not to have been given a copy of the partygoer's manual either.

We sat silently looking out into the garden for a couple of minutes.

'It's a nice house, isn't it?' Christopher commented eventually. 'Have you been here before?'

'No'

'Me neither.'

Silence.

'My cousin lives in a house a bit like this,' he said.

'Oh yeah?'

'Except his has even got a swimming pool.'

'Really?'

'Yeah, but it's an outdoor one, in the garden, you can only use it when the weather's warm enough.'

'That's a shame'

'Yeah, but he lives down south though, so the weather's quite often warmer than it is here.'

'Right.'

'His dad – my mum's sister's husband – works in London, in a bank or something like that, so they're rolling in it, cash I mean.'

'Of course.'

'Different world innit, London and that.'

'Yeah.'

Silence.

'I like your jumper.'

I admired the way he kept trying to get the conversation going, and felt bad for letting it fizzle out. It was just that I had nothing to say about big houses and swimming pools. My experiences of those stretched as far as a school trip to Chatsworth House and the local leisure centre, which wasn't really comparable to Becca's house or the pool at Christopher's cousin's.

'I'm a bit warm in it actually. It's cooler in here than it was in the kitchen, but it's still a bit warm.'

'So take it off.'

'But I've only got a vest top on underneath'

'So?'

He averted his eyes as I peeled the jumper off as though I was stripping full naked. The vest I was wearing underneath was black and had 'cheeky' written across the bosom area in small white writing.

'What does it say?'

'Cheeky.'

'And are you?'

'Sometimes.'

Laughter. Then silence.

Christopher topped up my mug with lukewarm white wine and emptied the rest into his own Winnie the Pooh beaker.

'Becca chose this one for me because it has Christopher Robin on it.'

I smiled. I was feeling less nervous, maybe from the wine, maybe from the shared awkwardness.

'So the reason I'm wearing such a big, thick jumper...'

'Not any more!'

'The reason I was wearing it is because I told my mum I was coming to a sleepover at Becca's house and around now she thinks we're painting each other's nails, eating chocolate biscuits and giggling about boys.'

'Not drinking wine and talking to boys then?'

'Heaven forbid. Between the lie, the wine and the conversation with you, I'm due about sixteen million Hail Marys.'

'That's a serious sore throat.'

We laughed again and I told him all about why I'd lied to my mum about where I was going. Not just the stuff about being in trouble at school and my mum being sacked from cleaning at Mrs Wilkes' house, but all about the house where I lived; the small rooms, the swirly carpet that made your eyes go funny, the ornaments, the obsessive cleaning and tidying, the need for everything it its place. I told him how it had always been just the two of us and how me and Mum were close, but sometimes it was a closeness that was suffocating, as though we were the only two people left in the world and had to rely on each other for everything.

Christopher said nothing as I talked, but just nodded from time to time so I'd know he could hear and understand what I was saying. He waited for me to begin again each time I took a sip, or paused, or hesitated, topping up my mug when he could see that it was getting empty and looking straight at me to encourage me to carry on talking.

I told him that you never knew which Mum you were going to get from one day to the next. How, sometimes, she would be full of fun and ideas and energy. I told him about the time she'd woken me up on a Saturday morning and said that she'd taken the day off and we were going on an adventure. How we'd gone to the station with a plan to catch whichever train was next to leave and had ended up in Liverpool for the day, wandering round the Walker Gallery striking the poses of the figures in the paintings and sculptures and catching a Mersey Ferry just to ride there and back.

But other times, she'd be in a bad mood for no reason. She'd complain about having no money and working too hard. About how expensive life is. How expensive it is to have a daughter. How she might just one day fall over and never get up again. I told Christopher about the days when she took a nap in the afternoon and the weekends when she didn't get up until lunchtime and spent both Saturday and Sunday in her pyjamas. I even told him about the time we had cheese and crackers for tea, followed by biscuits for pudding and how much I'd come to despise tinned ravioli because it was the over-sweet ketchupy taste of her bad days.

Christopher just listened, nodding and changing his facial expression to show me he was still with me but saying nothing in response. Only once before had I ever even begun to tell anyone any of this, when I was best friends with a girl called Anna who'd left our school when her family moved to the South of France to run a B&B. I'd got one or two sentences in and Anna had responded with 'My mum's a bit like that, she yelled at me this morning just because I put the empty cereal packet back in the cupboard instead of in the bin. Mums should go to parent training college like teachers have to.' I'd laughed and closed the curtains on life in our house again.

But here with Christopher, with the noise of the party rumbling away behind us and the quiet of the dark garden in front on us, I shaped feelings into words like I never had before. If he'd been more skilled in small talk, or I had, or we'd both been less nervous or less on the edge of the party, those sentences would never have been formed and even the thoughts would have stayed buried.

Christopher topped up my drink again and poured the last of the second bottle he'd brought out from the kitchen into his own mug. He still said nothing and just looked at me and then into the garden, and I followed his eyes into the darkness. I'd finished talking and the current that had been sweeping my words along beyond my control had been interrupted. But Christopher was making no attempt to fill our new silence. Maybe he had nothing to say. Or perhaps he knew that some words are locked away so securely that they need time to work their way free with no distractions.

I looked into his reflection in the window. He returned my eye contact via the glass and took hold of my hand, just wrapping his fingers around it softly so that we were connected in a complete circle, physically in the real world of Becca's conservatory and out into our reflected images and their distorted double-glazed echoes, suspended in the garden.

'About two years ago, no, it's more like three, nearly three, because it was when my mum's Uncle Paddy died and that was a couple of weeks before Christmas, I went to bed but I couldn't sleep. Mum still had the heating on because she'd stayed up and it was really cold. You probably remember it was the year when everyone thought we might have a white Christmas and then it snowed just before but it had all turned to mush by the time we got to actual Christmas.

'So I was roasting and I couldn't sleep and I heard Mum come upstairs and I heard her go into the bathroom but I didn't hear any water running or the toilet flushing, just a kind of thwoop noise. I knew what it was because we'd had the brandy out earlier in the day with a knitting needle, piercing the Christmas cake and dousing it one last time, then rewrapping it in brown paper and putting it back in the tin to soak up the alcohol in time for Christmas. We do it every year; it's one of those Christmas traditions that's part of the countdown and hasn't changed since I was very little, except I don't have to stand on a chair now to plunge the knitting needle into the cake and she doesn't pretend that the brandy is 'magic juice'. She doesn't even knit: that's the knitting needle's only purpose in life, to make little worm holes in the cake.

'So I heard the cork stopper and I knew it wasn't right and when I got into the bathroom she was there with pills all laid out in front of her on the window ledge and the bottle in her hand. Taking a big swig.

'I don't remember what I said to her or what she yelled at me. It's like one of those dreams you have when you remember stupid details but you can't figure out what exactly happened in what order. I remember she was wearing her dressing gown with her clothes underneath. I remember that a shampoo bottle was knocked over and made a pink oil slick from one end of the bath to the other.

'And I remember grabbing hold of the pills and running into my bedroom and opening the window and throwing them out into the back yard where they hit the hard, wet ground like sugar sprinkles on a cake, with pink and pale blue pills scattered in amongst the white.'

Christopher said nothing. He just carried on looking out to the garden as though I was telling him about a programme I'd seen on TV the night before.

'She chased me in there, and tried to snatch the pills from my hand. She pulled at me to get me away from the window and pushed me to the ground and then leant out to see the pills starting to dissolve on the concrete flags.

'I remember her stepping over me then and going down to the back yard to try to pick them up and I had to follow her, in my pyjamas and my bare feet. And, as though God were watching and had decided to intervene, it had started raining hard, so by the time I made it through the back door that she'd left wide open she was soaked through and kneeling, pawing at pills that were already slimy and too soft to pick up with her panicked fingers.'

I never broke eye contact with Christopher in our shared reflection and he didn't look away either. He seemed repulsed and enthralled as we sat side by side in the confessional, with my unstoppable words tumbling like a landslide and his eyes punctuating my sentences every time he blinked with those luxuriant lashes.

'So I had to pick her up gently and get her to leave the mess on the flags and come back with me into the house. I had to find her a towel and help her get dry and ready for bed. I made her a cup of tea, which I put on the little table next to her bed, and I helped her to bed and kissed her goodnight and told her it would all be OK. I said 'goodnight God bless' like she's said to me every night of my life. And then I went to the bathroom and put the stopper back in the brandy and took it back down to the kitchen and into the cupboard ready for the next Christmas cake. I went out in the rain with the yard brush and swept what was left of the pills into the weeds by the fence, until everything was like it had been, apart from it wasn't sweltering anymore because I'd left the window open in my bedroom and the window ledge was wet through.

'The next day we got up for work and school as normal and she said nothing about it, so I didn't either. It's never been mentioned again since. She does that, just moves on without another word. Or maybe she's blocked it from her memory or convinced herself it didn't really happen.'

I turned away from Christopher's reflection to look at his actual face when I'd finished my story, perhaps it would look different or show me something I couldn't see in the glass. But he carried on looking straight ahead.

'Look,' he said, 'Out there on the lawn, can you see it?'

I looked out but didn't know what I was looking for.

'There,' he whispered, 'a fox.'

As soon as he said it, I could make out the fox, illuminated by the light from the conservatory, just casually walking across the lawn, loitering as if he had all the time in the world, sniffing the grass, confident that this was his space and he belonged there.

'It's beautiful, isn't it?' Christopher whispered.

'It's like magic, stepping out of the night, coming to put on a show just for us,' I said, and the fox looked like he'd heard me because he stopped ambling across the garden and turned to look right at us.

I looked straight into the mirrored darkness of the fox's eyes and, as he looked back at me, I stopped seeing a fox walking across an empty garden and saw my mum's face, all upset and annoyed that I'd shared her secrets with Christopher and betrayed her twice in a single night, first with my lie about the sleepover and then with my confession.

'Go on then,' the fox said to me. 'There's more, isn't there. You might as well finish it off. You may as well give Christopher the full warts and all of it. Why don't you tell him why I'm such a screwed up mess? Why don't you tell him what I told you?'

'There's something else,' I said, and he glanced away from the fox to look at me. 'My mum told me last week that she had me after she was raped by someone who gave her a lift home from church.'

The words were far too big for their little sentence. Christopher took a deep breath and looked back out into the garden but the fox had gone.

SEVENTEEN

We had to walk to church from school to see the Stations of the Cross. As school trips go, this was about as lame as it gets; no coach, no extras in your packed lunch to eat on the way there and no gift shop. We had to walk crocodile-style and we weren't even allowed to choose our own pairs, so I had to walk all the way next to Martha Buckley, who's OK but she talks all the time about nothing much, even when she was paired up with me, who wasn't even remotely interested in a word that came out of her mouth. I had Arthur and Christopher behind me though, so I could talk to them on the way, which was OK, except I had to keep turning round so that they could hear me and every time I turned round Martha punched me in the arm for not listening to her.

I also had Captain hidden in my bag and I was worried that people would hear the sound of the tin clanking against my lunch box in my backpack as we walked along. Even if it did make a noise, though, Martha's chattering and the constant hum of conversation in the supposedly quiet crocodile – 'they hunt by stealth, you know,' John-Joe once told me, 'that's why school calls it a crocodile because it's supposed to move along silently' – would easily camouflage the sound.

'Not the best crocodile in the world, are you Year 6?' said Mrs Drake as we stopped like a row of dominoes along the pavement outside the church gates, with some of the kids towards the back knocking into the ones in front of them because they hadn't realised we were stopping. Actually, we were nothing like a crocodile.

'Year 6!' Mrs Drake put down the box she'd been carrying all the way there and held her hand in the air with her palm facing forwards, waiting for silence in a gesture that looked more like she was trying to stop traffic. In Year 1, the teacher used to clap at us in a one-two, one-two-three-four rhythm to signal that we needed to be quiet. We had to clap the same rhythm back. That worked much better than the whole palm in the air thing, but Mrs Drake was new and she thought we were too old for clapping. The stopping traffic thing usually did work OK, eventually, in the classroom, but she hadn't much of a hope outside. Word was passing back through the line like Chinese whispers that Mrs Drake was doing the sign of silence and Miss Groves, the teaching assistant at the back, mostly to make sure no-one wandered off to the park on the way, was doing her best to send the message up the other way too. But you could see Mrs Drake was getting frustrated. And so were the people walking past. A woman came along with a dog and half the class bent to stroke it as she passed. She looked pleased when the first one or two did it at the beginning of the line, but by the time she'd slowly made it to the end of the crocodile she was glad to be free of us.

And still Mrs Drake stood there with her hand in the air, waiting for complete silence and saying nothing. 'She looks like Moses trying to part the Red Sea,' Martha whispered. It's possibly the funniest thing Martha has ever said and I laughed out loud.

'Is something funny, Jim?' Mrs Drake broke her silence to say my name.

Since we'd gone back to school all the teachers had been extra-specially nice to me. Not that they weren't nice to me before, I'm the kind of kid that gets my work done, keeps my books neat and puts my hand up to answer questions. All my school reports say nice things and I always get a treat after parents' evening because the teachers have said such good things about me. But since John-Joe died they'd all gone out of their way to be nice to me. John-Joe may not have

171

been the kind of kid that always listened when the teacher was talking and he sometimes couldn't be bothered doing homework, but all the teachers liked him, even though he was always asking random questions that no-one else would think to ask, usually without putting his hand up first. Maybe that was why they liked him. But Mrs Drake only started at our school that September, so she didn't know me very much and she'd never met John-Joe. She might have known that I had a brother who died, the other teachers must have told her that, but she didn't know him so she had no reason to be nice to me.

'Jim?'

Everyone looked at her as though she'd just blown out the candle on someone else's birthday cake or farted in the middle of the Our Father.

'No Miss.'

'So why I are you laughing?'

'I told him a joke, Miss,' Martha replied.

'I didn't ask you, Martha.'

Martha looked like she might cry. She had never been told off for anything in her life and now she had told a lie on her way into church and been snapped at by a teacher. Even at school where everything was at its most normal things were slightly off balance, it was like John-Joe dying had tipped something in the universe so that there was a bit of a kink.

The whole class was so shocked that Mrs Drake had told off the dead boy's brother and the world champion goody-two-shoes that they had all fallen silent, so she quit while she was ahead and didn't say another word. Instead, she put her finger on her lips and we automatically all copied her. Then she put her palms together in front of her chest as though to pray and we all did the same, walking past her into the churchyard through the heavy metal gates like a rabble of unholy altar boys and girls, with our grey and red school uniforms and our rainbow of back packs and school bags.

School church is not like the church we go to at home; it's the same priest though, Father O'Connor, who must spend a big chunk of every day driving from one church to the other in his bright red Ford Fiesta, with the rosary beads swinging to and fro on the rear view mirror every time he turns a corner. He's super-ancient and barely any taller than me, but he's kind and he always tells the children a cheesy joke when we go up to the front to do the Our Father. He must have a book of cheesy jokes for kids. Mum always says he's a good man and a hard-working priest. He definitely talks a lot and drinks a lot of tea, that's for sure.

They do all the same stuff in school church as we do at our church, they have the same dog-eared books for following the Mass and saying the right responses at the same time, we say all the same words and kneel and stand up and sit down in all the same places and we say the same prayers to the same God of course, but school church – St Anthony's – feels different.

Mum won't come here, that's why we go to a different church for Mass, St Chad's. She says it's clammy at St Anthony's and she can't breathe in there. She says it creeps her out, but Nanna used to go to St Anthony's, before she died, and it didn't creep her out.

It doesn't creep me out either but it does feel different. Not just because it's old and looks more like what you'd think a church should look like, with its carved wood and big paintings and a big golden dome over the altar. And not just because it's always cold, even when it's sunny outside, or because the heating constantly makes a noise that sounds like someone standing behind you and humming a single note as quietly as they can. It's not even because of the smell of old books and charity shops; it's just the feeling. St Chad's and St Anthony's both have all that extra space so that you feel small inside the building; I think they leave extra space above your head to make a buffer between us down here and God up there, so that our thoughts can be filtered and the unholy stuff can sink back down. But at St Anthony's, there's so much space you feel as though it's wrapped around you. The way sound works is different at St Anthony's too; when someone stands at the altar and tries to make themself heard to everyone, their voice gets sucked into the walls and into the air all around them and you haven't a hope of hearing a word if you're sitting at the back. But if you whisper something to the person next to you because you're bored of all the standing up and sitting down and waiting for the gaps to say 'pray for us', it's as if you had a microphone hidden in your shirt like a TV presenter and everyone on the next pew and the one after that and even the one after that can hear you.

Mrs Drake led us up the aisle then turned to face us and motioned for to us to sit down on the pews either side. I wondered if she was planning on making us spend the whole morning in complete silence while she communicated entirely through sign language. Or perhaps the way sound behaves abnormally at St Anthony's freaks her out too.

'Listen to that Year 6,' she said eventually, when the last of us was sitting down and the sound of rustling coats and bags thudding on the pews next to us had finished.

'Can you hear it?' This was clearly a rhetorical question.

'That's the beautiful, holy sound of silence and that's the sound I want to continue hearing while I hand round the clip boards and explain what I want you to do this morning. It's also the sound I expect to hear while you walk round carrying out the task.'

John-Joe was standing in the aisle next to me so I moved up a bit to let him sit down. Mrs Drake gave me the look as I shuffled along the pew.

'It's not even silent anyway,' said John-Joe, 'You can hear everyone breathing and you can hear the radiators.'

'Shhhh.' I forgot no-one else could hear him.

'I'll be doing any shhh-ing if it's needed, thank you Jim.' Mrs Drake was much stricter outside of school than she was in the classroom and she was bad enough in school. She was also super-keen on all the religious stuff; our class had never prayed so much or written so many prayers, even when we were supposed to be doing creative writing she had us writing about God and Jesus. And now a school trip to church where at least half the class went every Sunday anyway.

'Catherine and Rachel, can you hand everyone a clipboard please?' She opened the box that she'd rested on the pew beside her and handed Catherine and Rachel an armful of clipboards each, which had paper already clipped to them.

'If anyone has coloured pens or pencils with them you may silently get them out of your bags now because they will come in useful as you walk round the church doing your own depictions of the Stations of the Cross.'

'How are you supposed to open a zip on your bag silently or get a tin of pencils out of your bag without making a noise?' John-Joe rolled his eyes and shook his head and pulled his tongue out at Mrs Drake.

I just ignored him and took my pencil case out, moving the tin with Captain in it to the top of my backpack while I had the chance. I saw John-Joe looking at the tin but he didn't say anything. Rachel shoved a clipboard at me and I took it.

'Now, has everyone got a clipboard?' We all nodded as silently as possible and Mrs Drake nodded to Miss Groves to check we were all armed with our equipment while she gave us our instructions.

'Those of you sitting on this side of the pew will start with the first seven Stations of the Cross,' she gestured towards the wall where the depictions of Jesus' route to crucifixion were vividly portrayed in kind of 3D pottery pictures along the wall. 'You will draw your own picture of each Station and write a description underneath in the line provided.

'The rest of you,' she turned to the pews on the other side of the aisle, 'Will start with the last seven Stations of the Cross, which is not ideal but we can't have everyone in a crush on that side of the church all at once. There are seven boxes for pictures on each page and you should all have two pages, simply switch over the page on the front of the clipboard when you switch sides of the church. Please remember to number each Station – children on this side that means yours will start with number eight, children on this side,' she turned to face my group again, 'that means yours will start with number one.'

She looked around at a sea of confused and unenthusiastic faces. It didn't seem fair that some people were going to have to start from the end of the story and go backwards. It's not like any of us didn't know how it all ends – gruesome actually, it would definitely be rated higher than a PG in the cinema and here we were on a school trip expected to lap up all the blood and guts – but a story's not the same if you tell it backwards.

'If there is too much congestion at the particular Station you're drawing, it is fine for you to draw the Stations out of sequence but you must have them in the correct order with the numbers by each one on your sheet. Is that clear?'

Twenty-nine blank faces said nothing.

'Good. Off you go.'

'So does that mean I can start with number three as long as I leave space for numbers one and two and go back to them later?' Arthur asked me.

'Yes, that's right.'

'Thanks Jim.'

'Jim?' Mrs Drake stared at me.

'I was just helping Arthur, Miss.'

'If Arthur needs any help he can ask me,' she snapped back at me. 'Now off you go in silence please.'

John-Joe stood behind Mrs Drake pulling faces and saying 'Off you go in silence please.' She was annoying but he was being even more annoying.

Arthur stuck with me as we started drawing the Stations of the Cross, so I was sandwiched between him and John-Joe and it all got a bit claustrophobic. Arthur can be a bit clingy like that and he always assumes he's not doing his work right so he looks over my shoulder a lot to see what I'm doing. I don't mind usually, but in the church it was really starting to get on my nerves, especially when I had John-Joe in my ear telling me what I was doing wrong and how I should be doing it better.

'You haven't left enough room for the sky.'

I looked at him by way of asking him to elaborate. At St Anthony's even if I whispered to him Mrs Drake would hear me.

'Look, Jesus' head is almost at the top of the box and Pilate's going to be standing on that step so his head will be even higher and there'll be no room for sky.'

I was only on the first Station and just getting used to doing it. And, anyway, drawing's not my best thing, maths is more my thing. If John-Joe had been alive I would have thumped him at this point but I was afraid to touch dead John-Joe because, even though I could see him and hear him, if I tried to touch him he might not be there.

'I can just make it so that Pilate's not as tall as Jesus,' I whispered.

Mrs Drake heard me, of course.

'Jim, just so that you understand what I mean when I say silence, silence does not mean whispering to your friends when you are supposed to be concentrating on depicting the most special story ever told.'

'Sorry Miss. I sometimes mumble a bit to myself when I'm concentrating.'

'Concentrating is good, Jim, but mumbling is not good, you'll disrupt the others. Get on with it please, you should be on the next Station by now.'

'Mumbling is not good,' John-Joe repeated. Super annoying.

I drew Pilate like a semi-midget and, even though there was no sun shining on the picture on the wall I drew a sun in the sky just to prove to John-Joe he'd been wrong about the space left in my frame for the sky. Anyway, they were in Israel so there should have been sunshine in the picture. Like a lemming,

Arthur put a sun in his sky too, so Mrs Drake was bound to know he'd been copying me.

It was freezing in the church even though it was sunny outside and everyone was walking round in their coats, communicating with elaborate sign language and exaggerated facial expressions to overcome the barrier of silence that Mrs Drake had put up. It's amazing how much you can say without a single word. It's also odd how much you miss speaking and how unnatural it feels to stay silent when there are other people around, even when you have nothing to say.

John-Joe had plenty to say. According to him, every picture I drew had something wrong with it and, while the rest of the class moved from Station to Station, accompanied only by the sound of their shoes squeaking on the stone floor, their pencils scraping on the paper, the low hum of the heating and the irregular interruption of coughs and sneezes, I struggled to concentrate with John-Joe's running commentary on everything I was doing wrong.

'You've got the cross at the wrong angle, he'd never be able to carry it like that, it needs to be further back on his shoulder or he'd be tripping up over it.

'Look, he has to balance the cross bit on his shoulder because it's heavy,' John-Joe mimed being Jesus with a heavy, invisible cross.

I needed him to shut up. I had to get on with doing the drawings, deal with the irritation of Arthur standing about two centimetres from me so that he could constantly look over my shoulder and try and figure out how I was going to get Captain out of my bag so that I could hide him somewhere at St Anthony's where he'd be safe and looked after without upsetting my mum or being anywhere she could find him. I had to fix things.

'You're putting too much detail in,' John-Joe had nothing positive to say about my drawings, he just had a long list of the things I was doing wrong; like he could have done any better.

'You're never going to get round all fourteen stations if you're taking this long on each one. Look, you're just finishing Jesus falling for the first time, he's got to fall another two times before he gets to the top of the hill and then you have to draw him being nailed to the cross, dying and being put in the tomb. The rate you're going he'll already have come back to life again and rolled the stone away before you go back to school.

'If you just start with the cross and draw around that, that'll make it easier. It's all about the cross really, isn't it? I know it's Jesus' story and all that but the cross is the symbol, isn't it? It's 'Stations of the Cross,' not 'Stations of Jesus,' so If I were you I'd just draw the cross and then look to see who else is supposed to be in the picture.'

'Will you just shut up!' I had meant to think the words in my head but he was really getting on my nerves and they just tumbled out of my mouth loudly in the silence. Everyone stopped what they were doing and looked at me. Mrs Drake was standing next to me in a nano-second.

'Jim, what exactly is it that you don't understand about silence? Everyone else seems to be able to work quietly and diligently but you seem to think that normal rules don't apply just because you're outside school. But here we are in God's house, Jim, you need to show even more respect and more humility. This is not a morning off, it's a very special lesson in a very special place.'

I looked intently at the necklace she was wearing, which was a little silver bird with a twig in its beak anchored at either side by a chain. I hoped my bowed head showed regret and apology and I also wanted to avoid catching John-Joe's eye because I could see him on the edge of my vision, pretending to be Mrs Drake telling me off.

'It's a shame Jim, because you've done some nice work here, though there's not very much of it, is there? And it looks like you've been heavily influenced by Arthur's efforts, which is disappointing.'

Arthur mouthed 'sorry' at me but Miss couldn't see him.

'I'm afraid I'm going to have to ask you to sit out the rest of the session, Jim, and reflect on how you need to behave in church. I've never seen you here at Mass, perhaps that's why you don't know what's expected of you in God's house.'

'We go to a different church, Miss.'

'Is that right? Well I'm disappointed to hear you shouting out like that in this church, Jim, so I'd like you to sit out the rest of the session over there and you can complete the task at home by looking up the Stations of the Cross on the internet.'

She gestured towards the bench and I took my clipboard and sat down. Gradually the rest of the class stopped watching me and continued drawing the Stations and walking round in extra-quiet silence.

Miss Groves took pity on me while Mrs Drake wandered round looking over people's shoulders and telling them they'd done good work or suggesting ways they could improve their pictures. She came and sat next to me and asked me quietly if I was OK.

I like Miss Groves, she was my teaching assistant in reception and Gabe was in her class last year. John-Joe was never in her class but she knew him because she's the kind of teacher who knows everyone and everyone's stuff; not in a nosey way just in an interested way.

I nodded quietly at her and she started to say that it must be difficult and how everyone misses John-Joe, which was nice of her, but Mrs Drake heard her, even though she was talking in the quietest of whispers and came to tell her off, almost as though she were one of the kids.

'Miss Groves, I think the children working on Stations eight to fourteen could do with some input, if you don't mind.' They smiled at each other like adults do when they're letting each other go first in a queue when really they'd like to elbow each other out of the way to be at the front but the world expects them to have better manners. Miss Groves stopped long enough to give me a proper smile and pat me on the back of the shoulder, even though Mrs Drake was standing there waiting for her to do as she'd been told.

When she'd gone and everyone was busy again drawing their Stations or supervising the pictures, I knew it was time to get Captain out of my bag and give him back to Jesus. It was easy to find the tin without too much rummaging because I'd moved it to the top when I took out my pencil case and it was hard and cold to the touch.

'What are you doing?' asked John-Joe kneeling up on the pew in front of me to peer at my backpack. I couldn't risk answering him or even showing him, in case Mrs Drake spotted me. I took the tin out of my bag and slid it onto my knee. I looked around to make sure everyone was still occupied, then slid it off my knee and onto the pew next to me.

'You can't do that!' John-Joe leaned forward to reach for the tin. 'Captain belongs at home with us.'

I looked straight at John-Joe as I quietly slid the tin off the pew and leaned down towards the floor, looking up the whole time until I felt it make contact with the tiles and carefully laid it flat. Then I sat up slowly and pushed it under the pew with my foot, making sure I worked it into the corner so that it sat snugly in the right angle of the wood where no-one would see it or trip over it.

'Why are you doing that? Captain is ours, he belongs at home with us. We resurrected him, He's like our version of Jesus waiting to rise up back to life.' John-Joe looked really upset.

'He upsets Mum, she wanted him gone,' I whispered, 'and I shouldn't have brought him back in the house because she'll never be OK while he's there.'

John-Joe looked upset but he nodded because he knew I was right.

'Jim, I thought I told you to sit there for the rest of the session in complete silence,' Mrs Drake was right next to me like she'd teleported over again. 'Enlighten me Jim, why is it you don't think the word silence applies to you?'

'Sorry Miss,' I looked at my hands for extra humility. 'I was just saying some quiet prayers for my dead brother, John-Joe.'

John-Joe smiled and gave me a double thumbs-up.

'Right, well, I suppose that does mean that you've remembered you're in God's house and understand how to behave here. You'd better get as many Stations finished as you can before we head back to school.'

EIGHTEEN

I hadn't noticed any effects from the wine while Christopher and I had been talking and looking out into the night, but once I'd finished speaking and he found he had nothing to say, a creeping fuzziness started first in my limbs and then in my head until I wasn't quite sure how many words had actually been spoken out loud and how much of it had been in my head. I wanted Christopher to take my hand and tell me it was all fine. I wanted reassurance, some kind of sign that he was OK with me telling him all that stuff. Maybe even a word to say that he was glad I'd shared my secrets and they would be safe with him. I reached out for him to take my hand but he either didn't notice or he didn't want to. He just sat, looking out into the darkness, his eyes searching the garden for the fox that had completely vanished.

'You two look like an old couple out for a country drive,' said Claire, bounding up behind us and slapping me on the back so that I was jolted out of my own space and back into the party. 'All you need is a picnic blanket over your lap, a Tupperware of sandwiches and a flask of milky tea and you could be parked up at a beauty spot admiring the view and reminiscing about your courting days.'

I turned and gave her the little laugh and amused expression she was looking for: she was funny; she just wasn't very good at choosing her moment, or reading the mood. Or she didn't care.

'So, have you snogged her yet?'

Christopher was still looking out into the garden when Claire spoke. He turned with painful slowness to look at her, trying to process what she'd said as though she'd asked a question about theoretical physics in Japanese.

'What?' he said, eventually.

'We've just been talking actually,' I said, trying to fill any dead air space where she might otherwise be able to squeeze her embarrassing question in again. 'Actually, it would be more accurate to say that I've been talking and Christopher's been listening. He's a great a listener. You're a great listener.' I turned to him trying to convey something of my panic that he might repeat what I'd told him if she asked him, while still trying to appear relatively normal and cheery to avoid being distracted by the unfamiliar fuzziness in my head.

'Talking is it? Well each to their own, I suppose, I prefer snogging myself.' She let out a huge guffaw, which seemed to surprise even her with its volume and made everyone else in the conservatory sit up and look at us as though they were noticing us for the first time.

'Are you both OK for a drink?'

My mug was almost empty again but I didn't want any more.

'I think there's still some in here,' said Christopher, handing her one of the part-filled bottles he'd brought with us from the kitchen. 'I'm dying for a pee actually.'

Christopher stood up and Claire blocked his path as though she were marking her opposite number at netball.

'Was it something I said?' she asked.

'I just really need a pee, so, unless you want me to make a puddle on the floor, I suggest you let me pass.'

She didn't move.

'You're into that, are you?'

I wasn't sure where the animosity between Christopher and Claire was coming from. Claire stepped out of his way.

'Have one for me while you're there, will you?' she said as he brushed past her.

'Actually, could you bring me a drink of water?' I added. 'You can use this if you like, just pour away what's left in there, unless you want it.'

I stretched out my arm to give him the mug, but Claire snatched it from my hand before he could take it and gulped what was left in there.

'Waste not, want not,' she chirped, handing the mug back to him. And we both watched him walk back through the conservatory to the kitchen, closing the door behind him.

'So,' she asked, as soon as Christopher was definitely out of the room. 'What's the story? Why haven't you snogged him? I thought you liked him?'

'I thought you thought he liked me?'

'What?'

'Never mind, I do like him. Actually I like him more than I thought I would.'

'So why haven't you snogged him? Hang on a minute, when you say like him do you mean fancy or do you mean just like?'

I opened my mouth like a fish, with no noise coming out.

'Well, it doesn't matter either way really. I handed him to you on a plate. I agreed with him that he was going snog you, more than snog maybe if you got on all right. I set it all up for you and here you are *talking* like you couldn't do that every day at school. What did you even talk about anyway? The fucking weather? The fucking vintage of the cheap plonk you've been necking?'

The Claire that had been my mentor and my partner in crime a couple of hours ago had become the voice of my subconscious, telling me what a pathetic loser I was. She looked the same but different: an angry, ugly version of herself who fired words like bullets and didn't blink.

There was a chasm where her words had ended and mine had not yet begun and I was aware of the stares of curiosity filling that space as the remaining people in the conservatory stopped speaking to listen.

'Claire,' I said standing up so that she and I were face to face instead of her leering down at me. 'The thing is, I'm new to all this, as you know. And I'm really glad you brought me and invited me and arranged for me to get together with Christopher and all of it: I'm really grateful. But we just got into a conversation that turned into something a bit too heavy for party chat, I suppose. I'm no good at flirting...'

She snorted at that and her reaction put me off my stride.

'Look Marie, all you needed to do was agree with everything he said and laugh at his jokes and you'd be there. It's not rocket science. Everyone can fucking flirt. But I can just imagine what you were like. You probably bored him half to death with your pseudo-intellectual bullshit and made him feel like snogging you would feel like snogging a teacher or the librarian or something.

'I went to a lot of effort. A *lot* of effort. I made this happen for you Marie. I cleared it with your mum, I cleared it with Becca, I set everything up with Christopher and here you are, sitting on your own, looking out of the window imagining what life would be like if you actually lived it. Well, you carry on peeping in at the rest of us if you want; I'll see you later.'

Before I could say anything else, she'd gone, leaving the door between the conservatory and the kitchen open so that the noise from the rest of the party filled the room like smoke.

I sat back down in my seat, looked back out into the garden and waited. I was only half waiting for Christopher, which was good because he didn't come back and I didn't know what I would say to him or what I'd do if he reappeared. I sat there, Claire's failed Pygmalion experiment, reprimanding myself for not doing everything differently, for not being different. As the noseying onlookers gradually stopped staring at me and returned to their own conversations and intimate moments I sank into the background, wondering as I merged with the darkness of the garden whether I could have done things any differently, or if this had been fixed for me since birth.

I moved to a chair that someone had left empty. I'm not sure how long I spent there. I may have slept, I may have just drifted off into a place in my own head where thoughts start to form and then get lost again like the shapes you see in clouds. I was there long enough for the sting of Claire's words to ease off with the effects of the wine and for both to be replaced by a feeling that nothing really mattered and nothing was real.

The noise of the party had died down and I considered going to look for Claire; there was a niggling feeling sitting somewhere behind anything that made any sense that I should go and apologise to her because that was what she expected and that would make things right. But I didn't want to see her and be reminded of how disappointed she was with me. Having let everyone down – Claire, my mum, Christopher – I just wanted to escape from my own head and my own skin, rewind to before it had all happened and start again so that I could do it all properly this time.

Instead of looking for Claire, I opted for some fresh air and opened up the patio door into the garden. It was cold outside but the cold felt good as it wrapped itself around me and I breathed it in deep. It had looked really dark in the garden from inside the house but, now that I was part of the darkness, the conservatory seemed much too bright and its light made it easy enough for me to find my way across the patio to the steps and then the grass. I looked for the fox. Maybe I could ask him some questions about what to do next. Perhaps the fox would become my mum again and sort everything out for me the way mums are supposed to.

I didn't see the fox. Maybe he was bored of me, or maybe he had never been there at all. But I heard a voice.

'What's this? Some kind of dare? Who can be the first girl at the party to catch pneumonia by wandering round the garden wearing next to nothing in the early hours?'

It was the boy that had got me the mug and poured me my first serving of red wine in the kitchen, a lifetime ago. He was sitting on the swing, his own mug on the ground by his feet, looking ridiculously large in the wooden frame of Becca's mini play park.

He was right, I'd left my jumper in the house and I couldn't even remember where my coat might be; I was standing in the dark, in a vest top, in the garden of a girl I barely knew, talking to a boy I just about recognised.

'You're right, I should go and get my jumper. It's inside.'

'It's OK, you can have my jacket.'

He'd taken off his hoodie before he'd finished the sentence and handed it to me.

'It'd be rude to refuse, you know. This kind of chivalry doesn't happen every day. Certainly not from me. I love that jacket; it's just on loan, I'll be wanting it back.'

He watched me as I put it on, zipped it up and put the hood up, shivering with the transition from cold to warm.

'You look like ET riding the bicycle across the moon with the hood up like that,' he smiled.

'You do know that in no way qualifies as a compliment, don't you?'

'Actually,' he gestured for me to take the seat next to him on the swings, 'ET is very cute and adored by millions around the world.'

'Just like me, then.' I sat, flinching at the cold and damp of the hard seat. 'I can barely move for fan mail every morning. We've actually been through six postmen this year because they've all got back injuries from the weight of all those letters.'

He laughed. 'You're funny.'

'Yeah? Most people say funny but mean peculiar.'

'I like peculiar.'

'There you go, you did mean peculiar when you said funny.'

'Nope, I meant funny. I like funny and I like peculiar.'

I was still shivering from the cold in my bones but his compliment made my face burn. Here I was, tired, dishevelled and out of place, wearing someone else's hoody and talking to a boy, a good looking one that could have chosen pretty much any girl in the party to join him on the swings, and he was flirting with me. And I was flirting back. Surely I'd morphed into someone else or tumbled into a parallel universe.

'How come you're not inside, with everyone else?' I asked him.

'I just needed a break. A bullshit break. They're all so full of shit and so desperate to be liked. And to be like each other. If you say anything about anything they're so quick to agree and tell you they loved that film or they've been to that holiday resort or they'd love to do that. It's all so boring.'

'So what are you doing here then?' The words came out more spiky than I'd intended.

'Oohhh, quite the little interrogator aren't we?'

'Sorry,' I blushed even harder, I was back into my own skin and my knack of blurting out the wrong thing because I wouldn't recognise the right thing to say if it jumped out of a bush in front of me and danced a jig.

'Don't apologise, you're right. I've asked myself the same question. The answer is, I think, I haven't found anything else. I'm bored of this, I don't really like it, but what else is there? Stay at home watching TV with my parents? Jump on some alternative youth bandwagon?'

'You could be a Goth. You'd never have to worry about your outfit matching ever again if everything you wore was black.'

'Newsflash: I don't spend any time worrying about that now.'

I looked at what he was wearing, just jeans and a T-shirt and trainers and the hoody that I had on, nothing unusual or different.

As though he could read my mind he responded to the thought.

'That's just it, you see, I'm one of them. I'm trapped in this boring merry-go-round of parties and nights out where everyone pretends they like each other and everyone pretends they give a shit about each other but really they're all just wrapped up in themselves and desperate to get you to validate their existence by liking them back. It's like you get points for turning up, for who you talk to, who you cop off with. And there are extra points for who you avoid and who you mess about and how gutted they are afterwards.'

'Points?'

'They're unofficial and no-one's actually keeping count but everyone knows where you are on the leader board.'

'So where are you?'

He laughed again. 'You love those killer questions don't you? You're like my Gran; no filter.'

'Thanks.'

'Welcome.'

He bent down to collect his mug off the ground and downed whatever was left in it.

'Your mate Claire is the worst.'

'She's not really my mate.'

'Newsflash: she's not really anyone's mate.' He paused to put the mug down again. 'Claire will talk to anyone, be nice to anyone, be nice about anyone and shag anything that moves if she thinks it will get her points on the leader board. The sad thing is, it pays off. She has to keep working at it; she's got to make sure she plays the right games with the right people at the right time.'

'Sounds exhausting.'

'It's a way of life. She's like a bird, flitting around filling her nest with all kinds of things just because her instinct tells her to.'

'Like a magpie collecting shiny things,' I suggested.

He paused for what seemed like the longest time and looked straight at me. His eyes looked like they had been cut out of his face and were part of the darkness behind him.

'Exactly,' he said eventually. 'Claire is just like a magpie, and if the shiny thing she finds turns out to be not quite shiny enough, she just drops it and moves on to look for something else.'

I looked back towards the house. There were just dribs and drabs of people in the conservatory now, mostly sleeping.

When I turned back to the boy on the swing he was still looking at me. He stood, raised me up off my swing, pulled me towards him and kissed me like in a film; one of those kisses that starts really soft and slow like he's checking to see how solid I am, as if my face were ice he needed to walk on. And when I didn't break but kissed him back he drew me in tight and pressed hard.

'Let's go in the summer house,' he said, gesturing towards the fancy shed at the bottom of the garden with his eyes.

'What if it's locked?'

'What if it's not?'

He took my hand and led me across the garden, with the ground getting muddier and more squelchy on the slight incline towards the summer house. He took hold of the door handle and paused for added drama as he turned it.

'Open Sesame,' he exclaimed with a flourish as the door opened easily and he bowed like a doorman at a swanky hotel to let me in before him.

'It's a bit dark,' I said tripping over something as I walked in.

He switched on a lamp by the door and closed it behind us.

I'd tripped over a box of summer games, tennis racquets and croquet mallets.

'Who actually plays croquet?' I said, turning to show him the mallet.

'People with enough garden and enough social ambition,' he responded, moving forward to take the mallet out of my hand and put it back in the box.

He kissed me again and put his hand up inside the hoody I'd borrowed. It was icy cold against the thin fabric of my vest and I jumped back.

'Your hands are freezing.'

'All the more reason for you to warm them up, Grandmother.'

'There you go again, comparing me to your gran.'

'Far from it.'

He looked straight into me again and, unable to cope with the eye contact for more than a couple of seconds, I looked around the room.

There was a desk at one end, a big, old sturdy thing like the one in Mrs Edgar's office. There was a framed photograph of Becca and her parents on the desk, a lamp, a notebook and a pot of pens, and behind it, on the wall, there was a whole lifetime's worth of pictures, framed and mounted like a gallery. I walked over to it for a closer look.

'I can't resist a nosey at other people's pictures.'

He followed me to the desk.

'Becca's mum's writing a book,' he explained. 'I think she comes in here to write.'

'What kind of book?'

'I don't know, you'd have to ask Becca. I think it's about when Becca was ill, you know, when she was a little kid. I don't know if it's a story about a kid being ill or a book all about what happened to Becca and how she got better and everything, but it's definitely something to do with her illness.'

The pictures above the desk were all of Becca, some with one or other of her parents, some alone and some with doctors or nurses. They showed various states of illness, from the puffed up face of a helpless sleeping thing in a hospital bed to a smiling little girl giving a double thumbs up as she was being wheeled out of hospital in a wheelchair. In the centre of them all there was an embroidered motto in a frame, like the Bible verses on Mrs Edgar's calendar, but not from the Bible. It read: 'Life is short. Live, laugh, love every day.'

'It's a bit cheesy isn't it, but it's true though, eh?'

He had followed my gaze to the motto and was standing really close behind me with his hand on my hip.

'My grandad popped out to book a cruise for him and my Nan the day after he retired and came home to find her dead in the kitchen with a pan of soup still bubbling away on the stove and the bread half-buttered. They'd waited all that time for the right time to have the holiday of their lives together and then it was too late, just like that.'

I turned to see if I could read his face and check whether the story about his grandparents was true or just a line but he was kissing me before I could read anything, and the feeling of needing to live now was already squeezing all conscious, sensible thoughts out of my head.

Before I knew it we were on the sofa at the other end of the room, a tangle of naked limbs, tongues, hands. I was in the moment and not really in my own body or in the physical space at all.

When he'd finished and he'd peeled his body slowly away from mine, we lay wrapped together using his hoody for a blanket and he slept while I lay trying to make out the detail of the pictures on the wall. Perhaps that sequence of events that seemed to have begun when I found the vibrator in Mrs Wilkes drawer had really started when Becca got cancer.

He was still asleep when I decided to make a move, wondering where Claire was, what my mum would be like when I got home, how I was going to get home. I eased myself off the sofa and collected up the bits of clothing spread around the room, eventually finding both boots and bending to zip them up.

'Are you heading home?' he whispered.

'I think I'd better find Claire. And my jumper and my coat.'

'OK,' he answered and pulled his pants and his jeans on, standing up groggily to open the door for me like a gentleman.

'See you, then.'

He kissed me in the doorway. 'Yeah, see you soon,' he answered.

I looked back at him as he closed the door behind me, and I walked across the grass to the conservatory.

I never saw him again.

NINETEEN

Once Captain was out of the house, I couldn't see John-Joe anymore. I could still talk to him but he didn't answer. The last time I saw him was when he was being really annoying in the church. He wasn't there at school when we got back from the trip. He wasn't there to pull faces when Jenny made us do our homework and he didn't even turn up at bedtime or chat to me while I was brushing my teeth. I still used his toothbrush though; he'd given me permission to do that and if he wasn't going to come and claim it back then I was just going to keep it.

That first night it was nice having Dad all to myself without John-Joe interrupting. I felt a bit guilty for thinking it but for once I could concentrate on what Dad was saying. He was telling me about how we're all descended from Vikings and how everyone thinks it was the Romans who were the clever ones that built all the roads and the baths and everything but actually it was the Vikings that made us into farmers and makers of things. He promised we could go to the Viking museum one weekend, maybe just the boys because Anna was too young to be interested in Vikings. It sounded great when he talked about it and how we'd be able to dress up like Vikings with real swords, but as soon as he'd gone and I was all on my own with just the lamp and the empty bed beside me I missed John-Joe because he loved dressing up and fighting games. Being a Viking was never going to be the same without him.

The next night I really missed him. When he was alive, I seriously wanted a bedroom of my own without all John-Joe's mess and noise in it. Without him waking me up when it was still officially night time to tell me some nerdy fact that he'd just searched up on the internet or keeping me awake by asking me what I wanted for Christmas when it was only July and we hadn't even broken up for summer yet. But now our room was like looking at a photograph of a day you can't remember when you can see that you must have been there because you're in the picture but you don't have the feeling of experiencing it.

I waited for him to come back and I even said prayers for it. I wrote a letter to Father Christmas too, even though it was only the beginning of November and I'm a bit too old to still believe in all of that. I thought about going back to St Anthony's and finding Captain and bringing him back. Getting the magpie out of the house had made absolutely no difference to the way Mum was, she was just the same ghost of herself as she'd been before, and now John-Joe had vanished.

I felt sure he would come back for my birthday though. My birthday is two days after Mum's and it was nearly two weeks after I had left the tin in the church. Jenny had taken us to her house to make cards for Mum the weekend before her birthday and we also made fudge to give her as a present. Gabe got bored because Jenny said the fudge mixture was so burning hot that only I was allowed to stir it in case Gabe tipped the pan over or let the fudge splash on his skin.

Gabe hates it when he gets babied like that just because he's the youngest (apart from Anna who's obviously too young to stir fudge) but then he makes it worse for himself by acting like a complete baby just because he couldn't stir and ruining the whole thing. I liked making fudge with Jenny and she never normally invites us over to her house (I'm not surprised, it's a bit of a mess actually) but she'll probably never ask us to do anything like that again after he nearly screamed the place down.

Obviously, it was me that sorted everything out in the end by telling Jenny that we should let Gabe be the first to taste the leftover bits of fudge out of the pan once it had cooled down.

He said he'd leave me some but there was practically nothing but the smell of sugar by the time he'd finished.

We gave the cards and the fudge to Mum before school on her birthday and I found a cup in the back of the cupboard with Mother written on it so we took her a cup of tea in that and some breakfast in bed. She smiled at the cards and she even tasted a bit of the fudge and declared it delicious but said she'd save the rest for later because it was a bit early for fudge.

'It's not too early for me,' Gabe grinned, so she let him and me both have a piece as long as we promised to brush our teeth for an extra minute.

Dad gave her a big bunch of flowers and a necklace that you can put a picture inside. She let me open it to have a look inside but there was no picture in it.

'I thought you might want to choose which pictures to put in yourself. When you're ready,' said Dad and Mum started crying then and didn't say anything else.

'Right boys, if you've finished that fudge you need to get those teeth brushed.'

Dad tried to usher us out of their bedroom but Gabe just opened his mouth wide to show him that the fudge was still dissolving slowly on his tongue. It's exactly what John-Joe would have done. Gabe never used to be like John-Joe but since the accident it's like Gabe has figured out that we still need that clever, cheeky boy in the house so he's behaving just like him.

'Just chew it or there'll be no more later. We need to leave your mum in peace to enjoy her birthday breakfast, get your teeth brushed and your shoes on, give this stinky item a nappy change, grab the packed lunches and go.'

'Aww but Dad…'

'Aww but nothing, Gabe. If you don't hurry up and get in that bathroom I'll get you to change Anna's nappy and she's done a massive one, I think.'

Gabe ran across the landing and I followed him. Wishing John-Joe were here. Wondering if John-Joe would turn up to talk to Mum once we'd left for school. After all, it was her birthday and she missed him more than any of us. Even more than me.

But when we got home Mum didn't seem like she'd been talking to John-Joe, she didn't seem like she'd been talking to anyone. Jenny said she'd gone upstairs for a nap but when I went up to see her, it looked like she'd been in bed all day. She was still wearing the same pyjamas.

'Are you coming downstairs Mum? Jenny's made a cake. I mean, I know she's always making cakes but this one is for your birthday and it's pretty awesome with loads of chocolate on it. I think she's brought you a present too. And you get to choose which takeout we're having. I was thinking maybe fish and chips because I'm going to choose pizza from the delivery man when it's my birthday on Friday and we probably don't want to have the same thing twice in a week?'

She smiled at me as though she was trying to remember who I was from a long time ago.

'Fish and chips sounds great,' she said. 'I'll text your dad to ask him to pick it up on his way home.'

So I went downstairs, pleased that she was looking forward to fish and chips and eager to share the news with Gabe who loves fish and chips from the chippy. Jenny let us look after Anna and watch TV while she laid the table ready and she'd brought Christmas crackers even though Christmas was still a few weeks away because she said she didn't see why they couldn't be a thing for any party meal, not just Christmas. She has some good ideas sometimes.

After ages, when it was nearly time for Dad to get home from work even, Mum still hadn't come downstairs and Anna was getting grizzly, even though Jenny had given her a bottle and put her in the bouncy chair where she could see the cartoon we were watching.

'Did Mummy say she was coming down?'

'Yes.' I thought about what she'd actually said. 'Well, I think so.'

'You boys keep an eye on Anna for a minute while I just check where she's up to. And don't touch the cake. If you so much as breathe in the vicinity of that cake I will know.' She pointed her fingers at us like a wicked witch and she was only half joking.

I thought Jenny would be downstairs with Mum any minute but when the cartoon finished they were still both upstairs and I was dying for a wee. Dad says I'm not supposed to leave Anna on her own with Gabe because he can be too silly and forget to look after her or forget that she's only a baby and do stupid things like try to share his crisps with her or show her his football tricks and kick the ball around right near her head.

'Gabe, I need you to stay just where you are on the sofa while I go to the loo. Just leave Anna there and I'll be back in less than a minute, you can count if you like.'

Gabe started counting 'One pink elephant, two pink elephants…' as I raced up the stairs while he timed me.

When I came out of the bathroom I could hear Mum and Jenny talking and I paused on the landing to listen.

'You might think it's your birthday and your choice to stay in bed avoiding all the joy your family want to give you, but you're a mum and that means that birthdays are not just your celebration they're for the whole family.'

'But the whole family is not here, is it? John-Joe isn't here.'

'Marie, this will sound harsh, and it is. The whole thing is bloody harsh and bloody unfair. I know it's a gargantuan effort for you to breathe, never mind put one foot in front of the other. I know what grief is. You never knew me before I lost Robert. You never saw us together, so you don't know how much I lost when he went. Believe me, I know how much you just want to lie down and never get up again. I know it, and I completely understand, but those boys downstairs are still here and they need you and it's not their fault. So you need to pull yourself together and get on with their life, even if you can't get on with your own.'

'Don't tell me you completely understand,' I could hear my mum getting out of the bed.

'How can you completely understand when you have never lost a child? I thought losing a child before you even had chance to get to know them was awful. Horrendous. It was. But losing John-Joe and all the special things he was; that fully-formed boy who always had an answer for everything, who was brave and clever and funny and full of cuddles and tickles, that's worse. Knowing he'll never have the adventure of growing up and experiencing the world and that I'll never get to share that with him, that's the worst kind of unfairness, the worst kind of punishment, the worst kind of loss.'

I stood on the landing wondering how I was ever going to fill the gap that John-Joe had left and be all of those things that she missed.

'You're right. It's awful, it's unfair, it's tragic but it's happened and you can't change it and neither can any of us. You might feel like you've lost everything Marie, but you haven't, you still have two wonderful sons and a beautiful daughter and a husband who loves you and is a great dad to your children and has been quietly, desperately looking after you all. While John-Joe's death has been happening to you it's also been happening to them. And just at the time they need you most you've curled yourself up under a blanket of grief and left them with the loss of a mother as well as the loss of their brother. James has been there, with a giant roll of duct tape, trying to fix the cracks wherever they appear, but he can't do it on his own, Marie, he can't just keep doing it on his own.'

'He has you to help,' Mum whispered.

'And I am here for all of you,' Jenny said calmly, 'but I'm not their mum. I can feed them and help them with homework and take them to the park and all those things that I would have done if I had ever been fortunate enough to have three lovely children like that of my own. But I can't be their mum because only you can do that. You need to do that, Marie.'

'I don't know if I can.'

I don't know what they said after that, or what they would have said, because Gabe appeared at the top of the stairs and was really cross with me.

'How am I supposed to time you when you take so long and the numbers get way too big for me to keep counting. You said you'd be a minute but you were much more than that because I got to hundreds of pink elephants and I've lost count now so I don't know how long you were but you were ages and I'm bored.'

Jenny stepped out of Mum's bedroom.

'What are you two ruffians doing up here when you're supposed to be looking after Anna?'

'She's asleep,' declared Gabe. 'And she's actually zero fun because she doesn't even do anything apart from laughing and crying. I wish John-Joe were here.'

He said it just as Mum stepped out of the bedroom and we all stopped as though someone had pressed the pause button on the remote control.

'We all miss John-Joe,' Mum said. 'And I'm sure John-Joe misses us, wherever he is. I…' She paused, she seemed as if she had known what she was going to say next but it was as if someone had snatched the words from her brain before they'd had chance to make it all the way down to her mouth.

Luckily we heard Dad's key in the door and his voice yelling 'Grub's up!' and he walked in carrying two bags of fish and chips. Gabe didn't wait to see if Mum was going to finish her sentence he just headed for the stairs at a sprint. He was carrying the bags into the kitchen while Dad took his coat off before the rest of us had even blinked.

They were lovely those fish and chips, not just because they were warm and salty and the batter on the fish was really crispy, but because we all sat together at the table and talked and laughed. When Anna woke up, Dad sat her on his knee and he even gave her a cold chip to eat, which she sucked on like it was the best thing anyone had ever tasted. Mum told him not to give it to her but he said a bit of potato wouldn't do her any harm and might help her sleep through the night.

Mum and Dad had wine and clinked their glasses together and then we all clinked our drinks in a toast to John-Joe and Mum cried, but only a bit.

'And what are you doing for your birthday on Friday, Jim?' asked Jenny, helping herself to more apple juice, even though she'd been offered wine.

'We haven't really made a plan, have we Champ?'

'Eleven is a bit too old for jelly and ice cream, I think,' said Mum.

At the mention of my birthday and doing something to celebrate, Mum suddenly switched from being normal but a bit sad, to being that shadow of herself that we'd started to get used to. She stood up and began clearing plates away, even though she hadn't even nearly finished hers and Gabe was still busy pouring another tonne of ketchup over his.

'We should do something though, eh Champ?'

'Maybe Jenny can make another cake?' I smiled at Jenny but had one eye on Mum, scraping leftovers into the bin and putting plates in the dishwasher. She came back to the table to collect Gabe's plate but there was no way he was letting go until he'd finished.

'Perhaps he could just have a couple of friends round for tea? Eh, Marie, what do you think?'

'We'll be having take-out pizza anyway, won't we Mum? So there'll be no extra cooking. We don't even need plates, apart from for the cake that Jenny's going to make for me.'

'Oh, yes, cake. Are you leaving some room for cake Gabe?'

Gabe looked up from arranging his chips in size order so that he could eat them from biggest to smallest, with ketchup smeared across his face like blood. Reluctantly he handed over his plate on the promise of cake and Jenny swooped down with a tissue to clean him up.

Mum brought the cake to the table and the sight of something so huge and delicious wiped the conversation about my birthday out of everyone's head for a minute.

Mum said she was too old for birthday candles.

'Nonsense, you're never too old,' said Jenny and Dad agreed so she let them put one candle in the cake and we all sang happy birthday while she waited to blow it out and make a wish. We didn't ask her what her wish was but I can probably guess. I knew what mine was going to be.

No-one said much while we were eating the cake and Anna was watching us all, opening and closing her mouth with longing, but as soon as we paused for air, Jenny said 'So what are you going to do for your birthday Jim?'

'I….'

'How about we invite a couple of your friends and go to the cinema?' suggested Dad.

'With me too, can I come?' said Gabe through a mouthful of cake.

'Of course you can come, we wouldn't dream of leaving you out. So the two of you, and me and two of your friends, we'll go to see a film, and have one of those massive hot dogs in the cinema. What do you think?'

'What about pizza?'

Gabe is quick off the mark when it comes to food, he won't be cheated out of any kind of treat.

'We can have the pizza on Saturday night instead. Jim? What do you think? Cinema and hot dogs just the boys and your mates? I'll throw in some fizzy drinks and a huge bucket of popcorn?'

I looked at Mum. She was putting what was left of the cake back in its tin.

'What about Mum?'

'I'll be here for presents in the morning and I'll see you after school but I'll stay here with Anna while you go to the cinema. We can't really have boys tearing round the house while we've got the baby here, can we? I think it's a great idea. Very grown up and eleven-year-old.'

I remembered my tenth birthday party then. How John-Joe had got angry with one of my friends because he'd said something mean about Gabe and then John-Joe had hit him in the kitchen and the other boy had gone at him like a prize fighter and given John-Joe a black eye.

'Thanks Dad. I've never had a cinema hot dog before.'

'It's a deal, you can invite your friends tomorrow and I'll make a plan with their parents.'

I was awake early on the morning of my birthday and looked across to John-Joe's bed in the darkness, hoping that he might be there to wish me happy birthday, but there was no sign of him. I switched on the lamp. Still no John-Joe.

It was nice though, when I got up. Dad made pancakes for breakfast and Mum hugged me so hard I thought I might suffocate. I got cool stuff and Gabe made me a card and wrote John-Joe and Anna's name in it as well as his own because, he said, they couldn't make me a card but he was sure they would want to give me one if they could.

I thought Dad would be taking us to school as usual but he left not long after breakfast because he wanted to get home early to take us to the cinema.

'Your mum will drop you off today,' he said and even though it was cold outside and a bit drizzly we walked and played I Spy on the way, with Gabe just guessing any old word that popped into his head whether it started with the right letter or not, and Mum taking Anna's turn as well as her own. It was just like the times before John-Joe died, except John-Joe wasn't there with his obscure clues that no-one could get.

Mum picked us up from school too and it took ages for us to get out of the playground with all the other mums crowding round to tell my mum how big Anna had got and ask her how she was. I could see that she was getting a bit upset so I had to step in and get us out of there.

'Actually, it's my birthday today and we really need to get home, don't we Mum?' I flashed my 'I am 11' badge at them just to prove it.

Mum smiled at them apologetically as we dashed away and then whispered 'thanks, you're a life-saver' to me once we were outside of the school gates.

Jenny was pretty much knocking on the door before we'd even got our coats off and she'd brought a birthday cake even more enormous than the one she'd made for Mum, which we still hadn't finished. It had Smarties all over it and she'd used all orange ones to make a number eleven in the middle of the coloured dots like a colour blindness test.

Jenny bought me a watch for my birthday too, which was really kind of her, and I was allowed to open it but I wasn't allowed to blow out any candles or cut the cake until Dad got home and my friends arrived. Gabe said it wasn't fair and started to steal smarties off the side of the cake when he thought we weren't looking.

'Off you go and get changed for the cinema, boys, while I make a cup of tea for Jenny and you can have a piece of my cake when you come downstairs. I have something else for you too, Jim.'

'What is it?'

'When you get down.'

Mum sent Gabe into the other room with his cake and Jenny when we got back downstairs, with strict instructions not to get crumbs on the carpet or chocolate down his clean clothes..

'I thought you might like this,' said Mum, handing me a small present once it was just the two of us in the kitchen. 'It's sort of from me but sort of from John-Joe. I know you sometimes wear it already and at some point we will have to go through John-Joe's things and decide what we want to keep and what's for the charity shop, but not quite yet.'

I opened it. I was the Mickey Mouse cap that John-Joe loved so much. The one from Disneyland that I wore sometimes.

'Thanks Mum.' I hugged her, partly to say thank you and partly because she was crying.

'Put it on then, let's have a look at you.'

I put the cap on and turned to look at my reflection in the kitchen window.

'Look! Look Mum, look at that!'

Outside there were hundreds of birds flying and swooping together, going first one way and then another, making shapes in the air and diving, then rising up as though they'd been practising a routine to put on a display.

'A murmuration,' whispered Mum, 'that's very special. A special birthday gift for a special boy.'

She hugged me again as we watched the birds together in silence. We both knew that the murmuration was John-Joe wishing me happy birthday.

Dear Father Christmas

I know you probably weren't expecting to hear from me again now that I'm eleven and most of my friends have grown out of thinking you can actually deliver presents to everyone in the world on one night and fit them all into one sleigh. I'm not saying I believe in it all either, but I still believe in the magic. I think you must be a bit like Jesus and the Bible – I wonder if the stories have got a bit exaggerated down the years and people have added stuff that's pure fantasy, like the beard and the flying reindeer and Mrs Christmas. You're probably not even married. You probably don't even like mince pies (and I know it's my Dad that eats the one we leave out for you because I've seen him.)

Anyway, let me get to the point. I don't believe all the extra stuff – that's like the tinsel and the fairy lights and all that – but you are the tree, Father Christmas, you are what's at the centre of all the Christmas craziness and when we strip it all back, there you still are, answering special Christmas wishes and making them come true.

I know it's a bit early but there are Christmas things in the shops so I don't think it's too early to ask, before you get booked up with Christmas wishes. This Christmas I have a big wish to ask for from you and I'm trying to make it realistic. As realistic as possible anyway. Really what I'd like is to have my brother back. I didn't do a great job of being his big brother because he died while we were playing a game and it should have been my job to look after him and make sure he didn't do anything stupid, but you can't be everywhere at once, as I'm sure you know. So if you could send him back, somehow, even if it was as something different (I thought I could keep him by keeping our dead magpie, Captain, in a tin under my pillow for a while but that wasn't the best idea I've ever had) that would be great. Maybe he could come back to us as a pet dog? Or another baby maybe?

Anyway, if you can't do that, here's the real wish (because I know the other one is a little bit magic sleigh and flying reindeer), please can you make our family back to normal? Gabe is OK, I think anyway, it's hard to know with him because he mostly just plays rubbish games and talks to himself just like he's always done, and Anna is fine because she's just a baby and doesn't know anything apart from when she's hungry or when to laugh when you play peek-a-boo. But my Dad is trying too hard to be normal and I think my mum has forgotten what normal looks like and I'm trying to keep everything going but it's really hard and I'm only just 11.

So, to summarise, like we do in the WALT in our books at school: I would like you to bring John-Joe back in some way or other if you can, and if you can't can you please use whatever magic it is you have to make things normal again.

Thanks Father Christmas and good luck with everything on Christmas Eve. Don't worry about eating all those mince pies because I reckon everyone's dads just eat them!

Lots of Love

Jim

PS: when I say can you make it normal, I don't mean like as if John-Joe was never there. We love him and don't want ever to forget him or even stop missing him, just to stop our whole lives being about that.

PPS: It's fine for Jenny to keep on coming round but just not all the time, if you can do that.

TWENTY

It was several weeks later, on Christmas Eve, when I realised I was probably pregnant.

Life had gone back to a version of normal and it seemed like the party and all that went with it had happened to another version of me in another life. I'd found my jumper and coat without too much effort but Claire had proved trickier to track down. It was still pretty dark in the house as I looked for her and most of the people that were still there were strewn on sofas and the floor, using coats and any discarded pieces of clothing they could find as blankets. I'd stepped over them and tiptoed between them, making several circuits of all the downstairs rooms before I finally found Claire behind a sofa, fast asleep with a rug on her as a blanket and her bare feet tucked under a cushion to keep them warm.

'Claire. Claire,' whispering her name had no effect. 'Claire' I whispered louder. 'Claire,' louder still and giving her first a gentle nudge and, as my volume increased, a progressively more vigorous shove.

Other people stirred and grunted their annoyance at me but Claire just lay there, wiped out and unresponsive.

'Look Claire, I'm going to go. I need to get home and... I just need to get home.' I spoke right into her ear.

'What the fuck are you doing, you weirdo? Can't you see that a person is sleeping here, like actually asleep?'

She opened one eye and used it to aim her anger straight at me.

'I just wanted to let you know I'm leaving. There'll be a bus or something to get home. It's nearly eight o'clock, they'll be running by now. I just thought I'd see if you want to come back with me now and, you know, let you know I was leaving so that you don't think I've vanished or anything.'

'Marie, I don't give a flying fuck whether you've gone home or been abducted by Mexican bandits as long as you let me fucking sleep.'

She closed her eye again and that was the end of the conversation and the end of the friendship, although it took a while longer for me to realise that we really weren't friends and she wasn't going to waste any more time or charm pretending that we might be.

Getting a bus was harder than I'd thought. I'd forgotten it was Sunday and I wasn't even sure which side of the road to catch the bus from, or which number I needed, let alone how often they would run. I found myself silently asking Jesus to help me or give me a sign as I tried to figure out the lists of numbers and unfamiliar stop names on the timetable at the bus shelter. He sent me a smartly dressed woman who offered help without me having to ask her.

'Are you all right, love?' she asked, and I wondered for the first time as she smiled at me what kind of state I looked. I patted down my hair and tried to appear as though I'd not been out all night as she spoke to me.

'It can be like reading the computer code for the lunar landings trying to make sense of those timetables can't it? And they come whenever they like anyway. What number are you waiting for?'

'I'm not sure.'

'Okay. Shall we see if we can figure it out then? If we club together we can use your teenage eyesight and my impressive experience of catching buses to read that list of numbers, crack the code and get you home.'

She asked me no questions about where I'd been or why I didn't know how to get home, but she offered me a humbug and a spare pair of gloves from her handbag, rummaging for them as she asked me where I was heading and checking that I had enough bus fare to get me there.

'I have a pass, I use it for school.'

'Great,' she said, with a mouth full of her own humbug. 'That's one thing sorted straight off.'

'And the even better news is that I think we can both get the same bus. I think if we both get the 256, I'll just get off a couple of stops before you, I'm going to St Anthony's Church, do you know it? Massive red brick gothic thing?'

I nodded. That was our church.

'So if I get off there, you'll know when to get off and how to find your way home? If you don't, I could come with you and walk back. I can go to the ten-thirty Mass instead of the nine o'clock one if you need me to walk you all the way home?'

'I'll be fine,' I assured her, 'You've been really kind. I'm so glad you were here.'

'My mother always said that faith will bring you help just when you need it most. I might get extra points in heaven for being your Good Samaritan today and,' she paused to lean into the road and stretch her arm out to hail the bus, 'you've helped the bus get here on time. Look at that, talking to you instead of watching the road has made it get here quicker, just like the kettle boils quicker if you empty the washing machine or wash a few pots while you wait.'

The bus was practically empty but we sat side by side chatting; her hardly drawing breath except to wait for the answer to any questions she asked me, and me wondering where kindness like hers comes from. After everything with Claire I found it hard to believe that her generosity was genuine, but I was too tired and too much in need of someone like her to do anything but accept it and be glad she was there.

'It's a trek for me, coming all this way on a Sunday and there's a church just round the corner I could go to, which would be a much more sensible option really. I do go there from time to time. I have friends who go there and the priest is lovely. But St Anthony's was my mum's church, she always went there, sometimes twice a day, and we went together every Sunday and then back to her house for breakfast. As she got older and more fragile, I made the breakfast or took her to a café, and did some little jobs for her round the house. It was just what we did every week: me looking after her when she was old, just like she looked after me when I was young, and the church standing there like it always has, connecting the two.'

The bus moved pretty quickly on the quiet Sunday morning roads but there were a lot of stops between where Becca lived and home and a surprising number of people with somewhere to go getting on and off along the way.

'When Mum passed away, you see, I missed her so much, and holding on to the old routine of catching the bus over to St Anthony's, sitting in the same pew, all of that, was a way of holding on to something of that life. Routine's important, don't you think? It's like punctuation in a sentence; you need that bit of structure to make sense of all the bits in between. And faith of course. Faith has helped me a lot. You probably think I'm a batty old religious nutcase.'

She laughed and I did too.

'I don't think you're old or a nutcase.'

'Bless you, sweetheart – what's your name?'

'Marie.'

'Marie, lovely name. I'm Theresa. I'm a good few years older than you and I quite often talk to myself, which I think might be a sign of creeping nuttiness.'

She laughed again and people on the bus turned to look at us as though enjoying time spent on a bus contravened some public transport by-law.

'I go to St Anthony's with my mum, too. But we go to the family Mass at twelve on a Sunday, or sometimes the ten-thirty.'

'Ah, so I might have seen you before at the ten-thirty – I go then if I've missed the bus or overslept. It'd make more sense for me to go to that one really, but Mum always preferred the nine o'clock, she said that was long enough to wait for breakfast. She was a conscientious Catholic, my mum, but practical with it.

'Speaking of practical, I'm in danger of missing my stop if I don't keep an eye on where we are instead of prattling on.'

She pressed the bell to ask the driver to stop.

'You know where you're getting off, don't you, Marie?'

I nodded and she stood up to go.

'Take care of yourself, love. I might see you at Mass some time. God bless.'

'Thank you.'

I'm not sure she heard my thank you as she stumbled to the front of the bus just as the driver braked for her stop. But she turned to wave as she stepped off and carried on waving until the bus had driven away.

I saw her again at church on Christmas Eve.

It had been a hard few weeks. It was business as usual for Mum and me; nothing was said about anything she didn't want to think about, so the incident at school and the 'sleepover' were never mentioned. She'd been drinking tea and watching a church service on TV when I got home.

'Did you have a nice time at Becca's sleepover?'

'Yes, it was good.'

'Off you go and get a shower and get changed then. You've got plenty of time for breakfast before Mass.'

There were no questions about what I'd done at Becca's or how I'd got home. No recriminations for the journey. No hints as to whether she knew I'd been at a party or what I'd been up to there. But I felt like she knew all of it, and anything she didn't know was easily decipherable in the guilt in every word and every gesture I made that day, from the smallest of blinks to the fakest of smiles. I was convinced she knew but she said nothing, that was our way and I was grateful for it that morning and in the weeks that followed.

Mum's birthday came and went with a modest fuss and a large cake. I got up super early on the day to bake the cake and have it all ready to give to her when she got up. I could see she was pleased, and she said it was a shame we'd not eaten it quicker when she had to throw the last stale bits away. She'd suggested that she and I go to the cinema together as a birthday treat. She was utterly delighted when I agreed and it was as though I'd given her a gift, even though she was paying. It was a struggle to find something we both liked the look of, so we settled for *Seven Years in Tibet* and agreed that seven years anywhere with Brad Pitt would be OK by us. It was special, like the mother and daughter moments you see in films. We even had popcorn.

School was harder. Claire was frosty on the Monday morning after the party; it was clear that she couldn't remember large chunks of the evening, including what she'd said to me in front of Christopher.

She may not have remembered the words but she definitely still felt the same about it all. She dropped small flavours of the same sentiments into conversations; little hints that seemed innocuous to everyone else but were said with a look or a smile in my direction to make sure I knew her comments were directed at me. She did what she could to make me look stupid and awkward at every opportunity; to leave me out of the joke, make sure I wasn't privy to any gossip and wasn't invited to anything that was going on outside school.

Christopher had been kind. More than kind, in fact: he'd been apologetic and eager to make amends.

'I'm sorry I disappeared off like that,' he said the next time I saw him after the party. 'It all got a bit intense, didn't it?'

'Yeah, I'm not surprised it freaked you out a bit. I'm rubbish at small talk and, as for flirting...'

He laughed.

'Exactly. Bottom of the class.'

'It wasn't really anything you said that freaked me out, you know. It was Claire turning up and smashing straight into the conversation. She was like someone turning the light on when you've been asleep in the dark and it just jolts you from where you were all comfortable and in the zone to something unpleasant that you want to escape from.

'She'd set us up you know and had kind of given me a mission to get off with you. Sorry, that sounds really... really... it's not nice. I'm sorry.'

'It's all right, I know Claire, I know how she works.'

'Exactly. But I'd been up for it. I'm not blameless, I'd agreed to it. But then I felt guilty when she turned up like that, like I'd betrayed you... That sounds stupid... Do you know what I mean? I felt bad. She'd ruined it, but I'd ruined it in the first place by having a plan and all of that.'

'OK.' What do you say to something like that? It was half apology, half confession, with a sprinkle of accusation over the top.

'So anyway, I thought we might start again. You know, do it properly this time, with no plans from Claire and no pressure and no five million people at a party.'

'OK?'

'So we can go on a date? Like, to the pictures or something.'

'Yes.'

'Or for a walk, not to the pictures, we can't talk at the pictures.'

'Yes, OK, a walk. A walk sounds nice.'

We'd agreed it on a Wednesday for the following Sunday afternoon and left arranging a plan with time and place until later, but it never happened. By the Friday, he was holding hands with Claire at lunchtime and avoiding eye contact with me in the corridor. Probably for the best really, all things considered.

I realised I was pregnant at Midnight Mass on Christmas Eve.

The church was crazy busy and we were standing in the side aisle close to the nativity at the front. Father Reilly, possibly the oldest man alive, had been talking about the miracle of the virgin birth and how, as we opened our presents and ate our Christmas dinner, we should remember the miracle of Christmas and how many miracles it brought with it, both at that special time of Jesus' birth and throughout the life of our saviour.

'So let's welcome Jesus into our lives once again this Christmas,' Father Reilly concluded, lighting the final candle on the advent ring, 'with the procession of the baby Jesus to his place in the manger, the most humble of beginnings for the king of kings.'

He nodded to the children who were standing waiting at the back of the church; the first an altar boy of about fourteen carrying a giant candlestick with a lit candle to light the way, and behind him a boy and a girl of about seven, the girl carrying a baby doll and taking her role of cradling it like a real baby very seriously. They began a slow walk up the central aisle towards the empty manger, where the static cast of parents, animals and shepherds had been gathering gradually over previous weeks, assembling for this showpiece finale of the birth.

As the candle, the plastic baby and the stand-in Mary and Joseph made their way up the aisle to the nativity, children left their seats and their standing-room-only spots around the perimeter to join the procession. I wished for those days when I would wait for the moment to leap up and join the children bringing Jesus into the world. The days when this silent invitation to join in and be involved in a miracle was such a huge part of the magic of Christmas. I still felt a ripple of resentment that I had never been chosen to actually carry the baby, despite hardly ever missing a Sunday at Mass, but as the church was filled with the sound of 'O Little Town of Bethlehem' I was lost in the nostalgia of it all and the feeling that I was part of a special promise of new life and miracles.

'How silently, how silently the wondrous gift is given...'

Perfectly choreographed in time to the words, the impeccably-groomed girl with her pigtails and her party frock laid the baby in the manger and, as I looked up from the plastic Jesus feeling uncomfortably warm and slightly nauseous from standing so long in the over-crowded church, I saw Theresa, sitting at a pew close by and smiling broadly when she finally managed to catch my eye and see a spark of recognition.

She waved at me and I smiled and raised my hand back.

'Who's that?' asked my mum.

I looked again at Theresa, then at my mum and then to the sleeping, plastic Jesus for some inspiration. But I found myself short of breath and short of answers and as I tried to draw in some air the nausea escalated, bringing a stream of vomit with the exhale, which covered my shoes and my mum's handbag and spattered across the coat and the long hair of the woman sitting closest to us.

The vomit-spattered woman sprang out of her seat. The children standing near enough to see what had happened exclaimed their 'eurrghhhs' without a hint of self-censorship and Father Reilly acknowledged what had happened with a calm expression of subtle distaste and a look towards my mum that communicated that she should do something. He didn't miss a beat however, and, as the singing stopped, the instruction to pray followed smoothly on from it without any reference to the private horror in our tiny corner of the church.

As the congregation bowed their heads to pray, my mum apologised repeatedly to the long-haired woman, offering her a scarf to wipe the vomit from her hair and referring to me as though I were a naughty toddler.

'I'm so sorry. So, so sorry. I don't know what's come over her. I don't know what she thinks she's doing. I can only apologise. What a thing to do.'

She looked at me accusingly.

'Apologise Marie, can you see what you've done to this poor lady's hair. And her coat, look what you've done to her coat.'

216

'I'm really sorry.'

'It's OK,' the woman reassured me. 'Are you OK?'

As we played out our mini drama in whispers, those seated nearest to us looked up from their prayers to follow our alternative Christmas story and the odd one released an audible 'tut' to let us know that talking during a prayer delivered on the most holy of nights was not the done thing. Even people sitting as far away as Theresa and on the other side of the aisle were glancing in our direction as our whispers echoed around the church, bouncing off walls designed to amplify praise to God.

We were saved by the transition from prayer into 'Come all Ye Faithful,' which was always the last hymn after the procession to the manger and I was grateful for the familiarity of the well-worn formula, which never varied from year to year, even though the audience was largely the same.

As the congregation called to the joyful and triumphant, my furious mother led me, carrying her soiled handbag, through the side door of the church, followed by the woman with vomit in her hair. There was a vestibule there with a toilet and enough separation from the echo chamber of the church for my mum to unleash her full disappointment at my behaviour and express her fury that I could embarrass her in such a way in front of Father Reilly, in front of the whole congregation and in front of Jesus, Mary and all the saints.

As there was only one toilet, my mum insisted that the woman go first to clean herself up, while she continued to explain the scale of her humiliation at my hands.

'And why were you sick? Was it something you've eaten? Have you been at the Quality Street?'

I wished that the answer lay in over-indulgence, or a bug, or food-poisoning, or alcohol, or anything except the answer that I knew to be true. The image of that baby born to a shocked and naïve mother being plonked in the manager kept coming back to me and made me feel nauseous all over again. Except this was no immaculate conception, this was new life created by me and a boy whose name I didn't even know.

The woman left the toilet with her hair wet and her coat slung over her arm, just as the singing stopped and Father Reilly began his final benediction.

'I hope you're feeling better soon, love. God bless and happy Christmas both of you.'

'Thanks,' I said, 'You too. Sorry again.'

She tiptoed back into the church.

'You're very lucky she was so good about it. You'd better get yourself cleaned up before everyone else comes out, see what you can do with my bag as well, will you. It's probably ruined but the sooner you give it a wipe the better.'

'*Then go in peace...*' the familiar words of blessing wafted in from the church and I took refuge in the toilet cubicle where the practical business of getting cleaned up and hiding from the congregation were the best defence I had against thinking about the actual mess I was in and how I was going to clean that one up.

I stayed locked away longer than I really needed to. Every time I thought about being pregnant a new wave of nausea came over me but there was nothing left to bring up. Most of the congregation would leave by the front entrance for the chance to chat with friends and shake hands with Father Reilly. Some seemed to think he was keeping count of who turned up at every Mass; perhaps he was. For some, though, the side exit meant a quick getaway and a head start on the queue of cars heading home. So I stayed where I was until I was sure that everyone had left and I could confine my shame to just me and my mum.

When I stepped out, she was standing waiting with Theresa, who'd hung back to see me.

'Oh love, and I was so pleased to see you standing there with your Mum, I was dying to say hello and then all this happens.

Never mind though eh? You're all tidied up now and these things are soon forgotten.'

'It's kind of you to wait. And thank you, for helping her with the bus that time.'

Clearly my mum had already quizzed Theresa on who she was and how she knew me.

'A very happy Christmas to both of you,' she said, coming over to me to give me a hug. 'You enjoy being together for Christmas.'

With that she was gone and I was forgiven. My mum transformed from angry and embarrassed to concerned and sympathetic as though Theresa had taught her the difference while I'd been locked in the toilet.

She had no idea what she was forgiving me for.

TWENTY-ONE

The routine of Christmas at home was the domestic version of the ritual of Christmas at Midnight Mass for us; it never varied in content or timings and there was no point even suggesting we shake things up.

We always walked home from Mass, no matter the weather, though in my memory it was always cold and crisp, never wet, and there was always a bright silver penny of a moon. I know this can't be true but that's the way memory works: it takes the best bits or the worst bits and fools you into choosing one or the other as the norm. So walks home from Midnight Mass were always full of that lovely Christmas feeling of being in a special bubble where everything was perfect and the bogeyman couldn't get you. Except this year. It was drizzling just like it had been the night of the party and the new moon in a cloudy sky made it dark and depressing outside, while all the houses we walked past looked cosy and full of Christmas cheer, with their glamorously-lit Christmas trees still blinking through the windows.

Mum's mood had lifted after her chat with Theresa and she linked arms with me as we walked, telling me I could open one present when we got home and then put out the mince pie for Father Christmas, as though the liturgy of our Christmas Eve and Christmas Day hadn't already been written years ago. As though I still believed in Santa and the need to re-fuel the reindeer with carrots. Usually there was comfort in embracing all that nostalgia but the bogeyman had already invited himself into my Christmas and was running amok through my brain, pulling thoughts down off shelves and sticking posters on the walls, all with the same recurring theme – what the hell I am I going to do now?

Amongst all that noise I had to pretend to be normal; as normal as I could with the scent of sick following me with every footstep.

'What a lovely woman that Theresa is. I can't believe I've never met her at Mass before. No children, though, and no husband. No family at all now that her mother has gone. Sad that, to be all alone in the world. Makes you appreciate being together, doesn't it? Doesn't it, Marie?'

'Yes, Mum.'

'I wonder if I should have invited her to ours? That would be the Christian thing to do wouldn't it? Don't you think Marie?'

'Yes Mum.'

'I should have got her number. I never think at the time, always afterwards I think on, when it's too late. I don't suppose you have her number do you?'

'No.'

'Perhaps she'll be at Mass tomorrow. We could ask her then. It might be a bit short notice for Christmas Day if we ask her tomorrow, well today really, and she probably has plans of one kind or another. She probably has friends or neighbours where she's already been invited. But Boxing Day, we could invite her to Boxing Day. What do you think?'

'Yes.'

'Yes what? Boxing Day?'

'Yes, if we see her. Boxing Day sounds like a good idea.'

Mum carried on talking to keep herself warm as we walked home and she put the gas fire and Christmas tree lights on as soon as we got in to 'make it cosy and Christmassy' while I got changed ready for bed and left my shoes on the back doorstep in the hope that the fresh air and the drizzle would wash away the scent of sick. Mum put her handbag in a plastic bag in the cupboard under the stairs, postponing the clean till morning, so even after I'd changed into my pyjamas and exiled my shoes outside, the smell of my secret still followed me round the house.

Mum had made me a hot chocolate in my special Christmas mug by the time I got downstairs, with marshmallows floating on the top. She'd also brought a mince pie to leave out for Santa on the matching Christmas plate; the plate and the mug were both a smiling Father Christmas face with a raised beard, cheeks, nose and hat to create a 3D effect. She had me put it in front of the gas fire on a tray with a glass of milk and two carrots.

'To a very happy Christmas!' She raised her mug of tea and clinked it gently with mine in a toast, then, as I drank, she raised hers to the face of the sailor with the yellow sou'wester on the wall, just as she always did, 'and a happy Christmas to you too, Uncle Paddy.'

I also raised my cup to Captain Paddy, in a toast to the uncle I had never met, who, in my imagination, looked just like that weather-worn sailor.

She handed me a present from the pile under the tree and watched as I opened it as though the contents would be just as much of a surprise to her as they were to me. It was a pair of slippers, sheepskin ones with soft, warm wool inside.

'Put them on then. I hope they fit. The man said I could take them back if they don't fit, but they should fit, they should be fine...' She didn't draw breath until I had them on. 'Perfect. Oh they're perfect. They'll keep you lovely and warm. Do you like them?'

I looked at my feet, I was a long way from being Cinderella adorned with a perfectly-fitting glass slipper by her adoring prince. They were utilitarian old lady slippers that had spinster of this parish written all over them.

'I love them,' I said. 'They are super cosy and comfy.'

'Brilliant. I'm so pleased they fit!' She gave little clap of delight, more pleased with the giving of the slippers than anyone could be by receiving the gift. I looked at the ugly things on my feet and thought of the patent shoes with a modest heel on the back doorstep, advertising my shame to the world. If only I'd stayed in the house with my slippers on the night of the party, there would be no churning in my stomach, no odour of vomit and no question racing round my brain on repeat: 'What the hell are you going to do, Marie?'

It was my turn to give Mum a gift and I reached for the one I thought she would love the most. I hadn't intended giving her this one on Christmas Eve but I felt so wretched and repentant that I needed to give her something she would treasure right now, while the world still had a possibility of righting itself again and I could still be the daughter she wanted me to be.

The gift was round and squishy and she opened it with agonising care and excitement. She started by trying to guess what was inside.

'You'll never guess, just open it.'

'I might guess.'

'You won't, it's nothing like the size or shape it looks like in the wrapper.'

She peeled off the Sellotape as though she might reuse the crumpled paper and I had to give her a giant yawn to remind her that it was well after midnight and long past the time we'd both normally be in bed.

I'd put the present in an empty cereal box with the top cut off and it was bulging out the sides. She pulled out two pieces, each wrapped in newspaper.

'Curiouser and curiouser,' she said, carefully unwrapping the first of the two items, a bone china saucer with a yellow rose painted on it and a gold rim. She smiled at me and unwrapped the second item, the matching cup with the yellow rose painted inside the bowl ready to be revealed as she drank her tea and the word 'Mother' in fancy gold writing across the front.

'Oh Marie,' she said, carefully placing the cup on its saucer by her feet on the floor and standing up to come and hug me. 'That's by far the most wonderful, thoughtful Christmas present I've ever had.' She was actually crying and her hug was so suffocating that I had to break free of it for fear I might be sick all over again.

'Look what you've done to me, I'm an emotional wreck! Thank you Marie, it's beautiful and I will treasure it.'

'I hope you'll use it.'

'I will, every day, starting with my first Christmas cup of tea in the morning. Now off to bed with you, there'll be potatoes to peel before church in the morning.'

It was one of those really perfect moments when you've done something absolutely and completely right. It felt like a sign that things might be OK after all. Perhaps I wasn't pregnant. Maybe it had just been the lack of air and the over-indulgence with so much chocolate and rich food in the house. What if the idea of being pregnant had only been the coincidence of seeing Theresa and the baby in the manger and feeling sick all at the same time.

I went to bed convincing myself that it had all just been a bit of an unfortunate embarrassing incident and we'd laugh about it years from now, maybe over a cup of tea with the Mother cup on the table between us.

But after a good sleep I woke up early, before it got light, and tried to remember when I'd had my last period. I couldn't remember while I was lying down, I had to get up and switch on the light and think back to when I could last remember needing to put tampons in my bag for school. I replayed the weeks in my head, going back through December and the cold snap at the end of November and Mum's birthday and the party to the very beginning of November and the stomach cramps I'd had during a maths test.

I went downstairs to the kitchen to find the calendar and counted back. It was nearly eight weeks since my last period, almost six since the party. I put the calendar back on the wall and filled the kettle.

'You're keen,' said my mum. 'Still got a little girl's excitement about Christmas, haven't you? I'll finish brewing up, I can't wait to use my new cup. You go and get your new slippers on, your feet will be freezing.'

She paused on her way over to the teapot to give me a kiss. 'Happy Christmas, Marie.'

We went to the nine o'clock Mass that year instead of the twelve o'clock. Mum said we might as well, given that we were up so early and she hoped to see Theresa and invite her over on Boxing Day. But Theresa wasn't there; perhaps it was hard for her to get there on Christmas Day or maybe she had better things to do, like have a lie-in and get ready for Christmas dinner with whoever.

I didn't know whether to feel relieved or disappointed. I'd had a half-formed plan to talk to Theresa about my predicament and see if she could help me or just tell me that things would work out and everything would be fine in the end. But, as I sat trying to convince myself that I couldn't smell vomit in the church, I began to wonder whether her absence was a sign that I shouldn't look to her for help. But if not her, then who? The problem would literally grow by the day and I needed to do something.

On Christmas Day, the prayers at church are all about giving thanks for the arrival of Christ and looking forward to when he'll come again. But I knelt and silently begged for help:

'I know that all life is precious and this was your creation, I know it was my stupid mistake and I should have thought about the consequences of my actions a bit sooner but please, please, *please* will you help me now. My mum doesn't deserve this and she won't cope with it. I won't cope with it either and all of that would not be fair on any child. Please fix this for me and I promise to be the best I can be every day from today for the rest of my life.'

My mum was watching me as I stood, unused to seeing me lost in prayer. She smiled at me and I felt guilt burn across my face at her assumption that I was full of the holiness of the season rather than filled to the brim with panic and regret.

Father Reilly made a point of shaking hands with both of us as we left the church that morning and wishing us a very happy Christmas. I was sure he knew.

'Feeling better today Marie?'

'Much better thank you,' my mum answered for me.

'All that rich food can be a bit much at this time of year, can't it?'

I looked for a sign on his face that he was being ironic but there was none.

'We've had a quick run round with the bleach this morning so no harm done,' he grinned. 'Thank the Lord for these tiled floors; they might let out the heat and make a pin drop sound like a bomb blast but at least they're easy to clean up.'

He and my mum laughed as I was forgiven by both of them for throwing up at Midnight Mass. I wished that all messes could be cleaned up so easily.

Christmas came and went with all the usual routine and anti-climax. We cooked a huge dinner and ate it, just the two of us, wearing party hats from the crackers and telling each other the jokes. Despite my best efforts to park the hugeness of my worries until later, the fortune telling plastic fish in my second cracker told me I was melancholy and it felt like the whole world knew what was wrong, apart from my mum who went straight from worrying that we'd done too many potatoes to debating whether the custard was too thick, then hunting for the Radio Times so that we could make sure we were watching the best film.

Boxing Day was similarly filled with too much food, too much TV and too little fresh air and we caught up with the obligatory photo of me standing next to the tree wearing a paper hat that we'd forgotten to do the day before. It was a tradition that my mum had kept every Christmas since I was a year old. The hats, the tree and the living room looked exactly the same on every picture; it was only me that had changed.

By Friday, the day after Boxing Day, we'd forgotten what day of the week it was altogether and went to the shops just for something to do to get us out of the house. I was just waiting for something to happen, waiting for a plan to come to me or for my mum to figure it out and say 'don't worry Marie, here's what we're going to do.' But at no point did I consider telling her. I didn't have the words to communicate something so huge.

So I reverted to plan B and when the week had finally dawdled to Sunday I got up early, much earlier than I needed to, so that I could be at church in time for the 9am Mass. I left my mum a note saying I'd been unable to get back to sleep and had decided to go to early Mass so that I could get through my homework in the afternoon. I knew she would never challenge the need to spend time on homework, especially now that I had mocks and then the real GCSEs coming up so soon.

I was way too early for Mass and decided to go and find Theresa at the bus stop instead. That way I could tell her all about it in the fresh air, away from the pious old ladies and Mary and all the saints.

She didn't seem surprised to see me.

'Oh, hello love, did you have a nice Christmas?'

'Yes thanks, did you?'

My response was automatic and insincere, much the same as Theresa's 'lovely, thank you' in return.

'Actually, it was pretty boring and a bit intense being stuck in the house just the two of us,'

Theresa laughed at my honesty. 'Ah yes,' she said, 'Christmas can be a bit like trifle, full of good things and a treat that you're supposed to look forward too but it's easy to have too much of it very quickly.'

'I hate trifle.'

'Me too.'

'I think I might be pregnant.'

'I see.'

Her step paused for the tiniest of seconds but she carried on walking as though I'd simply told her that it might rain in the afternoon.

'We came to the nine o'clock Mass on Christmas Day. I was up early anyway and Mum wanted to invite you for Boxing Day but...'

'I wasn't there. I always go to my brother's on Christmas Day. He picks me up in the morning and drops me back the day after Boxing Day. I expect you've had trouble sleeping with something like that on your mind. Have you told your mother?'

'NO!' This time the volume and horror in my voice stopped her walking and she turned to look at me.

'I can't tell my mum? How can I? She'd be horrified. She'd be angry, worried. She'd be so disappointed.'

'But you need to tell her.'

'How can I tell her? She's worked so hard to keep things going for the two of us all these years, how can I tell her that I've done something so stupid? I'm not one of those girls that goes to parties and goes out with boys and sleeps with boys, you know. If I were I probably wouldn't have got caught, I'd have been more careful. Like my friend Claire, she's slept with half the school I think, but this would never happen to her.'

'I see.' Theresa looked at her watch. 'We'd better keep walking, it's nearly five to. How sure are you?'

'Pretty certain. I've counted back and I've not had a period since before that party.'

'The night before you met me at the bus stop.'

'Yes.'

'And are you usually pretty regular?'

'More regular than that.'

'I see. And you were sick in church on Christmas Eve. Have you been sick again?'

'No, but I feel like I might be a lot of the time.'

'That could just be anxiety. We need to get you a test. We'll do it after Mass.'

We'd arrived at the big gates outside church and she squeezed my hand.

'Don't worry. One way or another everything will be fine. Trust in the Lord, Marie. I'm glad you've told me, love. Come on, let's go in.'

The nine o'clock Mass is shorter than the twelve o'clock, even though the liturgy is the same, because there's no invitation to the children to come up to the front and do the Our Father, but this morning the service seemed to last forever and I kept losing my place and missing the responses. Theresa joined in with the Mass as though we'd talked about nothing but last night's TV on our way here, but every time we stood up and sat down she turned to me with a smile of reassurance.

Father Reilly greeted us with surprise on our way out of church.

'Is your mother OK, Marie? We're not used to seeing you this early on a Sunday.'

'She's fine, thank you Father. I just wanted to come early this week so that I can get some of my homework done this afternoon. I've taken a break, you know, over Christmas and everything, but I need to get my head back into it.'

'Yes, of course, very important. Well done. I expect we'll see your mother later. And you have Theresa looking after you here. You're in excellent hands.'

He said the last bit to me but it was meant for Theresa, who shook his hand and thanked him, either for the compliment or the Mass or both, it wasn't clear.

'Come on, I'll take you to Boots,' she said, once we were through the gates, so we walked up to the high street together in silence.

The shop hadn't opened yet when we got to it and I wasn't the only one peering anxiously through the window for signs of life.

'It says they open at ten. That's only a few minutes. Let's go and get a cuppa and some breakfast. Have you had some breakfast? Then I can nip out and get the test and you can do it in the toilets in the café.'

'I'm pretty sure, you know.'

'I know, and I expect you're right but let's just make certain and then we can see about what to do next. I happen to know that the café over there does the best sausage barms of anywhere in the world. Come on, it's my treat, you're my excuse to carry on the over-indulgence.'

She patted her belly as though there should be signs of too much Christmas food and drink consumed over the past week but in fact she was very slim and looked like she'd never over-indulged in her life. We sat at a table by the window so that we could keep an eye out for when Boots opened, and the waitress, a girl of about my age with her hair cut longer on one side than the other, chirped 'coming right up' when Theresa ordered, before bringing us a huge teapot to share and setting down two mugs printed with the café's name 'The Copper Coffee Pot' and its logo of a steaming pot of coffee.

'You be mother,' said Theresa, nodding towards the teapot with no sense of irony, and I poured while she stared out of the window towards the chemists as though they might sell out of pregnancy tests if she didn't dash over there to buy one as soon as they opened.

Even though she wasn't speaking I needed to change the subject, I needed her to talk about something else so that the voice in my head that kept saying 'you're going to take a pregnancy test in a minute and it's going to be positive' would just shut up and give me five minutes off from worrying about what might happen next.

'So where does your brother live?'

'Ah, he emigrated over to the wrong side of the Pennines years ago now. Must be at least twenty-five years. He left for love, you see, and the love all worked out. He got married, they had the perfect family – boy, girl, dog, cat – and lived happily ever after. I keep my distance, really. I'm happy for them, and I adore the children – they're all grown up now of course, Adam has some high powered job for a financial services company in Leeds, no-one really knows what he does but he has a fancy title and a fancy pay packet to go with it, I think. And Miriam is in her final year at University and already set up with a civil service job in London after her finals. She'll probably be running the country ten years from now. You'll probably be telling your kids about the time you had breakfast with the Prime Minister's auntie.'

Even when I changed the subject my future children made it into the conversation, so I had to change it again.

'What about you? Have you got any children? Have you been married?'

She paused and the girl brought our sausage barms, huge things with a token bit of salad on the side.

'Help yourself to sauces. There's ketchup, brown, barbecue, and fruity if you're feeling really adventurous. They're on the table just over there. She pointed to a display of sauces, napkins and extra cutlery with a picture above it that read 'Have a great day'. She grinned at us then bounced off towards the kitchen again.

'Dig in then,'

'I'll just get some sauce. Do you want anything?'

'I'll have brown. No, make that fruity. Why not?'

I stepped gingerly around the tables, making sure I didn't knock anything or anyone on my way and made it back safely with a glass bottle of fruity sauce in one hand and a plastic bottle of ketchup in the other.'

'It's lovely to have an excuse to come here,' Theresa commented as I handed her the sauce. 'I used to bring my mum sometimes. She would have tea and crumpets while I had one of these.'

She held it up in front of her like a priest with the host but instead of 'body of Christ' she said 'It's a thing of beauty isn't it?' and took a big bite.

I started to eat mine too, and between mouthfuls and gulps of tea she gave me a full life summary. How she'd been engaged to be married to a friend of her brother, called Peter. They'd started seeing each other when she was twenty-two and he was twenty – her toy boy she said, smiling. By the time she was twenty-three they were engaged and they were planning the wedding. She had bought the dress, they'd booked the venue for the reception: a hotel she assumed I wouldn't remember because it had been knocked down to make way for a supermarket years ago. They'd been to have the serious chat with the priest about the responsibilities of marriage and bringing children into the world and had argued over the seating plan for three nights running until they finally had all the tables sorted.

'Then, six days before the wedding, while I was at home practising hairstyles for the big day, Peter got run over by a guy in a van jumping a red light. It was a pedestrian crossing, the red man turned to green and he just stepped out without looking they said at the inquest, just trusted that drivers would stop on red like they're supposed to. The driver involved got charged with reckless driving and went to prison for a bit, not for all that long though, considering what he'd done. And I had to un-organise everything and sit at home on my wedding day.

'Robert, my brother, was very good. He let everyone know and called the priest. And he was grieving himself, of course, Peter had been his friend. But then he met Michelle and moved away to Yorkshire and I was left here with Mum. Then her health started to go downhill and I poured everything I had into looking after her. And now she's gone too.'

I found myself crying and I wasn't sure whether it was for Peter, for Theresa or for myself. I felt sorry for Theresa. I wished things had turned out better for her and that she'd got her happy ever after, but, at the same time, her story made me think of what lay ahead for me: what if I ended up trapped with my mum until the end of time? Instead of university and a home of my own and a family one day, I could end up with just me, my mum, and my child, all crammed into that small house surrounded by ornaments and crippling resentment.

But Theresa showed no signs of resentment. She was too busy taking pleasure in the little things, like a giant sausage barm with fruity sauce.

'This fruity sauce is a revelation,' she said. 'Don't be upset for me. Peter and I had wonderful times together, lots of people don't even get half of what we had. And I've been able to keep him frozen in time and blissfully in love. He never went bald or got a beer belly, I never had to get upset because he was taking me for granted or staying out at the pub while I was at home chained to the kitchen sink and juggling the kids. We didn't get to have a life together like we'd planned but we had something fresh and beautiful that never decayed and there's a lot to be said for that. Now you finish your butty while I nip over to Boots and let's get your life sorted out, shall we?'

I'd almost let myself forget why we were there and, as she left to buy the pregnancy test, I even considered just leaving and pretending none of this was happening in the hope that it would just sort itself out. I wished I could swap lives with the waitress but wishing wasn't going to achieve anything.

The test was positive of course. I stood in the café toilet, double checking whether it was two pink lines for yes or no. No matter how many times I read the little leaflet, that second little line was definitely there and it definitely meant I was pregnant.

'Well?' said Theresa as I sat back down with the little plastic stick still in my pocket because I didn't know what else to do with it.

I just nodded, unable to speak for fear that saying the word out loud would release tears that wouldn't stop. Before, there had still been a tiny chance that it wasn't true and maybe it had been a blip in my periods or some kind of illness that had stopped them.

'So, do you want me to come home with you to be there when you tell your mum?'

I'd assumed she would know that the reason I'd got her involved was to help me get rid of the problem, not hold my hand while I confessed it to my mum.

I shook my head but it wasn't enough to communicate what I wanted to say.

'I don't want you to help me tell her,' I whispered. 'I want you to help me get rid of the problem so that I never have to tell her.'

There was a long pause while Theresa looked at me and considered how to say what she wanted to say. It seemed like the whole café went quiet as everyone waited to hear her response.

'But it's not a problem to be got rid of like a blocked drain or a cold sore, Marie. It's new life. It's a person and everything that person will grow up to be.'

So Theresa was happy to help me, but not in the way I wanted. Her idea of help was to support me in accepting my situation, not in changing it. She practically begged me outside the café that morning to let her come home with me.

'Or at least go and talk to Father Reilly about it. He's very good, you know. Very understanding. He will help you come to terms with everything. He can help you make it OK with your mum.'

I thanked her for the breakfast and walked her to the bus stop, assuring her I would think about it and pray about it. She said she would pray for me and gave me a hug as the bus approached. The hug was nice, it was comforting, but it wasn't what I needed from her and I didn't wait to wave as the bus pulled away, because that was the only way I could think of to punish her for not setting her own feelings aside to consider mine.

It was a horrible day after that. My mum was annoyed that I'd gone to Mass without her and even more annoyed when

I explained that the reason I'd been out so long was that I'd 'bumped into' Theresa and gone for breakfast with her.

'You knew I wanted to make friends with her and here you are cutting me out and keeping Theresa all to yourself.'

'I just didn't want to wake you, I know you don't get a lie-in during the week.'

'Well I wish you had woken me up. I'm sure it's very nice going out for breakfast but you shouldn't be expecting treats like that from virtual strangers and you certainly shouldn't get a taste for breakfast in cafés, I can assure you that won't be happening with me any time soon, especially not when we've got plenty of perfectly good food in the house that wants eating.'

She went out for twelve o'clock Mass at eleven-thirty and I went to lie down and think over my options. Go to the doctor on my own, find another adult to take me to a clinic, or tell my mum and let her decide for me what I should do next. The third one wasn't an option at all because all choice would be gone then. But number one was so scary and I was struggling to think of a new candidate for option two.

By 12.45 I had to make sure I was sitting at the table with my books spread out looking like I'd been hard at work the whole time she'd been away because that's what I told her I'd be doing. By the time I heard her key in the door I was sure she already knew, or that she would know soon. Theresa would tell her. Or Theresa would tell Father Reilly and he would tell her. I could hear her in the hall, putting her coat away in the cupboard under the stairs. She called hello through the wall. She went in the kitchen and then popped her head around the door.

'Do you want a cup of tea?'

Her mood had changed, lifted by her visit to church. She clearly knew none of what was going on with me.

'I'll make it if you like. I could do with a break.'

So I made a pot of tea and brought it in the Mother cup and we had crumpets with cheese on, done under the grill so that it oozed gooeyness into the holes. She assured me that it was good to take proper breaks from my revision and I just smiled, trying not to look guilty for the lies I was telling and the lack of any homework that had happened in our house that day so far.

I worked all afternoon though. I lost myself in Shakespeare and algebra until everything else was like the sound of an alarm clock in the next room when you're in a deep sleep; just a faint niggle in the background, not a noise that need bother you.

Like she did every week, Mum made a roast chicken dinner and when it was almost ready she came to drag me out of my sanctuary.

'You'll have to clear your stuff off the table now, love. I'll be putting the dinner out in five minutes.'

She asked me questions about what I'd been studying as we ate and it was nice to be normal and have a real conversation with true answers.

But eventually it was bed time and I was alone with no distractions and no plans and everything came crowding back in, bigger and fiercer than ever for having had a rest all day. As a child I had terrible night terrors, with wolves and snakes and ogres crowding into my bedroom in the dark and stopping me from sleeping. My mum would come into my room in response to my screams, turn the lights on to make the monsters vanish and sit at the end of my bed with the light on until I went to sleep. I wished for those times back, when she could turn the light on and make all the horrors in my head disappear but, light on or off, I would still be pregnant and my mum wasn't the cure for this monster; telling her would be the biggest ogre of them all.

I flicked through a mental directory of people I could turn to. Father Reilly? No. He might help me tell my mum but he wouldn't help me get rid and move on. Mrs Edgar? She might. Or she might tell my mum. It would put her in an awkward position. She might get the sack for keeping my secret and she was too nice for me to do that. Claire's mum? Claire's mum would definitely see it from my point of view. She'd probably be madly relieved that it was me in this pickle and not Claire. Who would have thought it? Claire's mum seemed like the obvious answer, the answer that had been right in front of my face the whole time. If my mum was the wrong person to tell, Claire's mum was the opposite of her so it must be right.

The light had been switched on and I slept. But I was awake again before it was light and something at the back of my mind, half-visible, half-obscured by sleep, was flashing red at me and stopping me from drifting back for another half an hour.

I couldn't get the image of Claire's mum out of my head, there in her hallway, still in her dressing gown with her toes half painted, chatting away until Claire came down the stairs.

If I told Claire's mum, Claire would know. And then the whole school would know. And then my mum would know. And then I would be both a teenage mum and forever that stupid girl who got pregnant while she was still in high school.

I ran to the bathroom and vomited yesterday's chicken dinner into the toilet. I was on my own and that was that.

Since it was early and the world was quiet, now seemed as good a time as any to get on with it. I waited outside the doctor's surgery with a couple of old ladies and a woman panicking because her toddler had a temperature and the medicine wasn't bringing it down. She gabbled at me so fast that I could barely understand her but she didn't want me to answer or be able to help, she just wanted to be able to share her panic with someone while we all waited for the door to open. I let the panicked mother and the early bird pensioners go ahead of me in the queue. A few minutes here or there wasn't going to make that much difference.

The receptionist said I could have an appointment at 8.45. It was a half hour wait but pointless going home and coming back again so I just took a seat and a cup of water from the water dispenser in the corner, which farted a big bubble back up to the top of the bottle as I walked away, prompting the woman that had been ahead of me in the queue to glance at me as though

I'd emitted the noise. The rewards for generosity are always less than you'd think.

I sat next to the panicking woman and staring child. He was hot and red in the face, unwilling to smile at me despite my best efforts and irritated by his mother's attempts to soothe him by stroking his hair.

'Barnaby McAllen' the doctor's voice called out over the tannoy from behind the wall next to us and the woman staggered towards the doorway, weighed down by her child and a bag stuffed with toys and snacks that were of no interest to him.

'Good luck,' I whispered to her, picking up her scarf from the floor to add to the pile and reaching out to turn the door handle for her because she had no spare hands to do it.

It was only when I sat back down with twenty minutes still to wait that I saw the poster right in front of me.

'Unwanted pregnancy?' It said. 'You're not alone. Speak to us about your options and let us help you make the right choice for you.'

It was as though someone had put it there specifically for me. They'd known I was coming. This was my equivalent of the census and the stable with the manger; somewhere there was a plan and it was all going to play itself out the way it had been intended from the start.

There were other posters and leaflets displayed around the place, of course, but they didn't apply to me, they were just a distraction. Headings like 'Coping with Cancer,' 'Arthritis – Your Questions Answered,' 'Your Smear Test Could Save Your Life'; as the minutes ticked down to my appointment I distracted myself with all the much more awful things that could be happening to me, to make myself feel better.

The woman with the feverish child came back out of the doctor's office. The toddler was now sobbing with genuine sorrow but hardly any noise. She looked concerned but calmer and I smiled a goodbye at her. She managed a limp smile back and, as soon as she was gone, I no longer thought of her as a real person but as a sign sent to show me how hard it would be to have this baby, not just when it was born but afterwards, for months and years. She and her poorly toddler were a message to stick to my decision to end the pregnancy, even if the doctor tried to persuade me otherwise.

In fact I didn't need to worry about the doctor trying to talk me out of it. When I finally heard my name called out to anyone in the waiting room that might be listening, Doctor Beverton was sympathetic and on my side. I hadn't seen her since I'd had an eye infection when I was eleven, and fairly rarely before that. My mum didn't believe in going to the doctor unless you'd tried every possible over-the-counter remedy first; a good sleep and a Lemsip was the answer to almost everything, but that wasn't going to work for this.

'Of course there are both physical and emotional implications involved in a termination,' the doctor said. She placed a box of tissues on the table next to me but I didn't feel like crying. Quite the opposite in fact: I felt like I was finally getting things sorted out and taking back control.

'If you're right about the dates, they can do a medical abortion, which is when they give you a pill to start things off and then another set of pills to end the pregnancy a day or two later. They'll probably want you to stay in the clinic and be supervised after those second pills and there will be pain – a bit like a really bad period pain – and there'll be blood, on that day and for few days afterwards.'

I just kept nodding as she explained with no drama and no compromise. It was like listening to a teacher say, 'Your homework will be collected on Friday and there'll be no extension to the deadline. There will be detention for anyone that doesn't hand their book in on time.'

'The emotional effects are much harder to predict,' the doctor continued. 'I've seen women who were very distressed at the thought of it respond very calmly after the event. I've also seen women who were certain and very matter-of-fact about it go to pieces afterwards. And it's not just the days and weeks after the event you need to worry about: sometimes women who cope well emotionally at the time are unable to reconcile themselves to their decision years later. Often, with girls your age, the decision to terminate a pregnancy becomes an emotional issue when they give birth to a planned baby years later and the full implications of their choice become clear for the first time, at a time in their life when they are most vulnerable.'

I said nothing. I understood her point and I could see how that might happen but I had enough to worry about with right now.

'How's your mum?' Doctor Beverton threw into the silence. 'I take it you haven't told her?'

'She's fine,' I said. 'Well, up and down as usual, if that's what you're asking, but fine. And no, I can't tell her. She'd be so angry with me and she'd make me keep the baby and she'd make me feel guilty for all the bother it would cause her for the rest of my life.'

'I see.'

'I just can't tell her. You won't tell her, will you?'

'I won't if you don't want me to, you're my patient and what's said in this room is confidential, but I would advise you to think carefully about whether to tell her. It's a big secret to keep. As we've already talked about, there are physical and emotional symptoms that you may find it difficult to hide from her immediately afterwards and you need to be mindful of the fact that this is a secret that you'll be keeping for a long time to come.'

She made it sound like I'd be keeping the baby under the bed and feeding it scraps I'd ferreted away in my pockets at the dinner table.

'I think when it's all over and I can just get back to normal and concentrate on my exams it will just be something I can put behind me. And anyway, I don't think my mum would cope either with me bringing a baby into the house or with knowing

I've had an abortion, so I don't really think that telling her anything is an option. I just need to clear up my mess and be less stupid in the future.'

The doctor smiled. She could see the sense in what I was saying.

'It's early, let's see if we can get you an appointment this afternoon for the first dose and then you can go back the day after tomorrow while you're still off school and have the whole thing over and done with by the time the new term starts. How does that sound?'

'Thank you.'

It was at that point that relief triggered tears, and I reached for the tissues she'd put in front of me while she leafed through a book on her desk to search for a number and pressed 9 for an outside line.

TWENTY-TWO

When Father O'Connor turned up at our house a few days after my birthday, I was sure that he must have found Captain under the pew and he was here to tell me off, or tell me I had to come to church and confess so that I could get my penance, or excommunicate me for blasphemy. Maybe Captain had started to smell and the whole congregation had hunted around on the floor for the cause of the stink. Or maybe a curious toddler at family Mass had been crawling around and found it while he was playing. What if he'd taken it out of the tin and screamed, or picked it up and shown his mum and she'd screamed at the sight of the bird's rotting carcass, just like my mum had screamed when she saw Captain pegged out on the washing line. More likely the cleaner had found it. Or God had told Father O'Connor it was there; priests are always praying, perhaps God tells them things when the rest of us are not really listening.

It was Saturday. Gabe, Dad and I had been at the park having a game of footy but we'd had to come home because we'd taken Anna with us in the buggy and she'd just cried and whinged the whole time. We'd ignored it at first and Dad had said she'd settle down and we should play on but it felt a bit mean to leave her there crying. She had proper tears and everything. I think she was missing Mum. Who knows what babies are thinking? Maybe she just doesn't like football.

We'd got back to find Mum and Jenny in the kitchen drinking tea, the washing machine was on fast spin but you could still hear Jenny prattling on about last night's TV and how the plot of EastEnders was getting a bit far-fetched. Mum didn't even watch EastEnders, but I'd realised that Jenny doesn't really mind whether you're interested in what she's saying as long as you look like you're listening. Mum just sat there sipping her tea and nodding while Jenny helped herself to another biscuit and carried on talking with her mouth full, just like she was always telling us not to do.

'Can I have a biscuit?' said Gabe, heading towards the plate of home-made biscuits on the table without waiting for an answer.

'You can get those muddy trainers off your mum's clean floor first, young man' said Jenny, as though they were her biscuits and her floor. Though, to be fair, it probably had been Jenny who'd mopped it while we were out and it had definitely been Jenny who'd baked the biscuits.

'Aww, but I'm starving,' Gabe complained, hesitating with the biscuit paused in mid-air half way between the plate and his mouth. 'And Anna has cried like a maniac the whole time we've been out. My ears are practically bleeding.'

'One biscuit, then out of those muddy clothes and into the bath,' said Mum. Everyone turned to her, surprised to hear her stepping in to over-rule Jenny. We'd got used to Mum being there but not quite being there. She was usually like a cardboard cut-out in the room; you could see her clear enough but she was quiet and kind of flat.

Gabe threw a triumphant look at Jenny and picked up the plate to offer a biscuit to me and Dad.

'Thanks Mum,' he said. 'Do you want one?'

She took a biscuit and put it on the table in front of her.

'Any chance we can give this grumbling item a biscuit?' said Dad. 'She might actually stop complaining.' Dad held Anna out in front of him as though he were going to drop her over the edge of an imaginary cliff or something with his arms outstretched and her legs dangling in thin air.

Mum leapt forward from her seat to catch Anna from the drop. 'Just give her to me. I'll take her. She might want changing.'

'Or just a cuddle with her Mamma,' I replied. 'Or some girl time. I think she's fed up of being with the boys. I don't think she's much of a one for football.'

Mum cuddled Anna in close to her chest, holding her with one arm wrapped around the baby's tiny, wriggling body and the other hand curled around her almost bald head. Anna stopped crying and watched me eat my biscuit, opening and closing her mouth every time I took a bite.

'I think she does want changing,' Gabe said, helping himself to a third biscuit before Jenny moved the plate and stood up to put the remaining biscuits back into the ancient-looking Quality Street tin. 'She is a bit smelly.'

'And a bit hungry too, no doubt,' said Dad. 'Jim, you go and get the bath running, Champ. Gabe, you get those trainers off. Jenny, thanks for your help this morning. I've got this now.'

'I was going to wait for the washing and get that sorted for you,' Jenny protested.

'Thanks Jenny, I don't know what we'd do without you but I'm on the case. Wash the kids, feed the kids, sort the washing and chillax. That's the plan, eh love?'

Mum was staring out of the window to where the cherry tree was changing to yellow and orange like a bonfire against the smoky grey sky.

'It looks lovely that tree, doesn't it Mum?' I said, watching it with her, missing her like mad.

She walked across to me and kissed me on the forehead. 'You're a good boy Jim. You're a blessing.' And she smiled a lovely, special smile just for me and I knew I'd done the right thing taking Captain out of the house, even if John-Joe had left with him.

Father O'Connor arrived while I was getting the bath running. Mum was busy changing Anna and Dad was in the kitchen trying to untie the wet, knotted laces on Gabe's trainers. Jenny let him in on her way out of the house and, even though she did call through the hallway to tell us she was leaving and he was arriving, we were so used to tuning out her voice that no-one listened.

Somehow, we all ended up in the hall at the same time and Father O'Connor was just standing there. He made us all jump. Even Anna started crying again when she saw him, but she's funny like that, she knows when everyone else is a bit anxious or upset and she just joins in. I had that racing heartbeat you get when you feel like you're going to fall off your bike or when you spot something out of the corner of your eye that looks scary, even if it isn't really. He raised up his arms to greet my mum with the baby – he loves babies – and the hallway was filled with the blackness of his suit with only his grey hair, pale face and the small cut-out of his white dog collar separating him from the general gloominess of the space.

I looked at Dad. He'd politely made cups of tea for Father O'Connor the couple of times he'd popped round just after John-Joe died but had managed to manoeuvre him out of the house pretty quickly. I was hoping he'd manage the same trick today. For the first time in ages, things had felt like they might actually get back to normal this morning. If not this weekend, then sometime soon. If not exactly normal, then at least as near to normal as it can be when your brother's died.

This morning Mum had smiled, not in the way we'd got used to where it looked like she'd pressed a button to turn the smile on and then it disappeared when she took her finger off the switch, but in the real, normal way smiles happen when you think something nice and your face changes without you even knowing you're doing it.

Just as she was learning how to do that again, the priest was here to remind us that something awful had happened and offer us God and faith and the prayers of all the saints and all the congregation in return for John-Joe. With him in the house we were going to have to think about what we'd lost instead of what we still had all over again.

I looked to Dad for a way to turn the dial back to normal but Father O'Connor had already wrested Anna from Mum's arms and was dancing her around in thin air in an attempt to stop her crying that was only making things worse. Mum looked at Dad to fix it too.

But it wasn't Dad who stepped in first, it was Gabe.

'Hi Father O'Connor, what are you doing here? Isn't Saturday your day off? Don't you have a football game to watch or library books to take back or something?'

Gabe has no filter and thinks that everyone spends Saturdays playing football, watching football, going to the library and eating bacon butties for lunch.

'Oh, I do like the idea of a day off on Saturday, Gabe,' said Father O'Connor, handing Anna back to Mum and clearly disappointed that his infant-whispering skills had not worked. 'The thing is though, being a priest is not so much a job as a way of life and every day is an opportunity to be with people and share the love of God.'

He reached out to pat Gabe on the head but Gabe just ducked out of the way.

'Actually, I invited Father O'Connor here,' said Dad. Gabe looked at me, I looked at Mum, Mum glared at Father O'Connor.

'I thought it might be good for you and Mum to have someone to talk to. I know you've got me and you've got Jenny...'

'Yeah, but it's hard to get a word in edgeways with Jenny,' Gabe interrupted.

'But sometimes it's good to be able to talk to someone who's good at listening and good at understanding. I mentioned it to Father O'Connor at Mass last weekend and he said he'd pop in when he was next in our neck of the woods.'

'Because we've not seen you at Mass much recently, Marie,' Father O'Connor picked up his cue, 'Even on a Sunday we've seen more of James and the boys and little Anna than we have of you.'

It was true. Mum had been having a lot of headaches on Sunday mornings recently or bad nights with Anna's teething that meant she needed to stay behind and have a lie-in while we all went to Mass. She's always been the one who made sure that we got there on time and, even if one of us was ill, it was Mum that had taken us and Dad that had stayed at home to keep the poorly one company.

'We've not seen you during the week either Marie. You know you're always welcome at both St Chad's and St Anthony's; either or. God doesn't mind.'

We were all still in the hallway, as though we were waiting for someone to finish the hoovering in the living room before we could go in. Mum was still standing on the bottom stair with Anna falling asleep now in her arms and Gabe was barefoot with his smelly football socks in his hands, swinging them round in a circular motion to give us all a whiff of his damp, sweaty feet. I was still in my football socks too, having left my football boots at the door, and Dad had one of Gabe's boots still in his hand with its knotted lace twisted round his finger. We were like one of those pictures that you have to answer questions about at school. 'Which of the people in the picture have been playing football? What evidence can you give for this answer?'

Mum looked like she was getting told off by the teacher and stood stroking Anna's hair, looking at Father O'Connor's shoes. They were black and fastened with Velcro, like school shoes.

'In fact, I don't think we've seen you in church since John-Joe's funeral, Marie,' Father O'Connor was trying to look into Mum's face and was sort of dipping his head in an attempt to catch her eye while she stubbornly focused on his shoes. 'Not that anyone's keeping count Marie, we're not, of course nobody is. And God certainly isn't. He wants to help you Marie. He understands you're hurt. He feels it. But he can only help you if you let him into your heart to help you heal it.'

There was a silence in the hallway when Father O'Connor had finished speaking that had become so familiar that none of us felt the need to answer him. We'd learned to wrap ourselves in that silence like a cosy blanket on a winter evening when the wind is raging outside and the rain is battering the windows. Cocooned in our blanket of silence nothing could be said that would upset anyone and no-one had to worry about what anyone else was saying. We were safe, protected, defended against all that bad weather. It was funny how much we missed Jenny's irritating chatter when she wasn't there.

But adults are programmed to remember their manners. 'Look, it's no good standing around in the hall chatting is it?' Dad said eventually. 'How rude of us not to offer you a cup of tea, Father. I think we even have some freshly-baked biscuits that the neighbour brought round, if Gabe hasn't eaten them all.'

'I only had two.'

'Three,' I corrected him.

'Is that bath still running, Jim?' Dad nodded towards the stairs and I ran upstairs to save the house from certain flooding.

Gabe appeared behind me more or less as soon as I'd turned off the taps and just started stripping off as though there was no-one else in the room.

'Dad says I have to have first bath and then it's your turn.'

'That's right, I did,' said Dad, appearing at the top of the stairs carrying Anna. 'I'm just going to put Anna down for a sleep while your Mum has a chat with Father and you two have a bath.'

'I bet he'll eat all the biscuits,' said Gabe, 'He loves biscuits. I've seen him eat loads of biscuits at school.'

'Just finish getting undressed for your bath,' said Dad. 'Jim, you keep an eye on him while I put this one down and then I'll swap you.'

He came back a minute later to find Gabe completely starkers and showing me how he could kick better with his left foot than his right by kicking an empty toilet roll tube into the shower cubicle.

'Goal,' he roared and ran round the bathroom.

'Bath,' Dad replied and pointed at the tub full of bubbly water.

'Jim, just check Anna has settled for me will you while I disinfect this naked article.'

So I left them in the bathroom and could hear them laughing as I walked down the landing to my parents' room where Anna still slept in her Moses basket by their bed. She was fast asleep and I was all alone, with Dad and Gabe laughing and chatting in the bathroom, Mum downstairs and John-Joe gone. Again.

I went to my room to try to talk to John-Joe. I thought if I called to him I might see him, or just hear him, or he might hear me. But even when I lay on his bed and wore his Mickey Mouse cap with the ears, there was still no sign of him. Nothing happened when I called his name or asked him if he was there except that my words sounded lost and a bit stupid in the empty bedroom.

I went downstairs to see if I could sit with Mum and Father O'Connor. Dad must have heard me because he stuck his head around the bathroom door and told me not to disturb them in the kitchen because Mum needed some time with Father because he could help her.

'I'll be done here soon, Champ, it looks like there is a boy under all that grime after all, so once I've rinsed half a tonne of mud out of the bath it'll be your turn.'

I carried on downstairs but instead of going into the front TV room and just putting the telly on while I waited for Dad to call me up for my bath, I stood by the kitchen door to listen. I expected to hear Father O'Connor saying something wise and reassuring like he does when we're in church. He's really good at that; I think it's his job and that must be what they train them to do at priest school, but he's definitely really good at his job.

But the only voice I could hear from the kitchen was my mum's and it was loud enough that I didn't even have to put my head to the door to hear her, I could just stand there on the other side of the door.

'I know exactly why John-Joe's gone,' she said, 'he's gone because God's punishing me for what I did all those years ago when I was too young to know any better. He wasn't there to help me then, when I needed him, was he? I had to do what I could to fix things by myself and of course I've asked myself a million times whether I made the right choice or not. Of course I have. It was the only choice I had Father and I trusted his forgiveness and I trusted him to accept that soul and understand. There's no forgiveness and no understanding though, is there Father? He let me think there was. He gave me all of this, and James, and Jim and John-Joe and Gabe and then he took my baby from me before it had chance to be born, just to remind me of what I'd done. Just to remind me that taking a life before it has chance to live is wrong and was never going to be forgiven. You'd think that'd be enough, wouldn't you?'

'Marie—' Father O'Connor tried to interrupt her but she wasn't going to let him respond.

'When those boys raised up that magpie to enact a resurrection I was freaked out, I thought the baby, the new baby, would be taken from me. They follow you, magpies, you know, Father, once they've marked you out, they have you.'

'Marie this is nonsense—'

'But when Anna arrived and she was fine and everything was OK this time, I thought he'd let me off. The magpie, Jesus, God, whoever. I thought that magpie resurrection was actually a good sign, like the real resurrection, a sign of forgiveness and a new start. But he was just fooling me wasn't he Father? He was trying to catch me off guard to punish me with something I hadn't expected. And then he took John-Joe to get his own back.'

'That's just not true Marie, God doesn't work like that. As you say, he's a God of forgiveness, a God of hope, but he can't always stop bad things, tragic things like John-Joe's accident from happening.'

There was a pause and I thought maybe Mum was thinking over what Father O'Connor had said and she would come out of the kitchen feeling better.

'He's a God of punishment too though, isn't he Father? Look what he did to his own son to teach us a lesson and now look what he's done to my son to teach me a lesson. Well I've heard him and I know I deserve to be punished but that's enough now. If he wants any more from me, let him take it, I can't stop it. But you let him know from me that I've paid my dues, more than paid them, and I'll not keep apologising and going back for more. You keep it, keep it all.'

'Marie, there is comfort in faith, there is new life in faith. I know you know that. When you lost your Mum, when you lost your baby, we saw you in church all the time. All those mid-week Masses you came to gave you solace. That comfort is still there for you now.'

'No Father, there is no comfort left for me in faith. There is no faith left in me.'

'Don't give up on God, Marie.' Father O'Connor sounded kind of upset. 'I know you're angry with him. I have felt angry with him too, so many times, and especially about John-Joe. But he is the parent and we are the children and we have to trust that he knows best and understand that sometimes bad things happen despite his love for us.'

'No Father, you're wrong. I made him angry by having all these children that I didn't deserve and John-Joe made him angry by re-enacting the resurrection with that magpie as Jesus. We might as well be worshipping our Captain as sitting in church waiting to receive the body of your Jesus, because John-Joe would still be dead and my poor lost babies would still be lost.

'All this time,' she went on. 'All. This. Time. I put my trust in God. I had real faith Father. Real faith. The kind where you wake up every morning knowing that there is some greater power at work and He will look after you. Through thick and thin.' Her voice was fading in and out now, I could tell that she was walking around. She does that when she's upset with us and she needs to give us a lecture about behaviour. She was probably waving her hands around a lot too.

251

'But I realise now that my faith has not been built on trust in a loving, forgiving God but fear of a bad tempered, angry God who might turn on me if I didn't behave—'

'No, Marie,' Father O'Connor interrupted, 'that's not what God is like, not at all.'

'With all due respect, Father, how do you know? How do you actually know? It's funny you should talk about God being the parent, because I realise now that's been exactly my relationship with God. Just like my relationship with my mother; constantly trying to please, always living in fear of getting something wrong or upsetting her and having to face the consequences.'

'Your mother got some things wrong, Marie. Perhaps God sometimes gets things wrong. But the thing they both have in common is that they love you and God will always love you.'

I wondered how priests always know what to say. How they don't get persuaded to switch sides like I sometimes do when we're arguing about who the best footballers are in the Premier League or which super hero is the strongest.

I could only just about hear what Mum said next. Maybe she was whispering on purpose, maybe she was turned away from the door. I pictured her by the sink, looking out to the garden and the tree where the leaves were falling from the branches like flaming blossom.

'It's not enough,' she said.

'Marie—' Father O'Connor began, but she interrupted him and she must have turned to face him because I heard the next bit really clearly.

'If God is a God of love and forgiveness, if He's there for me and my family no matter what, then He won't mind if I don't come to church or I don't pray or I don't take the sacrament, will He? Shall we see if He still loves me when I'm angry and empty and battered? Let's see if He comes and proves to me that He loves me or if He'll punish me again.'

'Marie—'

'Father, I have lunches to make for the children. It's been very kind of you to pop round but I'm sure you have lots of people to see, so I won't keep you.'

I tiptoed into the living room and put the TV on so that they'd think I'd been in there the whole time, too engrossed by the pundits' chat about the afternoon's matches to listen in to their conversation.

Father O'Connor popped his head round the door to say goodbye to me. 'See you later, Jim. You're doing a good job there looking after your mum. God bless you.'

I couldn't hear what Mum said to Father O'Connor as he left or what he said to her. The words were drowned out by a discussion of player selection and formation and I was distracted by the graphics of the numbered shirts spread out on a virtual pitch on the screen. But he must have hugged her because when she came into the room she smelt like Father O'Connor, slightly musty, slightly sweaty and a little bit of mothballs.

'Telly off and go and get your bath, Jim, there's a good lad. There'll be a bacon butty waiting for you when you're scrubbed up and handsome.'

She hugged me in the doorway and passed on the familiar scent of the priest.

We didn't go to Mass the next day or any more Sundays after that.

TWENTY-THREE

D r Beverton had tried to get me an appointment for that afternoon or the next day, but it was the following day, New Year's Eve, that I went to the clinic for my first appointment, carrying a bag of school books to back up my lie that I was off to the library to finish an essay while it was quiet.

'But it's quiet here,' my mum had said. 'And it'll be even quieter later when I go to work. I've got three houses to do this afternoon because they're having parties and they want it all perfect before their guests arrive. One of them even asked me to do again for them tomorrow, can you believe that? New Year's Day! I said I'd go the day after. In fact I'm doing them all the day after and a couple of regular Thursday jobs, back to normal by the end of the week. You might come with me Thursday, might you? I could probably do with a hand to get through the extra mess from the ones that have had guests.'

I tuned her out in just the same way that she tuned out my excuses

'OK. I think Claire and some friends are going to the cinema on Thursday to see the Spice Girls' film. I thought I might go with them. I mean, it's not booked or anything but if they are going, can I? I have some Christmas money so I can pay for myself.'

'Claire? Lovely. It would be nice for you to pick up with her again. And that other girl, Becca? You like her don't you? Maybe you could find out for me whether her mother's happy with her cleaner. It's a big house that one, easily three or four hours work a week, it'd be great if you could plant the seed of looking in my direction for a new cleaner with her mother. Anyway, do what you can. Off you go then love, see you later.'

I had to tick a million boxes to answer all kinds of questions at the clinic and they did a scan to check I wasn't more or less pregnant than I thought I was. Part of me was still hoping for a miracle where I'd have to apologise for wasting their time and promise to be more careful next time. But that particular apology wasn't needed.

'My name's Lorna, I'll be looking after you today,' said the woman who'd called me into her room, offered me a chair and put a box of tissues on the table in front of me. She asked the same question 600 times in a catalogue of different sentences, writing something down every time I spoke but taking care not to let me see what she'd written. She was nice, patient, and she wore a wig, which gave me a welcome distraction as I allowed my eyes to follow her fake hairline and wondered why someone like her might have no hair.

Eventually she left the room and came back with a glass of water and an ugly beige pill sealed in a blister pack.

'Once you've taken this your body will start to reject the pregnancy,' she said. 'Take your time.'

I sipped the water and remembered all the times my mum had mourned the life she could have had without me. By swallowing the pill, I could reject the pregnancy, reject that life defined by the mistake I'd made and avoid passing a genetic inheritance of bitterness down to a new generation. The thought summoned an image of me with my own daughter but I wouldn't let it in. I looked at the hairline, I looked at the pill and the water. Wig, pill, water. Water, pill, wig. And it was done.

'Well done, Marie. Are you OK?'

'I'm fine. I'm good. Is there a bin for the wrapper?'

Practical stuff. Where's the bin? Where's the sink? What time's my bus?

I went home via the library to make the lie less of a lie by doing the thing I'd said I would. That downgraded everything else to a sin of omission; I'd told my mum the truth this morning, I just hadn't told her the whole truth. The appointment card was in the back pocket of my jeans to remind me to come back two days later. 10am on January the second, my first appointment of the year. The card was there to remind me, but there was no question of forgetting.

It was after eleven two days later when they gave me the second set of pills. At first I had sat on the bed, looking through my books and writing notes as if I really was reading and understanding the words on the page, but I was just copying a list of symbols that had lost any meaning. There was just me and the pen and the lines on the page in a vacuum where nothing else existed.

But something else did exist and as it left me it refused to allow me to be distracted with notes and text books. It left with sickness and pain and blood and shivers and a throbbing in my head that made me feel as though my skull weren't big enough.

A woman came and checked on me, not Lorna, but a short round woman in a nurse's uniform and ugly shoes.

'I can get you some pain relief, lovey, there's no point in just coping with the pain when we have things that can help you.'

She squeaked out of the room with her rubber soles on the vinyl floor and came back with a little trolley and a syringe.

'There you go lovey, you'll start to feel a bit better in a few minutes. You might even have a little sleep. I can see you've brought your books with you but you probably don't feel much like reading those. I can get you a magazine from the waiting room if you'd like?'

I wondered what it must be like for her to meet people like me every day, for all this to be normal. To have a vocabulary full of euphemism and a routine list of little things that might make her patients feel a little bit better.

I said yes to the magazine and my body said yes to the sleep, just for half an hour or so but it was the best sleep in the world. I had my mum's voice in my head saying, 'sleep is the best medicine' and wished she was there to hold my hand.

It wasn't until they told me I could go that I realised the hardest part was still ahead of me. The achiness was temporary but the lying to my mum about it all was going to last for the rest of our lives and so was the telling myself I'd done the right thing.

I saw Lorna on my way out and she smiled at me with a look of vague recognition. To her I was an appointment earlier in the week; to me she would always be the person that was with me when I began my goodbye to my lost baby. My first goodbye to the first of my lost babies.

I was crazy tired when I got home from the clinic. Still a bit nauseous and achy, putting one foot in front of the other along the pavement from the bus stop as though I were operating someone else's legs.

My mum called to me from the living room as soon as she heard my key turn in the front door but I needed the toilet and a little minute to rehearse my 'everything's normal' face, so I dropped my bag by the front door and ran up the stairs with a thudding that must have been almost as loud in the parallel hallway next door. She was standing in the doorway to the living room, calling to me from the hall.

'Marie. Marie I need a word.'

'Sorry, I'm really bursting,' I called down to her from the top of the stairs. 'I'll be down in a minute.'

Our bathroom had no lock but I closed the door behind me, sorted myself out and held off with the flush to give myself an extra couple of minutes before I had to go back downstairs. I looked at my face in the mirror of the bathroom cabinet; it looked just the same as it had this morning, yesterday, last week. My face looked the same but my heart was running at double speed and, however much I told myself that it was probably something trivial – a promise I'd made to be home earlier than this, sweet wrappers in my pocket that could have damaged the washing machine, the dirty shoes getting ruined on the back doorstep because I still hadn't cleaned them up properly and it had been over a week now – I was convinced that she knew. No amount of showing her the notes I'd made that morning or telling her how the whole cinema had been singing along at the film would convince her that I'd been first at the library, then watching *Spice World*.

I smiled unconvincingly at myself in the mirror, flushed the toilet, washed my hands and opened the bathroom door. My slow walk down the stairs sounded just as loud as the thud on the way up. The only other noise was the sound of my own breath and the tick of the clock in the kitchen that I never usually noticed.

As I reached the bottom of the stairs she came back to the doorway and stood sideways on, as though welcoming a VIP to an important function. As I walked through the door I saw Father Reilly sitting in the chair by the window and my mum closed the door behind me, trapping me in the small space with the two of them. If there had been any question mark over whether she knew, Father Reilly's tall, elderly figure backlit by winter sunshine dissolved any hope of paranoia.

'Hello Marie,' said Father Reilly. 'Why don't you have a seat?' He pointed towards the empty sofa as though I didn't know the way round my own living room.

I sat down, thinking about Theresa as she practically begged me to tell Father Reilly because he would help. And now, here he was, helping. I studied the swirls in the carpet. I knew that if I looked hard enough for long enough the swirls would begin to move and swish and they would carry me into the pattern; they would take me somewhere else where nothing said in this room would count. I knew it because I had done it before, that carpet and me were old friends.

My mum didn't sit down. The empty spaces in the room were filled by the black and white figure of the priest sitting studiously still and my small mother looking larger than her size as she stood and I sat. The carpet swirled around us and the scent of Palmolive from my clean hands tried to persuade me that everything was just as normal as it had always been. The sound of the clock in the kitchen had been shut out when my mum closed the door so my breath was all I could hear, and we all sat and listened to it for a few long seconds as my mother and her priest performed their roles, just as they had rehearsed, to an audience of ornaments and knick-knacks, with Captain Paddy looking on from his royal box vantage point on the wall.

'Did you get much study done in the library, Marie?' My mum began. I looked at the carpet. I thought about those TV dramas where Hercule Poirot gathers everyone together and makes them feel as uncomfortable as possible before finally unmasking the villain.

The thought must have made me smile.

'I'm glad you can see the funny side of this, Marie,' said my mum, interrupting her interrogation. 'Because, from where I'm standing, there's been plenty of funny business but nothing at all for any of us to laugh at.'

I glanced up. She was looking at me with an ugly face. I looked back at the carpet.

'What about the film, eh? Was it good? Did your friends enjoy it?'

I followed the swirls with my eyes, losing myself deeper and deeper in the carpet.

'Nothing to say, eh? No stories to tell of how the library was so busy or how you had Maltesers in the cinema? No? But you're usually so good with your stories, Marie. You're usually so quick to think of a plausible lie.'

'I think what your mother means,' Father Reilly interrupted, 'is that we know you weren't at the library or the cinema. We know where you were.'

My mum reached up to the mantelpiece, took down my appointment card for the abortion clinic and put it down on the coffee table so that it made a 'snap' like when a magician selects the card you were thinking of and places it in front of you as the big reveal.

'I thought I'd put a wash on before I went to work and picked your jeans up off your bedroom floor. If you'd put them back in your wardrobe I might never have found this, but since they were on the floor I picked them up for the wash. And since you're always leaving, coins and sweet wrappers and tissues in the pockets that could wreck the machine, I checked the pockets before I washed them and I found it. And there was I worried about something as easy to fix as a washing machine. I take it you've been to this appointment today Marie? I take it I'm a little bit late for this conversation?'

The small, dark, warm room got smaller, darker and warmer. There was nothing I could say that would get me out of this space, just as there was nothing that could undo everything that had got me here. My only option was to stay in the carpet and keep her and Father Reilly and everything else in the room outside of my head. If I didn't acknowledge it, it didn't exist and it couldn't hurt me.

But there's only so long you can do that. My mum wanted me to yell so that she could yell back and Father Reilly was there to mop up all the guilt and contrition.

'Marie! Maaarrrie! MARIE!'

I looked at her and hardly recognised her face. The burning in my throat made it hard to say anything and the words were quiet when they came. 'I'm sorry.'

'Sorry? Sorry for what? Sorry for getting pregnant? Sorry for not telling me? Sorry for killing that innocent child? Sorry for lying to me? Sorry for betraying everything you have been brought up to believe in? Sorry does even come close to what you should be feeling Marie. You should be deeply ashamed. I know I am. Ashamed and mortified.'

She collapsed onto the chair and sobbed.

'Sorry is a start.' Father Reilly said the words quietly, in a soft tone, but there was no gentleness in his voice. He spoke to offer reassurance to my mum, not forgiveness to me. I looked right into the sharpness of his small, round dark eyes. He stood and the blackness of his suit filled the window and brought the walls still further into the room until there was hardly any space for me to sit in and I was struggling for breath. I had to get out, even if it were just into the hallway, maybe I could go as far as the front doorstep and outside where cars were still driving along a road that was still there. Outside trees and grass and houses and people were all still there and nothing had changed.

I leapt up quickly and bolted for the door. As I reached to open it, my mum was there, fighting me for control of the door handle, pushing the door closed again with her foot and totally focused on preventing my escape. Behind her Captain Paddy looked on with his wise and wizened seadog face, smirking, with his pipe in his mouth. There was nothing an old sailor like him hadn't seen before.

As my mum pushed forward to take control of the door and I shoved back, her shoulder knocked him hard, pushing him along the wall, trapped behind her.

'What's that? What have you done?'

'It's just an ornament. Here let me get it.' Father Reilly was across the room in two steps and reached behind my mum to grab hold of Captain Paddy so that she could step away from the wall, her hand still clutching mine and the door handle.

As she stepped away from the wall and Father Reilly reassured her that the fisherman's head was fine, the little ring that had been fixed to the back of Captain Paddy to hang him on the wall fell to the floor with a talc-like shower of plaster.

'What have you done?'

She let go of my hand and the door handle to take Captain Paddy from Father Reilly, running her hand over the decapitated sailor's head as though she were reading braille. She was looking for cracks and she found none.

I wondered whether, when she asked what I'd done, she was referring to the abortion or Captain Paddy's fall from the wall but I think she meant both. The two were interchangeable and completely connected and they always would be. From that point, Captain Paddy's yellow sou'wester and ironic smirk would be the reminders of my sin. The physical damage I had done to him was symbolic of the harm I'd done to my baby and my mother.

Father Reilly handed her the little ring.

'You could try fixing it to the back again but if you drill into it you risk cracking it. The only other option would be duct tape or superglue, but it might be that neither would hold and you probably don't want to risk him falling on the floor. Apart from anything else, something like that falling onto you as you walked past could do you an injury. It's heavy for the size of it, isn't it?'

My mum took the ring from him and placed Uncle Paddy and the ring side by side on the shelf above the mantelpiece where he continued to watch us and with amused schaden-freude in his eyes.

'There, that will have to do.'

'Clearly he has sentimental value to you, but he looks good as new up there,' Father Reilly reassured her.

'Yes,' I agreed 'That's a perfect spot for him, he looks like he can see the whole room and we can see him from wherever we are.'

They both turned to me with a look that said 'who gave you permission to speak?' and I regretted reminding them that I was in the room.

'You've caused a lot of damage today, Marie, and a lot of hurt and a lot of pain. I suppose it's too late for us to do anything about it.'

I breathed the tears right back down into my gut and nodded.

'Perhaps we could pray together,' suggested Father Reilly. 'Prayer is the first step to reconciliation.'

So my mum and I knelt side by side at the coffee table with Captain Paddy looking on from the mantelpiece above us, the Christmas tree still trying to cling on to the Festive season in the corner and Father Reilly delivering a long and rambling prayer about forgiveness for mistakes, looking for strength and comfort in Jesus and choosing the right path. He delivered his message in a hypnotic tone that made me feel dizzy and disorientated. I began to feel myself swaying and had to open my eyes to avoid falling forwards and hitting my head on the table's glass surface, where the dark outline of Father Reilly's suit and the thin strip of his white collar were reflected as he spoke.

'Lord, we humbly ask that you forgive our weaknesses and we pledge to follow your example and strive to find a purer, more holy path in life. Help us take that path and support us as we follow it, protecting us from the temptation to wander or be distracted. Amen.'

'Amen.'

'Amen.'

My mum lifted herself up off the carpet. 'Thank you, Father.'

I found it hard to move and she took my hand to pull me up.

'Thank you, Father,' I echoed.

'Off you go upstairs, Marie. Take your bag and hang your coat up.'

I trudged up the stairs. I was tired and bleeding and relieved to be out of the living room. I sat on my bed listening to the low rumble of Father Reilly's voice and the familiar rhythm of my mum's responses until I finally heard the front door open and close again. The sharp footsteps of Father Reilly's black brogues petered out until the lack of noise left no evidence of him.

'Marie,' my mum called up to me from the bottom of the stairs.

Her tone had changed but my steps were punctuated by deep breaths.

'I thought we could do shepherd's pie for tea? If you can peel the potatoes for me while I get the mince on we'll have it ready in no time. You'll be needing plenty of protein to keep your strength up.

'I told Father Reilly you'd go to confession tomorrow. It starts at eleven,' she said as I followed her into the kitchen and she started getting ingredients and pans out of cupboards. 'Best to get there early, you don't want to be queuing. He's been very good. You could go to the library and get some more revision done after that. Unless you have other plans.'

I shook my head to say I hadn't.

'Right, well, that's sorted then.'

She looked like she might hug me, but she just handed me the potato peeler and told me that four biggish ones would be enough.

I didn't go to confession the next day. Neither my mum, nor I, nor Father Reilly ever spoke of it again.

Dear baby

I am sorry. Sorry that I didn't even consider that I might bring you into existence, sorry that I couldn't – didn't – allow you to grow and be born, sorry that all those things you were going to be will never exist. The colour of your eyes, the imperfections in your teeth, the way you laugh, your favourite foods, the million tiny habits that make you human were all lined up to happen and I destroyed them as quickly as I made them. I'm sorry.

Let me explain. I didn't make that choice on my own, not exactly anyway. It was my decision and the buck stops with me but it wasn't just me. I looked for help but I couldn't find any. I prayed to God and asked Mary for guidance – she was in my situation once, pregnant and scared for the future. Perhaps she would have made the choices I made if she'd been able to. Perhaps I wouldn't have made the choice I made if an angel had been sent to me to reassure me. The thing is, there was no sign that everything would be OK, and every sign that it wouldn't.

I was scared, baby. It all scared me much too much. Whatever you should have been was not the unwelcome burden of years of hard work and guilt. You weren't meant to be the embodiment of resentment and the constant reminder of my silly mistakes. You were meant to be loved and nurtured and encouraged and adored. You were meant to have another life from the one mapped out for you if you'd stayed with me.

So here's what I pray for you every day. I pray that your soul has gone back to heaven and that one of these days you'll be chosen as a special gift for a lovely family that will cherish you and help you to shine with all your gifts. And one day maybe I will meet you and you won't know me but I will know you straight away and the two of us will become friends and I will be able to tell you how very special you are.

But, for now my darling lost child, I have to say goodbye and I am writing this letter to you because I will never be able to hold you close and tell you how much I love you, or watch you play or help you with your homework or hug you goodbye when you head out into the world on your adventures. I am letting you go in the hope that you and I will be together again one day, in this world or another. I am letting you go with love and a million regrets and I will hold this letter close always because it is all I have of you.

God Bless xxx

TWENTY-FOUR

The blossom has come back to fill the garden with spring, just as it always has; a reminder that life continues and renews.

The trunk is still scarred where Dad started to chop the tree down; a reminder of all we've lost since we sat outside enjoying the sunshine and making cards for a dead magpie.

As the petals fall, Anna's enjoying crawling through the carpet of pink and Gabe and I play at making it snow for her by picking up handfuls and sprinkling them down until she giggles and stops crawling to sit and throw them back at us. She gets pink in her hair and stuck to her clothes and I've taught her how to blow the petals back up into the air again and make them fly on the breeze.

When I glance up I can see Mum watching through the window. From our spot under the tree at the far end of the garden, the window looks like a TV screen and Mum is the programme on in the background. Perhaps the window is like a cinema screen to her; whenever we're in the garden, if she isn't outside with us, she stands there, watching.

Easter was earlier than last year, right at the beginning of April, and Anna was allowed to try chocolate for the first time. She was quite keen on trying it for the second, third and fourth times too, until Mum told us off for letting her have too much and tidied all the chocolate away into a cupboard so that we have to ask for some if we want it. Since then it's been like our chocolate is in jail; she's been handing it out to us in a gazillion tiny instalments, so it will probably last until it's practically next Easter.

When I complained to Dad about how mean she's being with the chocolate he said it's a good sign that Mum's getting back to her old self. I pointed out that it's borderline theft and really mums shouldn't be allowed to steal what belongs to their kids.

'Don't worry, Champ,' he said. 'I'll make sure she doesn't eat it.'

We had an Easter egg hunt in the garden, just as always, but it wasn't the same without John-Joe. He was always super-annoying and competitive, making sure he found the most eggs even if he had to practically push us to the ground and step over us to get to them first. Mum always makes us share everything out equally anyway, so it doesn't really matter who finds the most but it wasn't really about the chocolate for John-Joe, it was about the winning.

This year, only I cared about finding the most. Mum walked round carrying Anna and helping her look, which wasn't fair because Mum knew where everything was hidden so, technically, Anna was cheating. And Anna didn't even know what the eggs were and she wasn't going to be allowed to eat them anyway, so there wasn't much point in her being there at all. Gabe was excited about finding the eggs before we started, but once he'd found a big one he just wanted to sit on the grass and eat as much of it as he could before Mum took it off him. That's the trouble with sharing them out at the end, there's no incentive to find the most.

Those are the days when I miss John-Joe the most, when the things we used to do as a team of three boys, with me theoretically in charge, John-Joe calling the shots and Gabe doing as he was told, are gone for good. Now I'm the leader for real, but the team has lost its centre. John-Joe was the star mid-fielder that could take a ball and run it the whole length of the pitch to score the winning goal, or plug a patchy defence with an instinct for being in the right place at the right moment. I'm more like the coach at Saturday morning football who gets lumbered with the beginners' group and constantly has to stop the game so that someone can re-tie his laces or go for a wee.

I missed him at Christmas too. And so did Mum. Dad keeps telling me that it's OK to miss him but sometimes missing John-Joe hits you from nowhere, like a ball kicked off the pitch when you're just standing on the side line waiting to be called on as a sub. I know Mum gets that too, a physical whack in the face of missing him so that she has to sit down or go for a nap. I know she's doing what she can to see those moments coming and steer them off course.

We went to see Father Christmas at the shopping centre, even though I'm too old and Anna's really way too young. It was embarrassing to be the oldest kid there and even Father Christmas (obviously not the real one – too young and too skinny behind his padded belly for a start) looked embarrassed so see such a big kid in his grotto. But Dad said it was important for Mum for us all to go as a family. It was tradition, he said, it's what we did. And anyway, it was Anna's first Christmas and it would be good to get a picture of her and her brothers with Father Christmas. We looked at each other when he said that and shared the urge to correct his sentence to 'two of her brothers'.

Mum went quiet in the car afterwards and went to bed with a migraine when we got home. She didn't come downstairs again until the next morning. Christmas has always been something we do exactly the same every year; as familiar as school or bedtime in its routines and habits, but, after that, Santa's grotto was the only Christmas tradition we stuck to.

The absence of John-Joe left a huge hole that Anna couldn't fill all by herself because she was the wrong size and shape. So instead of tip-toeing round the empty spaces and allowing us to notice them, Mum camouflaged them. It was as though our Christmas jigsaw had been mixed up with someone else's and we fitted new pieces together to make a completely new picture.

As well as adding Anna to our Christmas, we added Jenny. Usually she went to spend Christmas with her sister, Pat, in Basingstoke and came round the day before Christmas Eve with a Christmas cake and presents, but this year her sister and her brother-in-law were going on a Caribbean cruise for their fortieth wedding anniversary and Jenny wasn't invited.

'Funny place to go at Christmas,' Jenny said the day she pretty much invited herself to our house for Christmas. 'I'll be able to bring your presents and your Christmas cake round on Christmas Day now, though, and see what Santa's brought for everyone. There's always a silver lining if you look for it.'

Maybe it was the thought of the Christmas cake that had always been put out on the table but never eaten that made Mum think of switching old traditions to new ones. Or perhaps it was Jenny's talk of silver linings, but that was when Mum started chucking every new idea she could think of at Christmas, stopping just short of booking us all a Caribbean cruise so that we could surprise Pat and her husband while they sipped their Champagne.

'Actually,' said Mum, 'Instead of a Christmas cake with all that dried fruit and marzipan, perhaps you could make us a yule log this year? It gets expensive, all those ingredients for the fruit cake and it's a lot of work. I mean, I know it's a labour of love for you but I'm sure you'd love doing a yule log just as much.'

She was selling it to Jenny but Jenny was already on board. 'Yule log it is then.'

'What's a you log?' asked Gabe.

'It's a chocolate cake that looks like the branch of a tree with chocolate buttercream on,' Jenny answered before Mum could get a word in.

'That sounds a million times better than Christmas cake, why have we never had that before?'

'Well, we're having it now, and if Jenny's making it, I'm sure it will be the best yule log anyone has ever tasted.'

'I think so too, but if it's a tree what's Christmassy about that and why is it called a you log?'

Sometimes Gabe doesn't know how to quit while he's ahead.

'It's Christmassy because I'm going to put a robin on it and sprinkle it with icing sugar snow. I might even sprinkle glitter on it so that it looks like Jack Frost has been. As for why it's called a you log, that's because I'm going to make it especially for all of you.'

When she's not being really annoying and making us wash our faces, Jenny can be super nice. And that's why I didn't mind really when Mum said she should spend Christmas with us. Not just Christmas Day either, but Christmas Eve and Boxing Day too. She even invited Jenny to stay, so that it was a bit like going to Basingstoke for her, but not as far.

'She can literally walk from our front door to hers in less time than it takes to sing one verse of Away in a Manger,' Gabe whispered to me.

'I know,' I whispered back, 'but that's not the point.'

'If you're sure you don't mind? And the boys don't mind? And James?' Jenny said.

'Not only do we not mind but we insist, don't we boys?'

I'm not sure Gabe knew what insisting was and he definitely didn't look very enthusiastic about the idea but he didn't voice his objections out loud. I could see how much Mum needed to make this a completely different Christmas.

'We insist,' I echoed, nudging Gabe in the ribs. 'Don't we, Gabe?'

'We definitely do,' he agreed, then added 'But where will she sleep?'

'I thought you could spend Christmas in Jim's room and Jenny could sleep in your room?'

I was a bit weirded out by the idea of Gabe sleeping in John-Joe's bed, but he seemed really excited about it so the deal was done just like that, and Jenny joined us for fish fingers and oven chips to celebrate.

From there, everything about Christmas was different. Mum sent Dad to the charity shop with the box of Christmas decorations we used every year, including the ones we'd inherited from Nanna's house with all the baubles in their special boxes and Frankie the Christmas fairy.

'What about Frankie, don't you want to keep her?' I felt bad for all the times I'd said nasty things about the fairy and like I should stick up for the poor family heirloom. It wasn't her fault that time had been so unkind to her.

'Definitely not!' Mum laughed like I'd not heard her laugh for a long time. 'I'll tell you a secret, Jim, I've always hated that angel, it creeps me out. It always has, but it's just one of those stupid traditions you hang on to because you feel like you're breaking the rules if you don't. Like turkey, do you like turkey?'

'It's OK.'

'What about you, Gabe?'

'Not really. And I don't like sprouts. What's the point of sprouts? They make everything else on your plate stink.'

'Right, no turkey, no sprouts and no Frankie the fairy this year. We'll get a star and have beef and swap the sprouts for sweetcorn.'

'Can we have potato waffles instead of roast potatoes?' I'll give it to Gabe, he's really good at seeing his opportunity and going for it.

'I think that might be a step too far for Jenny but you can if you like. Why not?'

'And you log instead of stinky Christmas pudding for afters.'

'Perfect. When you get back from the charity shop the two of you can make me some Christmas menus if you like.'

She made us part of the switch like that, all the way along, from choosing what to eat to picking new decorations. We went out together to a garden centre with a Christmas shop and took it in turns to choose one each, then took it in turns to choose some for Anna.

'Dad,' I whispered while Gabe was busy getting Mum to eliminate one at a time from a shortlist he'd lined up, using eeny meeny miney mo, 'can we choose some for John-Joe too? I know he's not here and he won't get to see them but I think I know which ones he'd pick if he were here.'

'I think that's a great idea,' Dad smiled. 'But just add them to your picks, eh? Your Mum's doing really well.'

He didn't need to say any more. I made my turns one for me and one for John-Joe.

When the school holidays started, we decorated old shoe boxes with stickers and put our names on them.

'After Christmas,' Mum said, putting the first 'A' for Anna on the box she was doing, 'You can pack away your own decorations in your own box and then we can pick a new one every year to add to your collection. Then one day, when you're all grown up, you can take your own box to your own house to decorate your tree with your family.'

'And you can come round to visit?' asked Gabe.

'Of course, me and your Dad will be expecting an invite every year.'

'And you can bring the you log, or Jenny can?'

Mum just smiled at Gabe. 'Your box looks brilliant,' she said.

We didn't go to Midnight Mass so there was no Christmas Eve present waiting for us when we got back. Instead we had take-out pizza and Gabe made Mum and Dad promise that we'd do that every year as part of Christmas.

It was strange having Gabe sleep in John-Joe's bed: nice to have someone there again, but not the same as being in the room with John-Joe because Gabe just fell straight to sleep after Dad had finished reading him a story, even though he'd said he was going to stay awake to listen out for reindeer and see what Santa really looks like.

I stayed awake to talk to John-Joe, it had been weeks since he'd answered me and he was never likely to talk to me while Gabe was in the room but it was still nice to chat and fill him in on our new kind of Christmas and the decorations I'd chosen for him. People talk to Jesus all the time and he never answers or turns up at the end of the bed, so it's not as out there as you might think.

And like that, Christmas came and went, with all of us missing John-Joe and none of us saying so in words, just in the silences between the presents and the food and the crackers and the screwed-up-wrapping-paper snowball fights. Gabe spent most of the dinner putting pieces of sweetcorn in the holes of his potato waffles and cheating at pulling crackers with everyone, but Mum and Dad didn't mind. It was as though Christmas had been declared perfect in advance and no-one was allowed to imply otherwise.

It can't be Christmas every day though, and Jenny can't always be there like the grown-up in the classroom to make sure no-one misbehaves or gets upset. There have been lots of times when I've walked into the kitchen and found Mum crying. Sometimes I go up and give her a hug. Sometimes I walk away and leave her alone to miss John-Joe. I'm never sure which is the right thing to do because, when I miss him, sometimes I want a hug and someone to talk to about all the stupid things he used to do and his know-it-all annoyingness. Sometimes I just want to be left alone to wish he were still here.

He is still here really. He's in the blossom and the greenness that's come back into the garden. He's in Gabe's rubbish jokes and Mum's delicious lasagne. He's in the way Dad gives you the long answer when you've asked a simple question, and in the faces of all our friends at school. He is with us like Jesus was with the disciples after he rolled away the stone, hung out for a few days and then went back to heaven. When I left Captain in the church, he flew with John-Joe up to heaven, but heaven is all around us and John-Joe is right here.

Gabe moved into our room for good after Christmas because he said he liked sharing with me, and Mum said it would be good to move Anna into Gabe's old room,

I thought it would bother me much more than it did. I only said I didn't really mind because Mum wanted me to be fine with it, but it turned out I actually was fine with it in the end. Gabe has filled all the empty corners of the bedroom with his stupid questions and a million action figures that dive off the bed and have battles that no-one ever wins. In that pause between starting to wake up and being awake, when missing John-Joe makes my head heavy and my lungs tight, the way they are when you jump into the swimming pool, Gabe switches on a light and lets the air in. Sometimes with his gappy-toothed grin, sometimes with a not-very-funny joke, sometime with the actual lamp that still sits between John-Joe's bed and mine. Between Gabe's bed and mine.

It's not like Gabe's replacing John-Joe, he's just joined us.

Acknowledgements

Huge thanks – as both a writer and a reader – to the team at Bluemoose Books, for their passion for ushering new stories into the world, their encouragement and their relentless hard work and enthusiasm. In particular to Kevin and Lin for your patience, kindness and expertise.

Thanks too, to the Bluemoose community of readers and writers; it's a joy to be part of a network of booklovers cheerleading and supporting each other.

Thank you to the ladies at Manchester Women Writers; your wisdom and generosity have been so valuable, both in the writing of this novel and in life.

Libraries have also had a big role to play in getting this story from idea to finished novel. From the Manchester Women Writers meetings in Manchester Central Library, to my ringfenced writing time in Urmston Library while my daughter tapped and pointed her way through dance lessons nearby, Libraries are a comfort and an entry point to a million imagined worlds; I am grateful that they exist and hopeful that they always will.

Thanks to all the friends and family who checked in on how the novel was coming along and gently cajoled me to finish it. In particular, the real Mrs Edgar and my sister Lesley.

Last, but always first, thanks to Noah, Gideon and Ingrid, my children and my tribe, for all the times you've crept back out of the room when you could see I was writing, and for all the random chats.